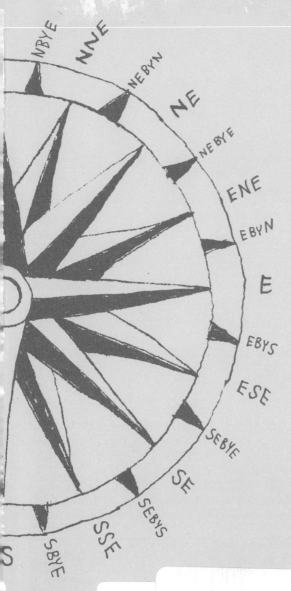

LAMPIE and the CHILDREN of the SEA

LAMPIE

and the

CHILDREN

of the

SEA

WRITTEN AND ILLUSTRATED BY
ANNET SCHAAP

TRANSLATED BY
LAURA WATKINSON

PUSHKIN CHILDREN'S

Pushkin Press
71–75 Shelton Street
London WC2H 9JQ

Copyright text and illustrations © 2017 by Annet Schaap

Original title *Lampje*

First published in 2017 by Em. Querido's Uitgeverij, Amsterdam

English translation © Laura Watkinson, 2019

Lampie and the Children of the Sea was first published
as *Lampje* in Amsterdam, 2017

First published by Pushkin Press in 2019

1 3 5 7 9 8 6 4 2

ISBN 13: 978-1-78269-218-8

N ederlands
**letterenfonds
dutch foundation
for literature**

This publication has been made possible with financial
support from the Dutch Foundation for Literature

The Bertolt Brecht quote in the epigraph is translated from
'Seerauber-Jenny' from *Die Dreigroschenoper* © Bertolt Brecht

Text designed and typeset by Tetragon, London
Printed and bound by CPI Group (UK) Ltd, Croydon, CRO 4YY

www.pushkinpress.com

For my sister Mirjam
For the children we were
For that one summer in the hay,
when we read and read and read…

"I want it," said the little mermaid, turning as pale as death.

"But you'll have to pay me too," said the sea-witch. "And what I ask is no trifle."

— *The Little Mermaid*, Hans Christian Andersen

And the ship with eight sails
And with fifty cannons
Will disappear with me

— *The Threepenny Opera*, Bertolt Brecht

CONTENTS

PART THREE   *The Boy under the Bed*

PART FOUR   *Summer*

PART FIVE   *The Mermaid in the Tent*

PART SIX   *The Stuff of Heroes*

Part One

THE LIGHTHOUSE

An island barely attached to the mainland, like a loose tooth on a thread, is called a peninsula. On this small peninsula, there is a lighthouse, a tall grey one that swings its light at night over the small town by the sea. It stops ships from smashing into the rock that is so awkwardly positioned in the middle of the bay. It makes the night a little less dark, and the vast landscape and the wide ocean a little less vast and wide.

In the house beside the tower, Augustus the lighthouse keeper lives with his daughter. They have a small garden and a little rocky beach, where something or other is always washing ashore. They often used to sit there all evening, with the light turning in circles far above their heads. Augustus would make a fire, and small boats sailed up from the harbour, carrying a crew of pirates. They came to sit around the fire and eat grilled fish and sing all night long. They would sing drinking and eating songs, sad songs and longing songs, and terrifying songs too, songs about the Secrets of the Sea, which made the girl both happy and scared, and so she would usually climb up onto her mother's lap.

But no pirates come sailing along any more, and her father has stopped making fires.

By the time dusk falls, the lamp must be lit. It is always the girl who lights it. Every night, she climbs the sixty-one steps, opens the rusty little door that covers the lens, lights the wick, winds up the mechanism that turns the lamp, shuts the door, and the job is done.

It was hard work when she was younger, but now her arms have grown strong and her legs can easily climb up and down the steps twice a day. Three times if she forgets the matches. That happens sometimes, and then her father always grumbles at her.

"It's almost dark and the lamp's not lit! What if a ship is lost, child? What if it runs aground on the rocks and it's all my fault? No – all *your* fault! Hurry up! Climb those stairs! Or should I just do it myself? I'm going to…" He's already getting up out of his chair.

"I'm on my way," the girl mutters, taking the matches from the drawer. The box rattles quietly. There's only one match left.

Must buy more matches tomorrow, she thinks. Don't forget.

The girl knows though, that remembering can be difficult. She always has so much inside her head: songs, stories, things she has to learn, things she wants to forget but that keep coming back. When she needs to remember something, she often forgets it, but she always remembers whatever she wants to forget.

As she climbs the stairs, she comes up with a little trick. What was it she wanted to remember? Oh yes. In her mind, she picks up a matchbox and then places it on a table in the middle of her head – with a little lamp shining onto the box, so that it will be the first thing she sees when she wakes up tomorrow morning. Or so she hopes. What kind of lamp? One with a shade of green enamel with a worn golden edge. Her mother used to have a lamp like that by her bedside. But that is one of the things she would prefer to forget.

Think of another lamp, Lampie, she tells herself.

Because that's her name. Lampie.

Her real name is Emilia. But that had been her mother's name too. And her father had always found it annoying when two people looked up as he called out the name, and then, later, he never wanted to hear that name again. So he calls her Lampie instead.

"You're not the brightest of lights though, are you, Lampie?" he always says whenever she forgets something or trips over, usually when she is carrying something like hot soup.

Lampie climbs upstairs with the last match. She has to be very careful. It must not go out before the lamp is lit, because then… Shipwrecks and an angry father. She is not sure which would be worse.

She twists the wick and fluffs it up, so that it will light properly. Then she takes the match out of the box and gives it a stern look.

"Do your best! I mean it! Or I'll…"

Or she'll what? What would a match think was the worst threat of all? Being blown out? Snapped in two? No, she knows what it is.

"Or I'll throw you into the sea," she whispers. "And you'll be so wet that you'll never burn again." Until it washes ashore, of course. On a hot beach somewhere, where it will dry out in the sun and…

"Lampie!" Her father's voice is so loud, even though it is coming from sixty-one steps below. "The light! NOW!"

Usually he has been asleep for ages by this time of day, snoring away in his chair. But not tonight. She strikes the match. A tiny, useless spark. And again. This time there is a proper flame and the smell of sulphur. That's good. She cups her other hand around the match and brings it to the wick. Come on! The flame hesitates a little, before growing bigger.

> "Flame, flame, burn hot and quick.
> Drink the oil and eat the wick!"

she quietly sings to herself, as she looks into the bright light. She could feel a bit of a knot in her stomach before, but it is starting to loosen now.

Close the door, wind up the mechanism, done.

"Matches, matches, must buy matches," she sings as she walks back down the stairs. Must remember to buy matches.

But still, she forgets.

And of course, the next day, there is a storm on the way. A bad one.

The weather has been perfectly calm all day, but now the seagulls are screeching restlessly and the dogs will not stop whining. They can feel the threat in the air, their owners say, looking anxiously up at the sky.

Late in the afternoon, clouds begin to gather on the horizon. The sky above the sea turns as grey as lead, and the sun goes into hiding.

No twilight today, it whispers. *I'm off.*

Everything starts to turn black outside.

Inside, a girl stands in front of an empty drawer, her face white with horror.

She has spent the whole day digging for mussels among the slippery rocks, because they taste so good and cost nothing. She also found sandworms for the chickens and driftwood for the fire, which she laid out to dry in the garden. Then she had a quick look for a special shell or a bottle with a message in it, but she did not find anything interesting. By the time she raised her head again, it was dark and she knew she needed to light the lamp. And that was when she finally remembered what she had forgotten, all day long.

Outside, the darkness falls in silence. The town has just a moment left.

A moment to dash outside and bring in the washing and fasten the shutters. To close the shops, to call the children inside.

"Oh, can't we play just a bit longer? Go on! Just a bit?"

"No, not even a little bit. Get inside, now!"

A moment for the old fishermen to nod their heads, their eyes gleaming as they mutter and mumble: "Yes, yes. It's going to thunder for sure. Like it did that one time, you know, and that other time when… When there was the Easter Storm, and the North Cape Storm in February, when the sheep went flying through the air and the ships crashed onto the beach." It surely won't be as bad as that, will it? Or will it? They slowly sip their milk. Everything was worse in the old days, they know, but maybe it could be even worse. Who knows, maybe they still haven't seen the very worst.

The wind begins to blow.

"Lampie? Lampiewhereareyou?" Her father's voice runs all the words together. "Lampieisthelamplit?"

"Yes, yes," mutters Lampie. "I'll just go and get some matches."

She puts her scarf on, grabs her basket and runs out of the

house. The wind tugs the door from her hands, slamming it behind her.

"Thank you, wind," says Lampie. It's always best to be polite to the wind. Then she dashes, slipping and sliding, through the garden, along the path, to the town.

The sea washes over the rocks, as the waves get higher and higher.

A narrow path of stones, as uneven as a set of bad teeth, runs from the peninsula to the mainland. Even at high tide, they stick up above the water. Lampie jumps from stone to stone. The wind blows into her face and pulls at the basket with the chamois cloth inside. The cloth is for wrapping up the matches to keep them dry, later, on the way back. Yes, she will have to come all the way back too. She tries not to think about that yet. That is not too hard, as the wind blows all the thoughts out of her head.

"Thank you, wind. Thanks again." She hopes that the wind is maybe a bit like a friend.

But then Lampie's friend tries to push her off the rocks and into the sea. Her shoes are already soaked through and are slipping on the stones. But there are wooden posts here and there that she can hold on to for a moment to catch her breath.

Not that far to go now, she thinks, but she can't see all that well. Sand is blowing into her face, along with other bits and pieces that the wind has picked up from the beach. Clumps of seaweed, branches, pieces of rope.

Presents, Lampie. Look!

She brushes them out of her hair. Dear wind, angry wind. I don't need them, thank you. I don't need anything. All I need is matches.

That makes the wind really mad, and it starts pelting her with rain. Within a few seconds, she is drenched and the wind blasts at her, making her even colder. She fights back.

"Stop it. Now!" she pants. "Get off, wind! Down!"

The wind is not a dog. It does not listen to her. It runs and jumps up at her again and again!

But there are the steps. Lampie slips and slides her way over to them, falling and bumping her knee, but then she grabs the handrail and pulls herself up. And there, finally, is the quay.

In the harbour, the ropes are all slapping against the masts. An orchestra: drumbeats, shrieking, and the first crashes of thunder. Lampie cannot hear her own footsteps as she runs along the quay. The storm tries to blow her down the wrong street, but she knows the way, even in the dark.

No one is out on the streets. The houses stand calmly, braving the storm. They are not afraid of being blown away. The trees brace themselves, losing leaves and branches. A metal bucket rolls by, rattling. All the shutters are closed, and all the shops are shut.

Down alleyways, down streets. When she is almost there, the rain turns into hail, and the wind throws handfuls of it into her face. Ouch, ouch! She shields herself with her arms and runs on. There is the street with Mr Rosewood's shop. The wind tugs at her basket one last time.

Go on, give it to me. Such a lovely basket to throw around, to blow so far, all the way to another country, or…

"Get off!" Lampie screams, holding on tightly to the basket. So the wind throws more hail instead.

But then she is there. There is the shop. The vegetable crates have been taken inside, the shutters are closed, the light is off. The door is locked. Of course it is, who would want to go shopping now?

"Me!" cries Lampie. "It's me! Mr Rosewood! Open the door!"

The wind even blows her voice away. She can barely hear herself. She pounds on the door with her fists. "Mr Rosewood!"

Fool, pipsqueak. Don't think anyone will hear you. I'll blow your voice away. I'll blow you away. I'll blow you in two. And I'll blow out all the matches you light. It'll be a breeze! Ha ha!

Her friend who is not a real friend rolls about, howling with laughter.

The wind's right, thinks Lampie. What am I doing? She's cold and her legs are trembling. Will she have to go all the way back now? Without any matches?

She screams one more time, at the top of her voice. "Mr Rosewooood!!!"

A small light appears, at the back of the shop. Someone walks to the door, carrying a candle. It is the grocer, Mr Rosewood, in a dressing gown and a scarf. When he sees Lampie, he hurries to the door, slides the bolt and opens up. An enormous gust of wind blows Lampie through the doorway. The shop bell rings away like crazy.

"Um, hello," says Lampie, shivering. "Do you have any matches?"

"Close the door, close the door!" shouts Mr Rosewood, and together they push the door against the storm until it clicks shut. Instantly, there is quiet. The hail clatters against the windowpanes, but that is outside. Lampie stands there, panting and dripping.

"What did you say, child? Have you come all the way from the lighthouse, through that storm?"

"We've run out of matches. And the lamp needs to be lit."

Mr Rosewood gasps. "It's not lit? Yes, of course it needs to be lit! Tonight of all nights! But you're not going back out into that storm."

"Yes, I am," says Lampie. "I have to." She tries to sound firm, but her voice comes out as a strange squeak. She wrings her scarf out a little and notices that her feet are standing in a big puddle.

"Come upstairs with me for a moment." The grocer lays one hand on her wet shoulder. "Dry clothes, warm milk. Child, you're freezing. You can't…"

She shakes off his hand. "I have to get back! Two boxes, please. Will you put it on our account?"

"That's insane!" Mr Rosewood shakes his head. "This storm will be the death of you!" But he is, above all, a grocer, a salesman, and his hands are already searching through the store cupboard. "Swallow Brand, right? Top Quality? But first you need to warm up. I mean it. Whoever would send a child out in this—"

"Frederick? Who's there?" Mrs Rosewood's voice, calling down the stairs.

"It's Lampie. She's here to buy matches."

"Lampie? From the lighthouse?"

"Yes. How many Lampies do you know, woman?"

"Send her up here!"

"That's exactly what I was going to do."

Tutting and sighing, Mr Rosewood takes off Lampie's soaking scarf, hangs it over an oil drum and gives her his scarf to wear instead. The wool tickles her wet cheeks.

"Take off your shoes down here and then you can get out of your wet things upstairs, and we'll…"

"No, thank you," says Lampie. "I need to get home." The scarf slips off and falls onto the floor but, without stopping to pick it up, she wraps the matches in the chamois cloth and puts them in her basket.

Then she hurries back outside.

Meanwhile Augustus is sitting at home, cursing.

He has emptied all the drawers onto the floor, pulled all the clothes out of the wardrobe. The floor is scattered with saucepans and shirts, with cups and dried peas. But there are no matches. Anywhere.

He curses Lampie and he curses himself. The fire has just gone out, and the stove is as cold as a stone. He hurls the useless hurricane lamp across the room. The hail rattles against the window. What should he do? There is nothing he can do! Absolutely nothing! And where has that child got to?

He hauls himself up there, limping on his good leg, up all sixty-one steps to the lamp room. She is not there either, and the wind almost blows him over the railing.

The waves crash against the tower. They are as high as a house, great green beasts that want to swallow everything and smash it all to pieces. He is not worried about his tower, but he is worried about the ships that will be blown into the bay in the pitch darkness. Above the storm, he thinks he can already hear the cracking and creaking of ships' bows being ripped open. And that is his fault. No, it's that child's fault, that wretched child. Where on earth could she be?

He peers out, trying to pierce the darkness. Please. Don't do this to me. Please, don't fall into the sea, come home safely. Please…

Scowling, he chases his thoughts away. Wishing is not going to help. What he wanted most of all did not happen. And the one thing he really, truly did not wish for, well, that *did* happen. No one ever listens to him.

So go on, thunder away all you like. Fine. Let the ships smash themselves on the rocks. Why should he care? Let the child blow away, that wretched child.

The wretched child is walking home through the storm. Or at least she is trying to.

She is no longer talking to the wind. They stopped being friends long ago, and now it is blowing right into her face.

She is making very slow progress. Stumbling across the town square, which is littered with branches and leaves, she heads for the quay, for the steps that lead down to where the path of stones begins.

Lampie swallows. The wind chases the sea over the steps, almost onto the quay. The path to the lighthouse can only be seen by the white foam splashing up as the waves break on the stones. Will she really have to go into the water? Will she have to swim?

She looks at the lighthouse, a darker silhouette against the dark sky. Her father is inside, probably pacing in furious circles, she can picture his face perfectly and how angry he is with her, she sees him stumbling, constantly looking at the door, she sees the door, the door knob, all she has to do is reach out her hand, she can already feel it against her fingertips…

Clutching the basket tightly, Lampie steps into the water.

At first it is not so bad, at first there are wooden posts and she finds her footing on the stones. The wind shrieks around her.

Hello, hello, my friend, are you back again? Have you really come to play this time?

Child, child, lighthouse child,

Are you as strong as the sea so wild?

"Yes!" screams Lampie above the storm. "Yes, I am! Yes, I am that strong!"

She struggles her way from stone to stone. The pitch-black water swirls around her, rising higher and higher, its cold biting into her calves, her knees, her thighs. Her heart is thumping.

But when she looks back, she is halfway there. The hardest part is still to come, but she has already done half of it.

"You see, wind! You can't…"

The wind rips the basket out of her hand. It blows it high, spinning it in a little pirouette above her head, just to tease her, and then carries it away, with matches and all. To another country with another beach, to another child, who will find it tomorrow. Lampie watches the little dot disappear into the dark sky. She screams in fury and immediately gets a mouthful of seawater. It is salty and cold, and she is already chilled through, and now she has lost everything. Her tears are salty too – she can't taste any difference.

She looks around. The lighthouse is as far away as the harbour, both out of reach for such a small girl in such a big sea. But she does not need to go home now, of course, not without matches.

The water rises higher and higher, and her feet lose their hold on the stones. She can swim, but she doesn't.

Fine, she thinks, then I'll come to you, Mother.

Her father is sure to be sad, but he was sad already. She lets herself sink.

She does not feel the cold bodies coming to swim beneath her in the water, the cold arms taking hold of her. Swirling green hair, like seaweed, billows in the waves.

Voices chuckle and chortle: "Oh my, a soul, a little drowned soul!"

Her head is lifted above the waves. She is pulled to the lighthouse island and dumped onto the stones.

"No two-legs in our water!"

That is where Lampie is lying now, beside her own front door, while out at sea a ship hits the rocks.

ROCK

And, as always, the next day the sun rises again. The water lies in the bay, perfectly still, as if slightly ashamed.

Waves? Us? No, of course not.

Storm? whispers the wind terribly quietly. *No, no, that wasn't me.* It brushes Lampie's face, like a hand stroking her cheek.

Mother? She is confused for a moment. Mother? Am I dead?

In her head she hears her mother laughing softly. *No, my sweet child. You're not dead.*

Oh. Lampie is almost sad. Really?

Really. It's not your time yet. Don't you hear the seagulls? Don't you smell the water? You're still here.

Lampie smells the salty water and hears the cries of the gulls. She feels the little stones sticking into her back and feels how wet her dress is. She opens her eyes a little and, through her lashes, she sees the lighthouse, high against the clouds.

She does not know how she got here, but she remembers everything else.

I was too late, Mother.

Yes, my sweet child. You were too late.

Is Father really angry?

Yes, he's really angry.

With me.

Yes, with you too. And me. And himself.

But there was nothing I could do about it! Lampie yells at the clouds. I tried so, so hard. I really did!

I know you did, her mother says. *You were very brave.*

But not brave enough.

Exactly brave enough. Only my child could be that brave. Come on now, go inside. You'll get poorly in those wet clothes.

Yes, poorly, says Lampie. She closes her eyes again, just for a moment. Very sick and then dead and then I'll be with you.

She sees her mother shaking her head. *That's not what's going to happen. On your feet, my sweet child.*

Lampie sighs and scrambles to her feet. She is stiff and cold and she can feel bruises all over. She climbs onto the doorstep and opens the door.

"Father?" The room is dark and the floor is scattered with the contents of cupboards and drawers. The stove door is open and her father's chair is lying on its back among the socks, the peas, the ash. She does not see her father though, just crumpled sheets in the bed.

She walks to the stairs, crunching and slipping. "Father? Are you there?"

Has he climbed all the way up the stairs? With his leg?

*

31

At the top, Augustus is looking out to sea, with his hands on the balustrade, which is red from the rust and white from the seagulls' droppings. Lampie walks over to stand beside him. Neither of them speaks; the mild breeze blows through their hair.

Down below, leaning on the rock in the middle of the bay, there is a ship. It is clinging to the rock like a sick child to its mother. The bow is splintered, the masts are broken and pointing in all directions. The sails hang limply, flapping in the wind. Planks and barrels and pieces of ship are floating all around. From the other side, from the harbour, comes the sound of shouting, and men in small boats are sailing back and forth.

Lampie feels herself turning ice cold. She bites her lip. This is her fault. This happened because of her.

She looks up at her father, at his greying red hair blowing in the wind, at the stubble on his chin. His eyes, too, are red-rimmed. Has he been awake all night? She tries to sniff his breath without him noticing, but all she can smell is salt and rust. He is furious with her, and she can understand why. Maybe he will never say another word to her, not for the rest of his life.

But then Augustus speaks.

"Listen to me," he says. His voice sounds creaky, as if he has not spoken for a very long time. "And remember this well. I was up all night, repairing the lens. The mechanism, I mean."

"Why? Was it broken?" asks Lampie. "There was nothing wrong with it yesterday."

Her father grabs her arm and squeezes, hard. "There's no need to go and look!" he says. "Just listen. Listen and repeat after me. My father…"

"Ow… um… my father," says Lampie.

"Was up all night…"

"Was up all night…"

"Repairing the lens."

"Repairing the lens. And who do I have to say that to?"

"To anyone who asks. And I didn't get it fixed until this morning, but by then it was too late."

"Oh, I see," says Lampie. "But…"

"Repeat the words."

"And you didn't get it fixed, um… until this morning, and…"

"But by then it was too late."

"But by then it was too late. But that's not true. It wasn't broken, so that's lying, isn't it? And… Ow!"

Her father glowers at her. "So what do you want me to say? That my child, this child here, forgot to fetch the matches, so all this is her fault?"

"No," squeaks Lampie.

"Well, then. So you know what you need to say, don't you?"

Lampie nods and her father lets go of her arm. "I, um…" she says. "So should I say that I helped and, um… passed you the screwdrivers and pliers and whatnot?"

"Whatever you like," says Augustus. "Suit yourself."

"Oh, and we can make our hands black, so that it'll look like we…"

Her father grabs her shoulder and gives her a good shake. "This is not a joke!"

"I didn't say it was," whispers Lampie. She looks at her hands on the railing, at the shattered ship. Did any sailors drown?

"Well, can you remember that?"

"Yes, Father."

"So repeat the words one more time."

"Um… my father, er… worked all night to repair the light, um, the lens, because it was broken and it wasn't fixed until, um…"

"This morning."

"This morning. But by then it was too late."

"Right, and that's what we have to say."

Her father's hand is still gripping her shoulder; it hurts a bit, but she does not mention it. She hopes this is his way of saying that he is glad she did not drown and that she is safely home again. And that it does not matter if she forgets something now and then. Everyone forgets things sometimes, eh? Including him. And that it is not her fault.

And maybe Augustus really does want to say all that.

But he remains silent.

Augustus sits in silence in his chair, his half-leg on a stool. Lampie brings him a cup of tea, which he does not drink, and then later some food, which he leaves untouched. She has learnt to leave her father in peace when he is like this, to stay in the shadows, not to draw too much attention to herself.

Because if she says something or makes a noise or laughs... It has become worse recently, and sometimes she is glad that he lost his leg, that she is faster than him, and that she can hide and wait until it is over, until her father has his normal eyes again and can see her clearly.

Augustus is so angry that he is shaking inside. And he is frightened too. That ship – this is really bad. Someone has to be blamed for it – he is well aware of that. And how does blame work again? Blame is a rotten egg that is tossed to and fro, from one person to the next, going around and around.

No one wants to catch it, no one wants to have that mess all over them when it finally explodes.

In his mind, he can picture it flying through the air. The person who has lost the cargo will throw the egg to the ship owner. The ship owner will toss it on to the captain. The captain will then fling it to circumstances beyond his control. An act of God! The storm! Those huge waves! That dangerous rock in the middle of the bay! But just you try taking a rock to court. Try squeezing it slowly until all the money has been recovered. All you'd end up with is sore fingers.

But who then? Who will catch the egg? Who will get the blame? Wait a moment. The lighthouse! It wasn't working! Negligence on the part of the town! The mayor glares at the councillor, the startled councillor stares at the harbour master, and the harbour master looks around for the person who… And suddenly everyone is looking in his direction.

The lighthouse keeper. Of course. That is where the egg needs to go. He sees it flying towards him, and it is about to burst. He can already smell the stinking muck inside it.

He really wishes he had something to drink, but he has finished everything. All he has is empty bottles and rusty water.

That afternoon, Lampie walks along the sea path to the town to buy a new packet of matches. She does not want to go, but it has to be done. They can't have another night with no light.

The harbour is busy. Big ships and small boats are mooring up and then setting off again. Pieces of wreckage are being brought to land, and crates and barrels. She hardly dares to look, but she does not see any drowned sailors. There are plenty of beachcombers and timber thieves though, loading all kinds of floating debris into their boats in the shadow of

36

the pier. Seagulls circle overhead and steal anything that can be eaten.

Lampie quickly makes her way through the hustle and bustle on the quayside, scared that someone will recognize her, will call after her: *Hey, aren't you?… Why wasn't the lamp lit last night? Have you people gone mad?*

The street with the grocer's shop is calmer today. Mrs Rosewood is standing behind the counter. She is a couple of heads shorter than her husband, and she looks at Lampie with small, cold eyes.

"Oh, so you're still alive, are you?" She does not sound too happy about that. "He went running after you yesterday, my Frederick. Did you know that? No, you didn't, eh? Didn't you hear him shouting? Of course not. Because of that storm. And the hail. He went out there to take you his scarf, would you believe? And of course he caught a cold himself, because that's what he's like. And you didn't even notice, did you?"

Lampie shakes her head. She can hear Mr Rosewood coughing upstairs.

"So now he's barking away in bed. And who has to look after the shop? And him as well?"

Maybe she should reply, "You, I suppose," but Lampie knows better than that.

"Two boxes of Swallow, please," she says. "And would you put it on our account?"

The grocer's wife leans over the counter. "On your account, eh?" she says. "Again. Do you know how much you already have on account?"

Lampie shrugs. She has a vague idea. It's a lot. Has been for weeks now. They have been so short of money recently.

Mrs Rosewood slides a sheet of paper over the counter to her. She pulls it out as if she had it ready and waiting. "There," she says. "Go on. Read it out loud. I think you might be shocked too."

Lampie looks at the words on the paper. Here and there she sees an E, the first letter of her name. Otherwise it is all just lines and dots, slowly blurring together. She does not want to cry. She does not want to talk to this woman. What she wants to do is to buy matches and then go home, light the lamp and crawl into bed.

Mrs Rosewood takes back the list and clears her throat. "Potatoes," she begins. "Two and a half sacks. Three gallons of milk. Three! Beans. Six loaves of bread, three currant buns… Why are you eating currant buns if you can't even pay for bread? That's what I'd like to know. And that's before I even get started on the alcohol. Just take a look at that!"

Lampie wishes she could just walk out of the shop. Mr Rosewood never makes a fuss; he always notes it down whenever she has no money. And sometimes he even quietly forgets to make a note. She sighs.

"I'll bring some money tomorrow," she says. "Honestly. But I need some matches now, Mrs Rosewood. The lamp has to be lit." Upstairs she hears thumping and more coughing.

"It certainly must," says Mrs Rosewood. "But why should we pay for it? Tell me that."

Lampie does not reply, because she can't think of anything to say.

Mrs Rosewood picks up the list again. "There are already three packets of matches on the list, the most expensive ones too."

Fine then, no matches, thinks Lampie. And that means another night of darkness, another ship on the rocks.

"Do you know how expensive—"

"Hilda!" Mr Rosewood shouts down. "Give that child a box of matches."

"Why should I?"

"Now!" Lampie sees big bare feet and blue striped pyjama bottoms coming part of the way down the stairs. "Have you gone mad?"

"Me?" shouts the woman. "You think I've gone mad? You must be talking about yourself! You gave your scarf away, you're giving half of the shop away, and now you're... No, stay upstairs. You're ill!"

Coughing, Mr Rosewood comes downstairs and into the shop.

"And without your slippers too," says his wife, pointing. "And without a scarf. For that little... But no, I'll just shut up, shall I?"

"Ah," says Mr Rosewood, with another cough. "Wouldn't that be nice?" He picks up a big box of matches and hands it to Lampie. "Go on. You'd better run." He places a hand on her shoulder and gently pushes her towards the door. "It's getting dark."

Lampie runs out of the door, past the rack of clinking bottles, but her father will have to fetch those himself – she is just glad to be out of the shop.

"I'm making a note of it, mind you!" comes Mrs Rosewood's voice from the shop. "So that's four packets of matches. Four!"

Up at the top of the lighthouse, she lights the big lamp. Her hands are shaking a little. She deliberately does not look at the ship, which is still out there. Her gaze drifts the other way, to the town, to the harbour, where the water is calmly licking at the quay. In the twilight, she sees something moving.

There, along the sea path, a line of people is approaching, almost black in the late evening light. They are men in big hats, with sticks in their hands. At the back is a woman in a dress. She trips and stumbles on the uneven stones, falling a little behind. As they come closer, Lampie sees who she is: the teacher from the school she went to for a very short time. Lampie can't remember her name. Slowly the line approaches the lighthouse.

Lampie feels a knot in her stomach. This is what they have been waiting for all day, she suddenly realizes. She quickly heads down the stairs, dashing over the smooth steps. "Father, some people are…"

"I've seen them," Augustus croaks. He is standing at the window, with his back to her. "Go to your room."

"Why do I have to —"

"And don't come out until I call you. You understand?" Her father follows her and slams the door behind her. "And remember what I told you this morning!" he whispers through the crack in the door.

What was it again? thinks Lampie. Oh yes.

Augustus leans on his stick. His leg is shaking, but he is not going to sit down; he does not want to be shorter than the men who are walking around his living room.

The fat sheriff has brought two deputies, just boys, with fluffy blond hair and pimples. They are striding around his house as if they live there, touching all his belongings. They are allowed to. And Augustus is not allowed to throw them out.

The woman in the grey dress does not touch anything. She just stands there, looking at him and at everything in the room as if it is too dirty to touch. She makes Augustus nervous.

What was it that he had come up with again? What was it that he wanted to say? Keep calm, that's the most important thing. Breathe slowly. Don't get angry. Stay polite. Say, "Yes, sir." Otherwise you'll only make things worse.

Yes, sir. Of course, sir. My sincere apologies, it'll never happen again. No yelling, no cursing. Hang your head.

He can't help thinking of Emilia, who always used to say that sort of thing to him: *Don't yell, Augustus. Don't kick chairs across the room, darling. And certainly not the sheriff!*

Now she's dead and he has to say those things to himself. He sighs. He is not very good at it, but he has to do it. For Lampie.

"My, my," says the sheriff. "What a thing. What a storm, eh? We won't forget that one in a hurry. And that ship. Smashed right into the rock, it did. Bang! Did you hear it?"

"Saw it," says Augustus. "You can see it from the tower."

"Well," says the sheriff, shaking his head. "Well. Must have been quite a climb, with that leg of yours. Bang it went. Crack! In two pieces! It's a blessed miracle no one drowned. Do you know how much it costs, a ship like that, Waterman?"

"No idea," says Augustus. He turns around and snatches something from the blonder deputy sheriff. "Hands off!"

It is Emilia's mirror, the mirror that has been hanging there on a nail, hanging there since... since for ever. It belongs there. He hangs it back up and sees his own face. It is very pale and his eyes are wide and scared. Keep breathing.

The deputy sheriff raises an eyebrow at his boss. *Want me to beat him to death?* is clearly what he means. *Now? Or shall I wait until later?*

Later, says the sheriff with a nod. *We have plenty of time.*

Keep breathing. Yes, sir. What was the question again, sir? Lampie had better stay in her room.

"Five thousand dollars is what a ship like that costs – at least." The sheriff slowly nods. "I don't have that kind of money lying around. Do you?"

Augustus gives a snort. "Not with what you pay me."

"That's true," says the sheriff. "We pay you. And would you just remind me what we pay you for?"

"To light the lamp."

"Exactly. You said it."

"Which is particularly important in a storm!" One of the deputies has come to stand beside the sheriff, and he is nodding his head, just like his boss. He is holding the drawer of cutlery from the kitchen.

"Exactly…" the sheriff says again. "Exactly. And what a storm it was yesterday. My goodness me." He rubs his hands. "So, tell me, *was* the light on yesterday?"

"No, sir."

"And why not?"

Augustus sighs. He has already told them twice. "Because the lens was broken, the mechanism. I worked all night to…"

"Oh, yes, that's what you said."

"And it wasn't fixed until morning. And by then it was…"

"Too late," the sheriff says, completing his sentence.

"Um… yes. And I'm sorry. And it won't happen again."

The sheriff brings his face close to the lighthouse keeper's. Augustus can smell that he's had a drink. Oh, he could really do with one himself right now.

"My deputy has just been upstairs," says the sheriff. "That lens is working perfectly."

"Yes, it is now! But it wasn't last night, I had to fix the whole—"

"Does that happen often?"

Augustus shrugs. "Sometimes. That thing's old."

"And did we know about that? Have you ever reported it to the town hall? Sent a letter? Requested a replacement?"

43

"What? You expect me to be able to write now? I'm a lighthouse keeper, that's what I am."

"Yes, that's what you are. With only one job to do. To light the lamp. And then put it out. So, *did* you light it yesterday?"

"Of course."

"With a match."

"What else?"

"But it wasn't on."

"That's what I'm telling you, that was because of the—"

"So you said, yes. The mechanism, blah, blah, blah."

Augustus's eyes flick to the door of Lampie's room. Did he just see it move? Stay in there, child. Please.

"Augustus Waterman, did you send your daughter Emilia to fetch matches yesterday evening? When it was far too late? When it was already dark?"

"I swear I did not." Augustus spits to reinforce his oath. As it hits the floor with a splat, the grey woman in the corner gives a disapproving sniff.

"So how is it we heard from Mrs Rosewood that your daughter went to the shop last night and her husband gave her a box of – and I quote – 'Swallow Brand Top Quality matches'?"

"You'll have to ask her." Augustus can now clearly see the door moving. Don't come out, he thinks. Stay there. "I didn't send her."

The sheriff looks around the room. "Actually, where is your daughter? Blown away? Drowned? Run off?"

"No, she's, um…"

"I'm here." The door opens and Lampie steps into the room.

Her father takes a threatening step towards her. "Get back in your room, child. Go on! Stay out of—"

"No, no, the child is staying here." The sheriff lays his hand on Augustus's shoulder. Not in a friendly way, but more like a threat.

"Tell us what happened last night, little girl."

Lampie takes a deep breath. She has done her very best to remember what to say. Now here goes.

"My father," she says, "worked all night to repair the lens, because it was broken and, um, then he didn't get it fixed until this morning and by then it was, um…"

"Too late, eh?" says the sheriff helpfully. "Goodness me, what a story. And then you went to buy matches."

"No…"

"That's what Mrs Rosewood says."

"Oh," says Lampie. "Oh yes, that's right, then. Or no, it was earlier, it was just before…"

"Why was that? Had your father forgotten? So he sent you? In that storm? You should be ashamed of yourself, Waterman."

"No," says Lampie quickly. "No, it was me who forgot, it was my fault, it was all my fault." Her cheeks are bright red but her eyes are determined. She is going to help her father. He does not have to do this all alone.

"Your fault?" says the sheriff. "Are you the lighthouse keeper?"

Lampie shakes her head.

"And where was the lighthouse keeper?"

"He can't walk too well with his leg, not all that way," says Lampie. "And he was… he had… He was tired."

"Shut your mouth, child!"

Lampie sees her father's fist opening and closing – which is never a good sign.

"Let your daughter finish, Waterman. Tell me the truth, little girl. Tired? Or drunk?"

Lampie gazes at him nervously. Lying to a sheriff is not allowed.

"Well? Answer me. Drunk? Too drunk to work?"

Lampie looks at her father and then at the sheriff and back again. "Um…" She nods her head and then tries to shake it at the same time. It doesn't work. "Ye-no…" she says. "Or at least…" She can't remember what to say and what not to say. "But that doesn't matter anyway, because I always help him. I help him every day. It's just that yesterday I forgot the matches, so it was my fault that…"

Augustus can see a red mist in front of his eyes. From far away and long ago, he can hear Emilia warning him: *Don't do it, my love. You'll only make things…* But he doesn't know if things could actually be any worse. His own daughter is handing him over to the sheriff. That jumped-up sheriff and his deputies are walking around his house as if it belongs to them. That woman in the corner is looking at him as if he's the most disgusting thing in all creation. He tightens his hold on his stick.

"Right, you lot! You can all GO! TO! HELL!" A huge voice comes out of his mouth, and he whacks the table with his stick, so hard that the cups jump up and one of the deputy sheriffs shrieks. The blonder one has Emilia's mirror in his hands again, and Augustus knocks it away from him. The mirror shatters, the pieces flying everywhere. And now he wants to whack the sheriff's head too, and that stupid face with the big cow eyes, but you don't hit a sheriff, that would be really stupid. What does he care though? Everything is already…

46

"Stop it!" Lampie cries, in her mother's voice. "Stop it, Father!"

And instead of the sheriff, he hits her.

Whacks the stick into her cheek, which flashes white and then glows red, and a trickle of blood comes from her ear, but his anger still isn't over and he raises the stick for another blow, but...

"Scandalous!" The voice of the teacher whose name Lampie can't remember echoes around the room. "Scandalous. How dare you?" In two steps, she is beside Augustus, pulling the stick from his hand. "Your own child. You brute!"

She turns to the sheriff and his men. "And look at you, just standing there. He could beat his own daughter to death and you'd stand by and watch."

"Oh, Miss Amalia, we really would never..." begins the sheriff. "We would have, we were just about to..."

"Yes, when it's too late, yes. Always just too late, eh?" She turns her eyes to the ceiling as if someone up there agrees with her. "I have told you about this before, sheriff. And now you have seen it for yourself. But I simply refuse to stand by and watch any longer. Not me. Not for another minute."

Lampie puts her hand to her cheek. This is going to hurt really badly later, she can already feel it. But right now everything inside her is still glowing with shock. She did – and said – completely the wrong thing. She tries to catch her father's eye. She wants to say, "I was only trying to help," and she wants him to look at her and to see her again, which is what always happens after one of his outbursts. Sometimes it takes half an hour, and sometimes a few days. But he is always sorry. He doesn't say so out loud; he can't do that. But he says it with his eyes.

Before he can look at her though, Lampie feels a cold hand on the back of her neck, pushing her forward, into her bedroom. Miss Amalia. That is what she is called – Lampie has remembered now.

Miss Amalia follows close behind her; she has to duck as she passes through the doorway. The feathers on her bonnet brush the ceiling.

"A few dresses," she says. "Underwear, nightdress. Socks."

Lampie just looks at her. She has no idea what the woman means.

"And something for Sundays, of course." Miss Amalia turns to look at Lampie's shelf of clothes. It is just a sorry little pile. Impatiently, she snaps her fingers. "Give me your suitcase. I'll pack it for you."

"I don't have a suitcase," whispers Lampie. She doesn't understand. A suitcase? Does she have to go back to school now?

"Or a basket? A bag?" Lampie shakes her head. With quick hands, Miss Amalia searches through the items on the shelf. She sighs with irritation as she tosses it all onto Lampie's bed. Her little dresses, her badly knitted socks. An old flannel nightdress.

"This one too?"

"Do I have to go away?" asks Lampie. "Do I have to sleep somewhere else?"

"Yes, child." Impatiently, Miss Amalia stuffs the clothes into a pillowcase. Which is also old and worn.

"You can come with me for now. Until we find a solution." She drags Lampie back through the doorway and into the living room.

The sheriff and his men are moving things and carrying them around. They have taken everything out of the cupboards and piled it all up untidily in the corner. Pans, cups, the bread bin. The rug has been rolled up roughly and placed on top. One of the deputies comes in with two angrily cackling chickens and releases them into the room. Shards of Lampie's mother's mirror lie all over the floor. Her father is slumped in his chair, looking at the floor, not at her. He is still angry – he must be. She picks up a shard of mirror.

"No, no, no, child, put that down. You'll cut yourself," says Miss Amalia. She grabs Lampie's arm. Suddenly Lampie remembers how Miss Amalia used to hit children on the fingers if they fidgeted or giggled. And that it was actually quite a relief when she had to leave the school.

"Did you drop it?"

Lampie nods at Miss Amalia like a good girl, but clamps her fist around the piece of glass. It gives her fingers a little nip.

Mother, she thinks. What on earth is happening?

"Come with me." The woman takes her by the wrist and pulls her to the door. "I'll see you tomorrow, sheriff. Gentlemen."

The men tip their hats. "Miss Amalia," they mumble.

"Oh, and you're most welcome," she says pointedly.

"Oh, of course, of course," replies the sheriff quickly. "Thank you. Whatever would we do without you?"

"I often wonder that myself," says Miss Amalia, pulling Lampie outside and into the night.

Lampie looks back over her shoulder one last time. Her father is sitting in the shadow; she can hardly even see him now.

He does not look up.

Lampie lies with her eyes wide open, staring into the darkness. Earlier, Miss Amalia made up the couch for her to sleep on and tucked in the stiffly starched sheets around her. Then she turned off the light and said, "Now sleep well, child." But Lampie cannot sleep.

The room around her smells strange, of soap or something that is even cleaner. There is very little in the room: a table with straight-backed chairs, a cupboard, a cross on the wall and a big clock in the corner that ticks really loudly, all night long.

She wriggles one hand out of the tight sheets and lays it on the pillow beside her cheek. Not against it – that would hurt too much. Her tongue keeps touching the spot on the inside of her cheek where the skin feels broken and it tastes of blood. And in her mind, she keeps seeing her father. How he looked and what he said and then what he said next and what he did after that. If only she could talk to him for a moment. Just listen to him breathing or snoring. She'll be able to go back home tomorrow, won't she?

Home to a house with no furniture. Had they taken everything with them?

Oh, but that wouldn't be so bad. They could always sit on boxes and eat off wooden boards. She could look for things on the beach. When she is home and everything is back to normal. When she has said exactly the right thing to her father and he is no longer angry with her. When she has worked out what that right thing might be.

She squeezes the shard in her other hand, under the sheet. Mother, I don't know how to put this right.

Ssh. Go to sleep, my sweet child. Tomorrow is another day.

In the dark she hears a sound and something heavy jumps onto her legs. With soft paws, a cat walks over Lampie and nudges its nose into the cheek that does not hurt. Luckily it does not smell of soap, just of cat. The cat lies down next to her head, purring. She can feel its warmth and its soft fur against her cheek, all night long.

And her mother is right: the next morning is the start of another day.

"When can I go home?" Lampie is sitting at the breakfast table, her plate full of little squares of bread. She is not hungry.

"Home?" Miss Amalia peers over the top of her teacup at Lampie – and at Lampie's cheek, which is very swollen. She shakes her head a few times. "It's just as well you're out of that place."

Lampie tries to hide her cheek behind her hand. "But when can I?..."

"I have an appointment at the town hall later today to decide that."

"To decide what?"

"What to do with you. What is best for you."

"I want to go home."

"So that we can weigh up all the interests. Particularly your own, of course."

"I want to go home."

"What a child wants is not always the best thing," says Miss Amalia, eating her bread with dainty bites.

When Miss Amalia has left, Lampie goes to the bathroom and takes a look at herself in the mirror. It's quite a bruise. The edges are already turning green and the skin of her cheek is red and swollen. Luckily she is not at home. Luckily her father does not have to see this.

I am absolutely furious with your father, says her mother's voice inside her head.

Yes, but, Mother, says Lampie. He really didn't mean to do it. *I'm sure he didn't.*

And he must regret it.

I hope he's howling with regret, her mother says angrily. *My poor child. Your poor cheek.*

The cat winds around her ankles. Lampie lifts it onto her lap and strokes it all morning, strokes the warm fur until it crackles.

Miss Amalia is cheerful when she comes home. She has a letter that explains everything, she says. She unfolds a sheet of paper and puts it on the table in front of Lampie.

"Take a look," she says. "Everything is coming together very nicely."

She unties her bonnet and takes it out into the hallway.

Lampie looks for a while at the white paper with the black letters on it and strokes the cat on her lap. After a while, she hears the water in the kettle singing, and Miss Amalia comes back holding a tray with tea and cups on it.

"So, what do you think?"

"When can I go home?"

Miss Amalia puts the tray on the table. "That's all in the letter."

Lampie can feel herself blushing. She strokes the cat even harder and looks at the table.

"Oh, of course," says Miss Amalia. "You didn't attend school for very long, did you? Oh dear. On top of everything else! Well, it's too late to do anything about that now." She takes the letter from Lampie. "I'll just have to read it out to you."

Lampie would like to listen, but it is not easy. She keeps thinking about everything, all at the same time, about now, about before, about those two weeks at school, years ago, in that packed and stuffy classroom, where she could not understand what was being said and felt so worried. Just like now. So when can she go home?

"Five thousand dollars," she suddenly hears Miss Amalia say. "More than that, even. And those... belongings of yours are not going to raise five thousand dollars."

Lampie gasps and sits up straight. The cat jumps indignantly onto the floor. "Five thousand dollars? But we don't have five thousand d—"

"Of course you don't," says Miss Amalia. "No one has that much money. And that is why you need to work to earn it. That's all there is to it. You can work, can't you?"

"What am I supposed to do? Where am I supposed to work? Can't… Can't I just work at home?"

"No, that would not do. Absolutely not."

"Or here? With you?"

"Here?" Miss Amalia chuckles. "The very thought of it. Of course not. I just told you. You're going to be working at the admiral's house."

"Where?"

"At the Black House, just outside town. You must know the place. Such a wonderful coincidence that someone came into town yesterday to ask if…"

"The Black House?" A song starts playing inside Lampie's head, an old skipping song from the marketplace.

> *In the Black House, the monster's home*
> *Where the beast does live and roam…*

"But there's a monster living there!"

"Don't be so ridiculous," Miss Amalia says, pouring the tea. "The admiral is a highly respectable gentleman. Highly. Otherwise we would never consider sending a child there." She pushes a flowery cup towards Lampie. "Come on, chin up, it's perfectly normal for a girl of your age to go out and work, isn't it? Besides, I've made sure that you will have one free Wednesday afternoon per month, which is not bad at all, so you should be grateful to me and—"

"But how long do I have to stay there?"

Miss Amalia starts calculating. "If we say a dollar a day, then that's five thousand days. But if you do your bit and your father does his, that'll be half each. And half of five thousand is only?…" She looks at Lampie as if she is back in the classroom.

55

But even if Lampie's head had not been full of panic, she still would not have been able to work it out.

"Twenty-five hundred days!"

"Th-that's such a long time," stammers Lampie.

"It's only seven years."

Seven years? That is terribly, horribly, endlessly long.

Miss Amalia stirs her tea, tinkling the spoon in the cup. "And seven years?" she says with a smile. "That's nothing at all if you consider the grand scheme of things."

Lampie tries very hard to consider exactly that, but all she can picture is vast long stretches of days. Days without her father, without the lighthouse, without everything she knows. In a house with a monster. She pushes her tea aside and shakes her head.

"No, I can't do it."

"I'm afraid you have no choice, child." Miss Amalia folds the letter neatly and puts it back in the envelope. "Now, drink up and fetch your things. We shall head over there at once."

Lampie starts crying. She can't help it. She cries into her tea, she cries as she packs up her belongings, as they go outside. She cries as Miss Amalia pulls her along and she cries all the way through the town, past the harbour, through the alleyways and up, further and further away from the sea, until they are outside the town and heading along the road through the forest. Then she runs out of tears.

From far away, the wind carries the scent of the sea. And something else: the sound of hammering. Big nails are being knocked into wood.

Lampie does not know this, but the sound is planks of wood being nailed over the lighthouse door. Augustus is inside and can no longer leave. Locked up with enough matches for seven years, which he has to use to light the lamp every night.

"With this leg?"

"That leg of yours is none of our concern, Waterman. And don't forget to turn off the lamp every morning."

"You don't need to tell me that. I've been doing it for ten years."

"You made your daughter do it – that's not the same thing." The sheriff chuckles at his own retort. His deputies laugh along with him and go on hammering.

"And what about my food? Am I supposed to eat matches?"

"We'll make sure someone brings food every evening. But don't expect anything special," the sheriff says with a snort.

Augustus presses his face to the small hatch in the door. He can just about squeeze his nose through, but nothing else.

"And what about my daughter?"

He does not receive an answer.

"What about my daughter? What's going to happen to her? Eh?" There is nothing Augustus can do, except for spit at the men through the hatch. Great gobs of hate. "Hey, I asked you a question!"

The last nail receives a final whack and the men quickly pack up their things. Pulling faces, they wipe off the spit. Then they head down the sea path and back to town.

Augustus swears at them as they go. "Answer me! When am I going to see my daughter again?"

The sheriff goes on walking. "You're going to have to earn it first, Waterman!" he calls back over his shoulder. "And then we'll see."

The Black House was built just outside the town, on the top of a cliff, so that it could look out over the sea. But the trees around it have grown higher and higher in recent years, so high that all you can see out of most of the windows is a few branches and the leaves of the black ivy that grows all over the house. Someone really should take the shears to it, but no one ever does. The ivy is full of rustling and full of life; owls live there and spiders, beetles and bats.

Are there any people living inside? There is no sign of it. Angry, stern, the house stands with its back to the sea, its shutters closed, its doors bolted, a high fence with sharp points all around. *What happens here is no one else's business*, it says. *So keep out.*

> *In the Black House, the monster's home*
> *Where the beast does live and roam…*

Lampie stumbles along the bumpy forest road. Miss Amalia is much taller than she is, so she has to run a little to keep up with her. The pillowcase with her clothes inside keeps banging against her legs and almost making her trip.

And in her head she hears the song over and over:

> *It'll bite off your arms,*
> *It'll bite off your head*
> *The floor will be red*
> *And you will be dead.*

Then they are standing in front of a fence. It is tall and rusty and overgrown with climbing plants, nettles and all kinds of greenery. Miss Amalia rattles the gate. It does not open.

"Oh, fiddlesticks…" she says angrily. She rattles it again. "And there's no bell or anything. How are we supposed to get inside?"

The bushes move and a man appears on the other side of the fence, a thin man in a big leather coat. Without saying a word, he opens the gate and, after the two of them have entered, he locks it up again with a grinding creak.

"Thank you most kindly," says Miss Amalia in a loud voice. Birds fly up out of the bushes, startled by the sound. "Say thank you, Emilia."

"Thank you," mumbles Lampie, but when she looks around, the man is no longer there.

They walk between the tall hedges to the house. Miss Amalia rings the doorbell, her other hand resting heavily on Lampie's shoulder. Far away, down a long corridor, they hear it ringing. They wait, but no one comes to the door. Impatiently, Miss Amalia rings again. They hear the bell, followed by some howling and barking. An angry voice. But no footsteps approaching.

"My goodness!" Miss Amalia's fingers drum irritably on Lampie's collar. She tries to peer through the letter box and, when that does not work, she takes a couple of steps back and looks up at the front of the house. "I can quite clearly hear that someone is at home."

Lampie looks along with her: three floors of black windows peer back through the ivy. They look like angry eyes.

Go away, child, says the house. *What business do you have here? Secrets dwell in this place, dark secrets and monstrous…*

"Excuse me! You in there!" Miss Amalia has bent down to the letter box. "Can someone come and open the door? I'm standing out here with a child!" She turns and glares at Lampie, as if it is all her fault.

Maybe there's no one at home, hopes Lampie. Then maybe she won't have to stay. She can earn the money another way, back at home, or in a shop, perhaps at Mr Rosewood's, if she is very neat and careful and…

Inside, a key turns and the big front door slowly begins to move, groaning as if it is an effort. A woman's face appears in the gap between the door and the doorpost. The face looks angry and its eyes are rimmed with red.

"Jolly good, it's about time," begins Miss Amalia. "Good day to you. I have come to—"

"We don't need anything," mumbles the woman. "Maybe next week." She starts to shut the door.

"Wait just one moment!" Miss Amalia blocks the door with her outstretched arm. "I'm not some tradesperson. I've come to bring the child. This child, to be precise. Emilia Waterman. It's all been agreed and this letter is—"

The woman tries to close the door again. "This is not a good time," she says. "Anything but, in fact."

Miss Amalia flaps the white envelope at her. "This letter is for the admiral and I would like to—"

"The master is not at home."

"So when will he be at home?"

"No idea. Not for a while." The woman tries, yet again, to close the door. "I told you, now's not a good time. This afternoon is not a good time."

"Not a good time, not a good time…" Miss Amalia simply pushes the door open. "The least you could do is let us in. We've had quite a walk. Come on, Emilia, get a move on." She pushes Lampie past the surprised woman and into the Black House.

Lampie steps into the corridor. It is cold inside. A long row of doors disappears into the darkness. The wall feels cold and wet to the touch, and when she brushes her hand against it, it leaves dirty white marks on her fingers. Miss Amalia gives her a slap.

"Stop that! What a terrible impression you must be making!"

The woman in black does not look at Lampie or at her fingers. She takes the letter from Miss Amalia and walks off down the corridor, with a blank expression on her face.

"I'll give it to him," she says. "To the master. When he's home. But he isn't now. And now is not a good time."

"That may well be," says Miss Amalia, her voice booming along the corridor. "But I'm leaving this child here in your care, um… Mrs… er?"

"Martha, Martha's my name. Now I'll thank you to leave." She angrily shoos the visitors away, but Miss Amalia is not finished yet.

"And I am sure, Mrs Martha, that you will provide her with food and a place to sleep. Won't you? And maybe something else to wear, as the child owns nothing but rags. There's no shame in that, but it's not very nice to look at, of course. Will that be a problem?"

Martha looks at her in surprise. "You're not leaving her here, are you?"

"Oh, that's all in the letter. Now make sure you work her hard. She's perfectly capable, and hard work never killed anyone."

"A child? I don't need a child. What am I supposed to do with a child?"

"Well…" Miss Amalia stares at the ceiling. Cobwebs are climbing up the lights, and the corners are black with them. "It looks as if you could do with some help. Couldn't you? With the, um, spring cleaning, shall we say?"

Martha flushes with fury. "That's not… It's because…"

"This is none of my business," Miss Amalia says, sweeping her hand around to take in the dust, the dirt, the cracked tiles. "It just seems to me that any extra hands would be welcome."

"I'm all on my own!" Martha shrieks. "They've all left, no one stays here, especially since…" That noise comes again, from far away down the corridor. Howling or barking or something.

Lampie feels in her pocket to see if her mother's shard is still there. She slides it over her fingers. No, Mother. Really, truly. I really don't want to stay here.

Martha takes a few steps towards the sound. "Stop it!" she shouts. "Lenny, keep them quiet!" Silence falls and she shuffles back to them, shaking her head. "I keep telling you. This is not a good time!" An angry tear rolls down her cheek. "We have to bury him and I need to get changed. I can't bury him wearing this, can I?" She points at her fraying apron. "And I always have to do everything!"

"Well, isn't this handy then?" says Miss Amalia cheerfully. "I'm certain Emilia here will be able to help you. She's a good child."

She gives Lampie's shoulder a few little pats. "Right, then. I'm sure you'll do just fine here, Emilia. The seven years will fly by."

"What? Who? Seven years?" Martha stares at Lampie and then at her companion.

However much Lampie dislikes Miss Amalia, right now she would like to cling to her and ask if she can go back with her, back to that clean house with that nice cat.

"What if there really is a monster here?" she tries. "What if it eats me?"

Miss Amalia bursts out laughing. The sound echoes off the walls. "You really are such a baby, Emilia. Work hard, do your best, and all those little worries will vanish from your mind." She turns to the door. "No need to see me out," she says to Martha, who has made no attempt to do so.

Miss Amalia looks at Lampie one last time. "And there's no need to thank me either, child. Really. No need. That's not what I'm doing it for." She opens the door and steps out into the late afternoon light.

Lampie sees the light hitting the tiles and the hundred thousand particles of dust whirling above them. Then the door shuts with a bang.

When she turns around, Martha is gone and she is alone in the corridor. She has no idea what to do or where to go.

Part Two

THE BLACK HOUSE

Lampie looks around the kitchen. It is big and dark and really quite dirty. She found it by coming through the only door that was a little bit open.

No one is here, no monster, no Martha, no one at all. There is a fire giving off a little warmth, and the ceiling is low, with rough black beams. She can see a lot of dishes that need washing, on the table, on the draining board, even piled up on the floor. She could wash them and tidy up. That is the idea, isn't it? Should she just begin? Or should she wait? The sooner she starts, the sooner the seven years will be over.

She waits a while, standing first on one leg, and then on the other. Nothing happens. No one comes.

Lampie puts her pillowcase on a chair, picks up a cup from the table and walks over to the sink. Her eyes are already looking for a tap, a kettle, a bucket, when behind her the floor creaks and Martha comes in. They both jump, and Lampie drops the cup. The handle breaks off and the rest rolls across the room, stopping at Martha's feet.

"Oh, oh, I'm so sorry!" Lampie bites her knuckle. It is as if she can hear Miss Amalia complaining away: *What a terrible impression you must be making!* "I, I just wanted to do the washing-up and…"

The woman looks at Lampie as if she had completely forgotten about her.

Martha has, in fact, done exactly that. She paces up and down, muttering away to herself. There is suddenly a child in her kitchen. As if today hadn't brought enough trouble. A night of howls, burnt food, no one daring to go into the room upstairs. Including Martha herself, now that Joseph is no longer here. What on earth is she going to do without him? And now there is a child, this pale child with her black-and-blue cheek and her pillowcase.

"Shall I wash up, miss?" she asks. The very thought of it!

"This is not a good time! I'll explain everything to you, but not now. Not this afternoon. This afternoon we have to… We have to…" Martha wants to sit down, but she doesn't do that, and maybe she'd like to cry too, but she doesn't do that either. She would rather be angry.

"Yes, child? Why are you still standing here? Get out of my kitchen. Go to your room. Go on!" She gives Lampie a push towards the door.

"I don't know where my room is, Mrs… Um…"

"Martha! Martha's my name!"

"Martha."

"Oh… no. Of course you don't." Martha points angrily at the door. "Up the stairs, second door on the left, no, the third, take that one, the bed's made up. Now, off with you. We have to… I need to get changed. Why are you still standing there?"

The long wooden staircase creaks, and so does the third door on the left. Lampie stands in her room and looks all around. It's chilly and it smells a bit like mould. There is a chair, a table, a wardrobe.

So this is where she has to live. All on her own. For seven years. She shakes her head. She can think the thought, but she still does not understand it.

A window without a curtain looks out over the garden. She sees a large overgrown flight of steps and, beyond that, an explosion of hedges, bushes and gnarled trees, stretching their branches in every direction. Lampie can only make out a little bit of the sky. No distance, no sea. It starts raining, gently at first and then harder.

But there is also a bed, with a bedstead of gleaming copper and a soft white bedspread. So much softer and whiter than at home. Lampie runs her hand over it and turns back the cover. For the first time since she arrived, she smiles a little. So clean! Spotless!

"I'll wash my feet," she whispers to the bed. "So that I won't get you all dirty."

When she hears some noise outside, Lampie runs to the window. Resting her elbows on the window ledge, she looks down. Two men are leaving the building, carrying a black coffin. A small thin one in a big coat is carrying the front end: the man who just opened the gate. The back end is carried by a big, burly boy. The rain rattles on the coffin; the two men are soon soaked through.

71

Then Martha comes outside too. She has put up an umbrella and wrapped herself in a black scarf. She is gesturing angrily at the two men. *Go on! Get moving! Off you go!*

The little procession sets off, across the terrace and down the steps. The difference in their heights means that the men have to carry the coffin at an angle. Martha hobbles after them, trying to keep the umbrella over the head of the boy at the back, but her arm is far too short.

The other man almost drops the coffin and Lampie hears Martha shriek: "You idiot! Be careful!"

As she runs to the front of the coffin to help them to carry it, she drops her umbrella into the grass and the boy steps on it. Slowly plodding, the three of them disappear behind a hedge.

Lampie waits, but they do not return. The umbrella is still lying there in the grass. It gets darker and darker, and finally night falls.

She does not know how they light the lamps here. She cannot see any matches. The house is absolutely silent.

No one brings her anything to eat.

When Lampie's mother became sick, she lost her voice. She had already had difficulty walking for some time. First she had to lean on her daughter, and when that became too difficult she just remained sitting. She was finding it harder and harder to pick things up, and she kept dropping everything, and then one day she started stumbling over her words as well. Before long, she was unable to make herself understood. No one knew how it had happened. But nothing could be done about it. Strange sounds fell from her mouth like marbles. She sounded like a drunk, like a madwoman. So she stopped speaking. She lay with her head on her pillow and stared and stared.

All that time though, Lampie could hear her talking inside her head. And when her mother died, her voice stayed with her. She usually says nice things. Sometimes she is a bit stern.

Come along, she is saying now. *Nightdress on, wash your feet and into bed! Stop dawdling!*

73

Lampie does not mind it when her mother is stern. Then it seems as if someone is still looking after her a bit. When she goes to take off her dress, she finds the shard in the pocket. She strokes it a few times before placing it on the bedside table. As she bends down to untie her laces, she hears something out in the corridor. Shuffling, snuffling. She jumps and looks up, but then she can't hear it any more. Maybe it wasn't even there.

She does not want to think about monsters. Her head is full of things she does not want to think about. But now that it is getting dark and she can't see anything outside, she can't stop herself, and she thinks about it all: Her own bed. The sound of the sea around the lighthouse. Her father's snoring, at home in the night. She tugs at her laces, which are in a knot, and tries so very hard not to think about everything that it feels as if she can actually hear his snores. Or maybe it's real.

It is as if, far off in the house, someone is snoring.

Or maybe growling.

Mother? There isn't really a monster here, is there?

Her mother just laughs at her. *A monster? Of course not – what nonsense! Wouldn't it have gobbled up Martha and those men with the coffin?*

But what was inside the coffin? wonders Lampie. Could it have been a girl, a girl just like her? Is she the monster's next meal, a monster that only likes little girls? With claws and teeth, with hairy paws, a man with six arms and with no mercy… Lampie can imagine all kinds of things.

She tugs even harder, but the lace won't come undone. In the darkness she can't see the knot and her hands are too

74

shaky. It smells a bit different now too – like rotten fish that has been lying around for a really long time.

The only monster she has ever seen for real smelt like that. A fisherman had caught it and half the town went out to take a look: a foredeck full of a tangle of black snakes, with two big dead eyes at its centre. Everyone went, "Aah" and "Ooh" and "Eeuw", and the air above it was black with flies.

But if a thing like that were still alive… If those dead arms had muscles that could pull her down into the black night…

Stop it, Emilia! says her mother. When she says "Emilia", she really means it. *That's enough. Shoes off, wash your feet and go to sleep right away.*

Yes, but, Mother, I really did hear something. It might have been a monster.

Don't be silly. Monsters don't exist.

The growling turns into a gurgling, barking sound. Far away. Or is it coming closer?

Lampie does not dare to wash her feet now. She does not dare to take off her clothes. She does not even dare to lie in the bed, but crawls underneath it instead, wearing one shoe and one sock. If something comes into the room, maybe it won't find her.

She can't sleep. Again.

She rolls herself up around her fear, and lies there on the cold floor, listening. Sometimes the barking sounds far away, sometimes closer. One time she hears something prowling along the corridor, with heavy paws and tapping claws. When it comes closer, she makes herself even smaller and curls up in the corner, with her back against the wall.

She wishes she had checked to see if the door had a lock. Anything could just come into the room. But the paws walk by and the tapping disappears down the long corridor. Then it is silent.

So she goes looking for shells, on a beach inside her head. She finds some really pretty ones, pink and green, shining and wet. She washes off the sand and lays them out to dry on a rock in the sun.

By the time the whole rock is full, she has finally fallen asleep.

Lampie is awoken by a voice saying, "Oh". Pale light pours into the space between the bed and the floor. She sees legs walking past, legs in ribbed stockings and black shoes.

"Oh," says the voice. "So did I dream it? Or not?"

The legs walk to the window, someone gives it a rattle. It does not open.

Whose are those legs again? thinks Lampie. Why aren't I at home? Oh yes. Oh yes, Martha.

"Well, maybe it's just as well," says Martha. She walks to the chair with Lampie's pillowcase on it, picks it up and shakes it out. Lampie watches her clothes tumble out onto the floor. A ball of socks rolls away.

"Ah," mumbles Martha. "So there *is* a girl here. But where is she? She can't have been... Not on the very first night? Surely not..."

"Here I am," says Lampie, crawling out from under the bed.

Martha gasps in horror! As if Lampie is a snake, or a crocodile. Or a monster. Panting, she clutches her hands to her chest.

"It's only me," says Lampie.

"I don't like that kind of behaviour, young lady," says the woman angrily. "Sneaking around and hiding. You'd better not do that here. Do you understand?" She strides towards Lampie and looks at her clothes. "Did you sleep on the floor? In your dress? Tsk."

I was frightened, Lampie wants to say. I heard something. She wants to ask: is there really a monster? Is it free to run around? Is it going to eat me up? Is that why they sent me here? She wants to ask a hundred things. But the words suddenly seem strange in the morning light. And Martha looks so angry, even angrier than yesterday, if that is possible. And her eyes are still really red.

"Don't you have any other clothes?"

"Yes." Lampie points at the pile on the floor. Martha picks up a couple of things, a dress and a vest.

"Hmm," she says. "This clearly won't do. I'll make something for you. Yet another thing to worry about." Then she holds Lampie's chin, turns her face to the light and looks at her cheek. Lampie can feel herself blushing; she really wants to turn her head away. The cheek hurts a little bit more than yesterday, as is always the case with bruises.

"I've read the letter," says Martha. "This isn't what I had in mind at all, but it's what has been agreed, or so it would seem. Not with me, of course. But when does that ever happen?" She sighs. "I don't know if it's such a good idea. I really don't know, um… Amalia. That is your name, isn't it?"

Lampie gasps. "Emilia! My name's Emilia!" Amalia? The very thought of it!

"Good, fine. Well, there's breakfast in the kitchen, Emilia." Martha turns to the door. "Are you scared of dogs?"

"Um…" says Lampie. "Are they big ones?"

They are very big ones. When Lampie walks into the kitchen, they run towards her, stumbling and drooling, and barking their warm dog-breath into her face. She screws her eyes shut and lets them sniff her hands. The dogs could easily bite her fingers right off, but they don't. The big, burly boy, the one she saw in the garden yesterday, pulls them back by their collars and slaps them on their big, hard heads. They do not bite him either – they just lick at his hands, Lampie is relieved to see. They let him push them away and then they walk over to the fireplace, paws tapping, and drop down sluggishly onto the rug. Was that what she heard last night? Just dogs, just animals? Not monsters?

"This is my son, Lenny." Martha pushes the boy towards her. "Shake hands, Lenny." She says it again, louder, when Lenny blushes and keeps his hands at his side. "Well, go on!"

The boy towers over his mother, but he looks like a child. His cheeks already have stubble, but he is painfully shy and does not even dare to look at the girl. So Lampie takes the big hand herself and gives it a bit of a shake. "Hello, Lenny."

Behind her, someone else comes into the kitchen.

"Oh," says Martha crossly. "You've decided to show your face, have you?"

Without replying, the man in the big coat sits down at the kitchen table, picks up a bowl and pours himself a cup of coffee.

"This is Nick." Martha lifts a pan from the stove and brings it over to the table. "Apparently he is capable of speaking, but sometimes you wouldn't think it. Don't go running off when you've finished your breakfast, Nick. There's something I want to ask you."

Nick stirs his coffee and shows no sign of having heard her.

"This is Ama… no… Emi… What was it again?"

"Emilia," says Lampie. "Or, um… Lampie, that's what they call me…"

She wants to say, "at home", but her throat squeezes tightly shut.

"And porridge." Martha puts the pan on the table with a bang and starts serving.

Spoons tap against bowls and rattle in cups. Coffee is slurped down. Chew, chomp, clink – and no one says a word. The dogs by the fireplace whimper in their sleep.

Lampie does not quite know where to look: at the strange faces, the chewing mouths, or at the big blue eyes of the boy in the corner, who keeps glancing up at her and then back at his bowl? Martha feeds him as if he is a baby, and she gives Lampie a grumpy look when she sees that she is watching. Lampie stares back down at her bowl. At the stains on the tablecloth. At her spoon full of porridge.

Yuck. She does not say it out loud, but that is what she thinks.

It's porridge! says her mother inside her head. *You used to love porridge.*

Lampie does not believe a word of it. She lets the porridge drip off her spoon. Slimy.

I always used to feed you porridge when you were a baby. Don't you remember? Give it a try. Mmm!

On the other side of the table, the thin man is shoving great big mouthfuls of the stuff into his face, and it is dripping down

80

his chin. She puts her spoon back in her bowl. Not today, thank you. Her stomach is closed.

You have to eat something. Her mother does not give up. *Go on. A bit of strength for the day ahead.*

Day one, thinks Lampie. Day one of seven years. With breakfast here every day. With these silent people. With these scary dogs. With that disgusting porridge.

Come on, says her mother. *Whatever happened to my brave little girl?*

Lampie grits her teeth and tries to hold back her tears, but one escapes and falls into the bowl. Plop.

Because it is so quiet, everyone looks up.

Lenny gapes. His lips begin to tremble. "Oh!" he says, pointing, and he starts whimpering along with Lampie, who is so startled that her own tears immediately dry up.

"Oh dear…" Martha puts down her coffee and sighs. "Oh dearie me…" She unties Lenny's napkin and wipes away his tears. Then she looks at Lampie. "Just make a start, child, eh? What else can we do?" Lenny sniffs and gives a few more sobs. "You wanted to do the washing-up, didn't you?"

Lampie shrugs and then nods shakily. Not really, but she has to begin somewhere.

"Then I'll give you a bucket in a minute." Martha gestures to her son to blow his nose. "And eat something, child," she says to Lampie. "A bit of strength for the day ahead."

Lampie looks at her, and Martha looks back for a moment. Not unkindly. Then she turns to Lenny, who has forgotten that he was crying and has started banging his spoon into his porridge. Splashes fly up in every direction, and Martha has to wrestle the spoon from his hand. That is no easy task, because the boy is strong and splashing porridge is fun. Nick watches the struggle from the other side of the table. He scrapes his bowl, swallows the last mouthful and stands up. Giving Lampie a little wink, he turns around and silently leaves the kitchen.

"Wait a moment," Martha calls after him. "Nick, I wanted to… You need to…" But he's already gone.

Martha begins angrily wiping the porridge and tears from Lenny's face. And from the table, because it is everywhere.

It looks really unpleasant, but Lampie still takes a mouthful of her own porridge. And another one. It's not good, but it does warm her up a bit. And maybe it does taste just a little bit like home once used to taste.

And that is how Lampie's days at the Black House begin. Two, three, four days crawl by, more slow and dull than nasty and terrifying.

In the morning, after Lampie has washed up, Martha gives her a bucket, a brush and a mop and shows her where to start. Lampie brushes and mops the tiles in the long, draughty corridors.

The house is big and dirty, the wind blows through all the gaps, it is mouldy and smelly, and her cleaning does little to help. She can only mop a small area at a time before the dogs go traipsing over the clean tiles again with their grubby paws. She is still a bit frightened of them and so she quickly gets to her feet until they have lumbered past into the garden, where they hunt rats. Later, with even dirtier paws, they walk back to the kitchen, to chew on bits of rat and to fall asleep.

Sometimes Lenny lurches out of the kitchen to watch Lampie and get in her way. At first he stood still in the corner, but he is no longer as shy and so he comes to sit beside her, with his bottom on the wet tiles, watching everything she does.

She does not understand him when he speaks, but that does not matter. He splashes in the water and sometimes knocks the bucket over, but that does not really matter either. After a while, Martha comes to fetch him and takes him back to the kitchen table. He spends the whole day there, cutting up old newspapers. He snips them into pieces, going neatly around the columns, making a pile of letters and black-and-white photographs and, when he has finished, he puts them all back together again, like a jigsaw puzzle, to make a newspaper. Whenever a piece blows away or gets lost, he cries. Lampie helps him to look. She is good at looking, finding even the tiniest pieces in the dusty cracks between the floorboards.

In the afternoon, the girl is given another bucket and a clean cloth, and she wipes very old dust from lamps, ledges and windows. Cheeky spiders crawl over the duster and up her arm, to take a rest before beginning a new web. Lampie usually lets them do as they please, and all afternoon she feels an occasional tickle by her ear or in her hair.

They had spiders at home too, in the lighthouse, and their soft touch comforts her. She sings spider songs for them and releases them into the garden in the evenings.

Then she searches for a while to see if she can find a gap among the branches and the bushes, a place where she can see the sea, and the lighthouse. But she does not find one: the bushes are growing in all directions and the trees have branches right up into the sky. The deeper she goes into the garden, the more impenetrable it becomes. The garden stings her with its nettles and scratches her with its brambles, and soon she bumps into the fence.

I'll never be able to climb over that, thinks Lampie. If

I want to leave, how am I ever going to get out? The bars are slippery and high and impossible to climb. But after looking for a while, she finds a tree with a thick branch that reaches just under the tops of the bars. If she is very careful, maybe she can climb over to the other side, drop down onto the ground, hoping she does not land awkwardly, and...

She jumps as a bunch of seagulls suddenly flies up behind her, shrieking. Lampie turns around and walks back, across what used to be the lawn and is now the weed patch, past the pond in the middle, where a thick layer of rotting leaves covers the water. The windows of the Black House are all dark. But up there, right at the top, where there is a kind of tower, she can see something moving. Or is she just imagining it?

Lampie stands still for a moment and looks, but she doesn't see any more movement. It must have been something like a curtain blowing in the breeze, or...

That tower, she suddenly thinks. Would that be high enough? Would she be able to look out over the trees and see the sea from up there?

Maybe. And if she asks, Martha is sure to let her go and look. Why wouldn't she?

Feeling a bit lighter, she walks back towards the house.

Down in the kitchen, the light goes on. Martha must be starting dinner. Probably porridge again – she hardly ever cooks anything else. Lampie sighs.

From his room in the tower, the monster watches her walk, a patch of white against the dark grass. He watches her until she enters the house and then he slides back down onto the floor. He does not know who that was, and he does not care either. The monster is hungry.

"But why not?"

"Because. You just can't. Now lay the table."

"Yes, but," says Lampie, "I really, really want to!"

Martha pushes a pile of plates into her hands. With spoons on top. "Look, get a move on, will you? Where has that Nick got to?"

Lampie watches her fussing around nervously. She walks from the sink to the table and back, drops forks, picks them up, puts them in the drawer, no, no, on the table. Even though there is no need. Lenny is calmly crumpling up bits of newspaper, the dogs are noisily chomping away on bones, and the food was ready long ago.

"Please?"

"Hey, stop getting under my feet and sit down at the table. No, fetch the milk for the coffee. There is nothing in that tower, so why would you want to go up there?"

"No reason," says Lampie. "Just because."

"Well then," says Martha. "The answer is no. Hurry up, I need some milk in my coffee or my day will be ruined." She pushes Lampie towards the pantry, which always smells so badly of fish.

Lampie stops. "I want to see our house," she says. "To see if my father—"

"Your father? The one who hit you? Why would you want to see him?"

Lampie shrugs. Because, she thinks, because, because. "Just for a little bit? Please?"

"Don't look at me with those big eyes." Martha turns her back on the girl. "I said no. No one goes up there. The room is locked and we've lost the key."

I bet it's not, thinks Lampie angrily, I bet that's not true. Her father always used to turn away like that whenever he was lying. When he said he didn't know where the money had gone, that she should just look harder for it. Even though she could smell on his breath what had happened.

She flings open the pantry door. It really stinks in there, like rotten old fish from the harbour that have completely gone off. Can't Martha smell it? She picks up the milk churn. Empty.

"We've run out of milk," she says.

Martha doesn't seem to hear. She is standing by the stove and stirring the pan so angrily that it is splashing.

"So you can just get that idea out of your head," she mutters.

Martha wishes that she could do the same, get it out of her head and think about something else, just for a moment. But all day she thinks about that room upstairs. She thinks about it, but she does not go up there.

Tomorrow, she tells herself every night. Tomorrow I'll go.

But she does not. All day long, she can smell the fish wrapped up in newspapers in the pantry. The smell is getting worse and worse. It really is time to take it up there. But she does not go.

She knows very well that she is only making it worse by not going. That she will make him angrier and therefore more dangerous. So she had better just grit her teeth and do it. Just go, and she can be back downstairs in no time. Open the door, put down the plate, close the door again. If she is quick, it should be fine.

But the afternoon comes, and then the evening, and she still has not been upstairs.

She could send that new girl though… Martha looks at her, helping Lenny with his puzzle, the tip of her tongue sticking out of her mouth. Such a little one, so skinny. It wouldn't be fair.

But life isn't fair.

She couldn't send Lenny, that would never work, and Nick…

He is never there when she needs him, and when he is there he does not do as she says. He sometimes goes for a week without turning up for meals, and she sometimes sees him sneaking around in the garden, doing goodness knows what. She can call him until she is blue in the face, but he will not come. No, Nick is no good to her.

So there is no one else. If she does nothing, then it will die. And if that thing up there dies, she can forget about her job, and about living in this house with Lenny too. And then what? She takes a swig of coffee. Bitter, her life has become bitter.

Maybe it is not dead yet, but weak and less dangerous. Maybe. She will go tomorrow. No, tonight. Maybe then she will finally be able to sleep.

The sea breeze blows around the house, the branches scratch at the windows. Lampie lies there, angrily listening to the sound. She really, really wants to find out if she can see the lighthouse from the tower, see whether the lamp is lit. She can picture her father limping up the steps. Or slipping, falling, and breaking his other leg. And she isn't there to help him.

Your father can take care of himself. Her mother's voice sounds stern.

No, thinks Lampie. She knows that he can't. What if the lamp isn't lit again? What if another ship...

Even if that is true, says her mother, *there is nothing you can do about it. You're here.*

I don't want to be here!

You are where you are. Go to sleep, my sweet child.

Lampie tosses and turns for a while, from left to right, right to left.

I can't sleep here.

Just give it a try.

I can't sleep when I can't hear the sea!

Then listen. It's there. It's always there.

No, it's not, says Lampie. Where is it? I can't see it anywhere.

But it's still there. Behind the trees. Very close, in fact. Just open your ears.

Lampie listens and she can actually hear the waves quietly splashing and crashing, far away at the foot of the cliff.

It's not the same.

No, says her mother. *It's not the same. Do you want me to sing the lullaby for you?*

No, thank you, says Lampie.

But her mother sings it anyway:

> *White ships, grey ships,*
> *Sailing across the sea,*
> *And a boat called the* Aurora,
> *Bringing you to me…*

The lullaby always used to help. But not now. Angrily, Lampie sits up. Why isn't she allowed to go up there?

She hears something, above her on the stairs. Was it one of the dogs, or did someone just scream?

Did he hear something? Is someone finally coming? The monster sits up.

No. It was just his imagination.

He is used to being alone, but it has been such a long time. The water is all gone. The food ran out long ago, but that does not seem as bad now. The worst of it is the thirst, the dryness. No, the worst of it is that they have forgotten him.

But that can't be true, can it? They can't really have forgotten him, can they? Someone is going to have to come upstairs at some point, aren't they? They haven't all left. He can hear the dogs barking, and he sometimes sees someone in the garden. They haven't all gone, so one day, soon, someone will have to come up to him, won't they?

And then he needs to be ready.

Ready for what, Edward? From far away, from before, he can hear Joseph speaking. Always the same lessons, the same words: *Don't bite, don't scream, don't let the monster out. You're not a monster, lad.*

Really? Then what is he?

A knight with honour and with might, a musketeer who knows no fear.

Well, not any more. Not at all. All he knows is hunger and fury and dryness and…

The monster pricks up his ears.

He heard something, just now, down on the stairs. Someone is coming up.

Martha's hands are shaking, and the plate and the glass are tinkling quietly. The fish is quite rotten by now and it stinks. Well, he should think himself lucky. He. It. She has no idea. She has lived here for so long, but she has never seen it. Heard it, yes. And dreamt about it, in long nightmares. Blood and scales and even worse. Of course, Joseph always came back downstairs in one piece and even spoke about it with a kind of affection.

Hmm.

But it got him in the end anyway. And those two men last week, the butler and the handyman, big men with big sticks, but they came back down bleeding and terrified. They ran straight out of the door. She knew she would never see them again. Not likely.

She puts her ear to the door and listens. Nothing. But it is in there, of course.

Quietly, she slides the two bolts, takes the key from her apron pocket and slides it into the lock. Something inside the room shuffles across the floor. She can hear it. It is very close.

"Get away from the door!" she says in her sternest voice. She hears it chuckling quietly. "Go on. Otherwise you'll get nothing."

The laughter turns into a hiss. But it does sound a bit further away.

"I'll open the door," says Martha. "But you'd better be careful or I'll… I have a stick!"

She does not have a stick. So stupid. She will have to remember it next time. Or bring the dogs. Only they don't dare come up here, they stay at the foot of the stairs, whining and pacing in circles, and they absolutely refuse to go any further.

"I've got a stick. I mean it! I'm opening the door… now!"

She hears her own shrill voice. Oh, that's really going to frighten him! She is an old woman with no strength, no stick, just a plate of fish. This is not a job for her. She feels angry with Nick again. This is men's work. Coward, coward.

Martha takes a deep breath, turns the key in the lock and opens the door a little way. It is pitch dark in there, and it stinks. Rotting seaweed, dead fish. Her breath is racing. Put down the tray, get out of there.

Out of the darkness, something slides towards her. She screams and jumps, stumbling halfway back through the door, dropping the glass, and the plate shatters on the floor. She feels sharp teeth in her calf and she kicks, kicks until it lets go, and then she scrambles out of the room, slams the door, locks it and limps along the corridor, down the stairs, away, away and down.

Never again. She is most definitely never going to do that ever again. So then… So then someone else will have to do it… Someone else… But not her.

Then what happens will happen, and she will just have to leave, and Lenny will have to… and she and Lenny will just have to…

She stumbles and sobs, the blood trickling down her calf and into her shoe.

Martha leaves the broken plate in the corridor. Tonight, once again, the monster will have no food.

Stupid, stupid, stupid, he is so useless, he can't do anything, he is such a pathetic monster.

What an opportunity, an old woman like that, and he let her kick him away as if he were a baby. And she didn't even have a stick.

Water gone, food gone, and now he has nothing. Just hunger and thirst. And he's dry, so, so dry.

He can feel his body shrinking and stretching and craving, he has licked up everything off the carpet, there is not a drop left now, not anywhere. All he can think about is water: streaming, bubbling, splashing like a waterfall, with him in it and everything in him drinking it up.

Ha ha, but that is not allowed. That has never been allowed.

You need to forget about it, boy. Rise above it. His father's voice echoes in his head. *Remember – you are not a fish. You can beat this. Mind over matter.*

He tries, he really does, but even his brain feels dried out.

Dry? You call this dry? The Kalahari, the Sahara – now that's dry. We travelled through the desert for seven weeks to reach the other coast. We drank sand for seven weeks and we laughed about it. That's what men do.

He tries to laugh but it just hurts his throat. Sand, what does that taste like?

Outside, the sea splashes, very gently, at the foot of the cliff. He crawls into the darkest shadow under the bed. Will anyone ever come upstairs again?

Probably not.

Because they're scared, of course.

So they should be. If they come, he will bite them. He's a terrifying monster, that's what he is.

No, you're not, lad. I know you. Joseph shakes his head.

Stop interfering, old man. You're dead.

Who knew people could drop dead, just like that? It wasn't his fault, it really wasn't.

Joseph suddenly fell onto the floor. He was talking, explaining something about wind directions and the compass. Edward already knew it all though, as he had finished all the books ages ago, but Joseph was coming upstairs less and less often, so he let him talk. It was nice just to listen and nod and to say something clever every now and then.

That's good, the old man would say. *That's good, Edward. You're making progress, lad. Before long you'll know more than me.* Or something like that.

But they did not get to that point, because in the middle of north-north-west, his voice faltered and he sighed, sighed out his life, he was gone and what was left slid onto the floor beside Edward, scaring him half to death.

It wasn't his fault. It really wasn't.

He shouted, shook him, screamed, but a hailstorm had started outside. The sea down below banged against the rocks, and he could not even hear his own voice. Joseph had stopped moving. Edward had put a blanket over him, because he was so cold, but that did not help, and he already knew that it wouldn't. Once the blood stops flowing and the heart stops beating, everything becomes cold and stiff. It's called rigor mortis.

That's good, that's good, Edward. You're so well read, lad. Next time your father comes home, I shall tell him, you can be sure of that.

But not any more. Not any more.

What are those? Tears? his father scoffs. Is that a runny nose? I do hope not. Men don't cry. You know that.

After the storm had died down, it was an entire day before they came. He had almost given up hope, but then he heard them on the stairs. They were frightened.

"You go first!"

"No! You! You can go first!"

He thought they were coming to help him. He put on his friendliest face, so that they would not be scared. He still believed they would feel sorry for him, that they had come to bring him something. Water, something to eat perhaps. Ha ha.

They came with sticks, such big men, two of them, both with sticks. And they just started hitting him.

He wanted to shout out: it wasn't my fault, it really wasn't, he just died! But they hit him and chased him away from Joseph's body.

He wanted to say: my food's nearly all gone, and my water, and every day I need…

But they just yelled: "Get back, you monster! You freak!" And they laid the old man on a blanket, as quickly as they could. "Jesus, Mary and Joseph! That monster was trying to eat him!" They both drew big crosses on their chests.

Of course I wasn't, he wanted to shout, I just wanted to make sure that he really wasn't moving, I would never…

But they kicked him, and again, because he did nothing to defend himself.

So then he started hissing and shrieking and biting. He bit them in the ankles where it is soft. They bled and shrieked, and that felt good.

But then they took away the blanket with the old man on it and slammed the door. He heard the bolts slide, and they were gone.

And then nothing, for a really, really long time. Longer than ever, until that old woman this evening, and now… No one will ever come again, of course. Now it is all over and he will die up here, of hunger, thirst, dehydration. He will never learn to walk, never stand on a ship, never get his sea legs.

He closes his eyes and falls into the darkness.

"Stop getting under my feet, will you?" Martha raises her hand, but Lampie ducks out of the way in time. She's used to it from home, of course.

She has never seen Martha like this before. There is a bandage on her leg and she keeps limping around, sitting down, standing back up, letting the tea water boil dry, jumping at the slightest thing: a dog barking, Lenny giggling, and then she lashes out. A slap for the dog, and a snarl for her son, who sits at the table with his lip trembling for the rest of the morning.

Lampie strokes his head and brings him tea and sandwiches, because Martha does not do that today either. The girl stays in the shadows as much as possible. In the afternoon, she heads upstairs with her buckets. Not that downstairs is clean or that she has nothing else to do there, but no one is paying any attention to her today, or telling her that it is not allowed.

It smells really bad upstairs in the corridor, just as bad as in the pantry, and it only gets worse as she turns the corner. The doors are wider here and the walls are covered with antlers on wooden plaques. There is also a rhinoceros's head, all grey and wrinkled. It has sad little eyes – and a long strand of cobweb on its horn. Lampie quietly opens the door beside the rhinoceros. She sees a room lined with shelves of stuffed animals and glass cases full of butterflies and beetles, all stabbed through with needles. Not a wing is moving. An empty tiger skin lies on the floor, and on the wall there are portraits of men in uniforms. They stare at her with angry eyes. *What is that child doing in here?*

Quickly, Lampie closes the door again.

She walks on, following her nose, to where the stink gets worse and worse. At the end of the corridor is a door with a staircase behind it disappearing into the darkness. That is where the smell is coming from. And somewhere up there must be the room she is not allowed to enter.

But shouldn't she go upstairs to tidy up? To mop up whatever's rotting away?

One time, when she was much younger, there had been a boat drifting just outside the harbour, a boat that was being bounced around by the waves and was going nowhere. It couldn't go anywhere, because its skipper had died at sea and his body now lay in the hold, while his catch was stinking on deck. It had been a magnificent haul – mountains of fish in the burning sun. The town's seagulls went crazy, flying in clouds above the ship and filling their bellies.

The old skipper had been called Pete. Everyone laughed at him a little behind his back, because he said strange things and never washed. He had always been smelly, all his life. He could never hire a mate to work with him either.

His ship stayed out there, floating beyond the harbour, with plenty of fish still left, and the wind blowing in the wrong direction. The whole town felt sick for two days.

The sheriff and his men finally rowed out to the ship and threw the catch overboard, along with the skipper. They tossed buckets and buckets of water over the deck, but the stench would not go away.

The harbour master refused to have the ship in his harbour, so they burned it out at sea. That stank too, even worse in fact. The smoke blew straight towards the town and lingered there for three windless days.

It became known as Pete's Revenge.

The townspeople walked around with cloths over their mouths, no one ate anything and Mr Rosewood had to throw away his supplies. Lampie's mother was still alive at the time and was unable to talk or walk, but she could still smell, and Lampie gave her wet cloths and bags of lavender, which did not help, and she was not sure whether to open the windows or to leave them shut. Her father never helped; he was always drunk, but drink did not help against the stench either, and it got to the point where no one wanted to breathe. But of course they had to.

Pete's Revenge. Yes, that is how bad it smells upstairs.

Lampie looks around. No one. On soft feet, she climbs the steps to the tower. Around the curve, there is another flight of stairs. Big dark drops have left a trail on the wood. It is blood, she knows it is, and she nearly turns back. Another curve, she has to go up again, and the stairs are becoming narrower and narrower. She has to let go of her nose, or she will not have enough air to breathe. Eeuw.

At the top of the stairs, in the half-light, she sees a door bolted on the outside. The source of the bad smell is lying on the floor: a broken plate with pieces of rotten fish. And something else. A key. A noise suddenly comes from below: Lenny shrieks, the dogs bark and Martha's angry voice calls her name. Lampie grabs the key, hides it in her dress and pelts back down the stairs.

After Lenny has had ointment rubbed into his hand, the tea has been mopped up and Lampie has made a fresh pot, Martha glares at her.

"Where were you? Did you go upstairs?"

"Only a bit of the way," says Lampie, with red cheeks. "I thought… The smell was so bad. I just wanted…"

"Let it stink," says Martha. "It's just how the house is. It'll go away." Then she roughly grasps Lampie's wrist. "You're not to go up into that tower. What have I told you?"

"I'm not to go up into that tower."

Oh, but she does go, of course. The heart wants what the heart wants – and the heart of a lighthouse keeper's daughter wants to see the lighthouse. The head of a lighthouse keeper's daughter can think all the sensible things it wants, but that does not help.

Her mother does not believe it is a good idea either. She has been talking and talking all evening.

Even if you do see something, what can you do to help your father?

Leave the man be, he's old and wise enough. Well, he's old, in any case.

There is something up there, Emilia, I don't know what it is either. But something. Something dangerous.

You said yourself that monsters don't exist, says Lampie.
That's right. They don't.
Well, then.
I am your mother, says her mother sternly. *And I really would rather you didn't. In fact, I forbid it, Emilia!*
Lampie stands up and takes a deep breath. "Yes, but do you know something, Mother?" she says. "You're actually… dead."
Her mother has no answer to that. Lampie feels her disappearing from her head, slowly and somewhat sadly. For a moment, Lampie feels miserable and lonely, but then she was miserable and lonely already. She is simply here. Simply alone.
Lampie sits down cross-legged on her bed and waits until it is completely dark. Her hands play with the key.

"Nick! Nick!" Martha's voice rings out across the garden, where no sound ever rings out. Startled birds flutter away; crows mimic her with their caws. "Nick!"

It is still very early in the morning, the sun has only just come up. And there is already so much noise.

She limps up and down the steps and shouts again, even louder. "I mean it, Nick! Come here! Now!" Her hands have become fists, ready to thump him. The man is no good to her. He is never around when she needs him. But this time he really has to come. "Nick!!"

Finally, the bushes part and the thin man in his enormous coat appears, unshaven, still sleepy. "What?"

"That monster…" Martha's voice trembles. "That monster!"

"Oh, woman…" Nick shrugs. "Monster… Just stop it."

"It's the girl, you fool. Listen to me! The girl, Emilia, she's gone, she's not in her room, not anywhere, she's—"

"Run away. Thought she would. Probably just as well."

Nick yawns and turns around, ready to disappear into the garden again.

Martha swears her worst curse. "Run away? How? Did she fly over the fence? All her things are still here, her shoes, everything. She's gone upstairs. I know she has! She kept saying she would. He's got her. Do you understand? He's got her up there."

"Oh." Nick scratches his head. "Ah."

Martha sighs. The way he's standing there, his arms dangling by his side, as what has happened slowly penetrates his thick skull. If she did nothing, said nothing, would the man ever act of his own accord? No. Nothing. Never.

"Don't you get it?"

"Yeees…"

"No, you don't. That child was brought here. Everyone knows she's here, the sheriff, that awful Miss Amalia, and soon the master will find out too, so she can't just disappear. It'll cause terrible problems. We can't just… We have to… There'll be such a fuss."

"And…" says Nick slowly. "She's a sweetheart."

"Yes, she's a sweetheart, and that monster or whatever it is will probably be eating that sweetheart all up, right at this very moment. Maybe he's already gnawing on her bones. He's wild, savage. Just look at my leg. And I don't want to go up there ever again. That's right – I said: never again! But we have to – and that includes you. For once you finally need to listen to me and do as I say!" She wants to grab him, to shake him, to yell in his ear.

But Nick says, "Wait." He turns around and walks away, back into the bushes. Quite quickly for him.

Martha slumps onto a cracked stone bench. She can't stand for too long, as her leg is so painful and she is so worried. That stupid, careless child. Martha thinks she's a sweetheart too, to be honest, so serious and so kind to Lenny. She can't be… It can't be true. But then, what else could have happened? It's ridiculous, having something like that in the house. If only the admiral would come home. Or not. Or maybe never again, in fact, and then he can't see what a mess she has made of things. And where has Nick got to? No one helps her. She can't count on anyone. She'll just have to do it herself again, but this time she'll take a stick, a big, strong stick.

Then the bushes part again, and Nick steps out. He strides up the steps. He is wearing a fur hat that is far too big for him, with a striped tail dangling down his back. There are large boots on his feet, and in his hands he has a long hunting gun. He walks to the kitchen door and nods at her to follow him. Martha limps after him, both surprised and relieved.

The dogs refuse to go unless Lenny goes too, and Lenny's too frightened. And Martha says he is not allowed to go, but he does not want to stay in the kitchen by himself. He cries and hovers around the kitchen table, making everyone even more nervous. Nick puts an arm around his shoulders.

"Listen, Lenny," he says. "We are hunters. We are going hunting. You too."

Lenny looks in surprise at Nick and then at his mother. Hunters?

"Hunters," says Nick, raising his gun. "Bang!"

Oh yes. Lenny nods seriously. Bang. He carefully accepts the carpet beater that Nick hands him and rests it on his shoulder.

"Bang," says Nick with a smile.

"No! No bang!" Martha is not happy. "He is not… No, Nick. Just the two of us should go."

Bang! Bang! Lenny shoots away enthusiastically. The dogs run around him, barking and drooling. Nick nods at Martha.

"Nothing will happen to him," he says. "I just need the dogs to come with us." He turns his head, with a swish of the tail. "Hey, Lenny? Let's go hunting, monster hunting! Let's go to the tower." Martha has never heard him say so many sentences in a row. "And ssh! Quietly, Lenny. Hunters walk quietly."

Ssh! Lenny replies, one finger to his lips. Ssh, dogs! The dogs immediately stop barking.

It's strange, thinks Martha. There's not much her son can do, but he can do that. She grabs the broom with the thickest handle and the hardest bristles, and she swallows hard.

"Nick," she says. "You do know you can't actually shoot him dead, don't you?"

It is a strange hunting party that makes its way down the corridor. A thin man almost disappearing under his fur hat, a woman with a limp and a broom, two big brown lumbering dogs, and a boy silently shooting away with a carpet beater. When they reach the stairs to the tower, the dogs realize where they are actually going, and they back up, whining and whimpering. Lenny hesitates too. No, surely they're not going there? Where he went once, just once, and saw something he never, ever wants to think about again. No, not there.

"Lenny," whispers Nick. "Hunters, remember?"

Lenny looks at him nervously. Still hunters?

Nick nods. "Yes. To help Emilia. The girl, she's up there, in that room. And we—"

"Nick!" hisses Martha. "Leave him if he's too scared! He doesn't understand! You can see that!"

What is going on inside Lenny's head? No one knows, because he can't talk. But he understands some things. Cutting, splashing, dogs, sweet dogs, a sweet mother. And since a few days ago: a sweet girl too. Who sometimes helps him. Who sometimes gives him a hug. And she's up there? And he's allowed to help her? He's never allowed to help, to carry anything, to do anything: Careful, Lenny! Don't do that, Lenny! Go and sit in your corner, cut something up and please don't touch anything. But now he's allowed to help. That is something he understands. And with a big grin he pulls the dogs up the stairs. Help the girl! He yodels with happiness.

"Ssh, Lenny! Remember? Quietly!"

Oh yes, ssh. Lenny nods and noisily sneaks his way up the stairs.

The light on the last landing is dim, and the door is open a crack. The smell of rotten fish fills the corridor. Nick signals for everyone to wait, puts the gun on his shoulder, lifts his boot and gives the door a kick. With a creak, it flies open. The room behind is dark and silent.

"Emilia?" calls Nick. "Are you there?" Still no sound.

"Oh God," whispers Martha. "We're too late."

Lenny holds the dogs by the collars, because they want to slink back down the stairs, away from here. They whimper and whine.

"Lampie?" Nick hesitantly puts one foot through the doorway.

A voice comes from inside the dark room.

"Ssh!" whispers Lampie. "Be quiet. He's sleeping."

Part Three

THE BOY UNDER THE BED

The lamp is lit. It is as if a weight falls from Lampie's chest.

The lighthouse is very small and very far away, a black line against a black sky. But the light is strong and it sweeps over clouds, waves, houses, over everything that Lampie knows so well. She lays her cheek against the cold glass.

At the door she had whispered, "Hello?" and, "Is there anyone there?" But no one replied – and nothing moved. (You see, Mother?)

On tiptoes she had crept to the window. She counted five windows in the almost round room. There were gaps in the curtains and through the fifth gap she could see a vague light moving – and then she had her answer.

She lifted herself onto the window sill behind the curtain, pulled up her feet and looked out.

So her father is at home as usual, and he can light the lamp, can somehow limp up the stairs every night. And get back downstairs, which is even more difficult. He can eat and sleep as usual.

Without her.

So he does not really need her.

Maybe he does not mind that she is here. Maybe he is thinking: Good riddance! That child – what use is she to me?

Or...

Maybe he is not living there at all, and they have locked him up somewhere she will never find him. In a cellar full of rats, with water and bread. Or not even that. And someone else is living in their lighthouse, a different lighthouse keeper, one with two legs and no daughter. Or perhaps he does have a daughter, one who is much cleverer than Lampie, who can read and write and always remembers the matches, and who is sleeping in Lampie's bed right now, under her checked bedspread. Or...

She does not know anything. She climbed all the way up here and she still does not know anything.

Something is moving in the room.

Something under the bed is moving and quietly growling.

Ah, so there is something in here after all.

She has to get out of here, to escape right away! Mother! Help!

But her mother is not there. What did she say to her? You're actually dead. Even the shard of mirror is downstairs, down two safe flights of stairs, next to her warm bed, by the chair with the pillowcase and the dry socks.

Jump down onto the floor, Lampie, and run, run downstairs!

But her feet refuse to budge. She sits on the window sill, too terrified to move.

Stupid, she's so stupid.

*

He's so stupid.

He fell asleep and someone came into the room. He does not know who or what, but someone is sitting on the window sill. Someone who is breathing.

Attack! Rip them apart! cries the monster in his head. *Face the enemy! Get up and fight! Stand up now and bite, bite, bite!*

But he cannot get up and he is so thirsty. He could drink an entire lake – and then another two. His throat is sore, his skin is cracking, he must have a fever or something.

Now is when it really matters, now his life is in the balance, and now he just stays there, under his bed. He is such a gutless coward.

It sounds more like groaning than growling, but Lampie is not entirely certain.

She has been sitting here for a while now, and she still has not been eaten. But there is definitely something there.

So there is a monster. A monster that fits under a bed.

But monsters don't exist.

"Monsters don't exist!" she whispers.

The thing under the bed laughs, softly hissing. Lampie gasps and pulls up her feet even higher.

So it really does exist – and it sounds like a snake.

There is a snake under the bed, and she is not even wearing shoes. How is she ever going to get to the door?

She thinks about Martha's leg with the bandage on it. About the trail of blood on the stairs.

She wraps her arms around her legs and makes herself as small as she can.

*

He can hear that it is only a child, just a girl, frightened and defenceless. He should be able to deal with her easily.

If he were not so tired and so hot, he would…

What, Edward?

Bite, tear, suck her dry? No, more like…

Ask for water, call for help, beg for…

No! Never! He is a monster, and monsters terrify people and make demands and threats: give me water, or I'm going to… What?

"Monsters don't exist!" she squeaks.

He just laughs. What does she know about it? Even his father calls him one, so it must be true.

I'm going to bite you in a minute, thinks Edward. I'm just going to wait for a moment, just rest for a little longer. He is so hot but so cold.

Inside her head, Lampie has been bitten to death long ago, but in reality nothing is actually happening. She can't hear him now.

But monsters are cunning. He is waiting for her to do something, of course. And then…

Well, he is going to have a long wait. She is not going to move a muscle, and she is good at keeping still.

Through the gaps in the curtains, she looks into the dark room. Where the light sweeps around the room, she can just about make something out. The floor is full of books and there are pieces of paper all over, covered with writing, torn and stained. On the walls are shelves with even more books, in crooked rows. An armchair, a low table with bottles of ink on it, a stool with the legs pointing upwards. In one corner is a dark shape, which looks like a bath. And in the middle, there is a big wooden bed with crumpled sheets on top of it. And a monster underneath.

A monster that reads books? A monster that can write?

She pictures it, scales and all, sitting at a desk in Miss Amalia's classroom, and the teacher slapping its tentacles with her ruler when it spills some ink and, in spite of herself, she giggles.

She quickly clasps her hand over her mouth.

Under the bed, the monster starts shrieking.

She is laughing at him! She is not scared of him at all. She is just laughing at him!

No one laughs at him!

He's going to, he's going to… He wants to let out his most terrifying monster scream, but all that comes out of his throat is a hoarse croak.

But he is going to get her. He can't see her, but she is sitting up there by the window, and there is nothing wrong with his hearing. He needs to wait for his chance. When she is sitting up there, he can't easily reach her, but look: she is already coming down by herself. Thank you, you stupid child. Now I've got you…

She is wearing socks, not even shoes, which will make it all the easier for a monster like him. He will bite straight through her bones. He will…

A weapon, she needs some kind of weapon. Lampie can't see a club or a stick anywhere, but there is a big flat book on the floor, and suddenly she is no longer frozen, but jumps off the window sill, grabs the book, and when she sees something emerging from under the bed – not big, much smaller than she had imagined – she takes the book in both hands and whacks its head, so hard that the book shakes and she falls onto the floor. But so does the little monster. It rolls onto its side and lies there.

He had not expected her to be able to hit so hard. He feels the blow echoing through his head, through his whole body, and he falls into the darkness of the night – and he is so tired that he just lets himself fall.

Beaten to death by a girl… sniffs his father from a very long way away. Very quietly, so quietly that he almost cannot hear it. And then he hears nothing else.

Lampie quickly scrambles to her feet and runs across the carpet to the door.

Hello, doorknob, I've been longing to see you. Hello, nice thick door that monsters can't get through. Hello, landing outside the room.

She holds onto the doorknob but turns around, just for a moment, to see what was actually there, under the bed.

The gap in the curtains is larger now, and the light from the lighthouse glides over books and papers and over the thin little creature lying among them on the floor. Its eyes are closed and it is not moving.

It's… it's actually a kind of boy, Lampie sees. A boy with a head that's a bit too big. His face is grey and scaly and his tousled hair looks almost green. He is wearing a dirty white shirt. And beneath that his legs have grown together into a dark tail. Like a fish's tail.

*

She stands there for a moment, just looking.

"Hey, little boy," whispers Lampie. "Hey? Fish? Are you dead? Did I kill you?"

There is no answer. She didn't hit him that hard, did she? Or did she? Very carefully, she walks over to him, her muscles ready to run away. She gives him a gentle kick with her sock. He does not move. He hardly seems to be breathing. She leans over and touches his hand. His skin feels dry and hot. So he is not dead then.

"Are you all right? Do you need anything? Food? Water?" At the word "water", the eyes suddenly spring open. Lampie steps back, her heart pounding. They are eyes without any whites. Gleaming black, like a devil's eyes, or an animal's. Then they shut again.

"That must have been a yes," she squeaks. "So you'd like some water?" She slowly shuffles backwards until she feels the door behind her.

"Fine. I'll go and fetch some."

Then she slips into the corridor, quietly closing the door behind her. Escaped.

Now down the stairs! Lock the door and get away!

But she stays for a moment to listen. She can't hear a sound.

She sees the big bolts on the door. They must be there for a reason. It is a dangerous monster, even though it looks a bit like a boy. A boy who is thirsty. Who has a fever. And she has promised to bring him water.

There is a tap downstairs with a bucket beside it. She knows all the taps in the house.

"I've brought some water for you." She puts the bucket down beside him on the ground. "Help yourself."

The boy does not move. He lies there like before.

Lampie fills the cup and holds it to his lips, but he does not drink. When she touches his hand again, it seems even hotter. His eyes do not open, even when she gently shakes him.

Lampie sighs. She wants to leave, but she can't. Something is keeping her here and making her do things she does not really feel brave enough to do.

She sits down beside him on the floor. His chest is going up and down very quickly.

He's going to die, she thinks. If I don't do anything, he's going to die.

She once found a baby bird in the grass, damp and fluffy, just out of the egg. And she found a young rabbit one day. She had to work out all by herself how to save them, endlessly dangling earthworms in front of the bird's beak and holding blades of grass by the rabbit's twitching nose. The bird died anyway. But the rabbit did not, at least not for a while.

Lampie stands up and takes some sheets from the bed. They are covered in dirt and mould. Carefully she lays a clean piece of sheet over the boy and pours some water onto it; maybe that will cool him down a little. She also places a wet cloth on his forehead, which is the hottest part of him. Then she drips the water from her fingers and onto his lips, as she used to do with her animals. It works. His lips open a little and he swallows.

"Well done," whispers Lampie. "That's better, eh, Fish Boy?"

His mouth gasps for more, and she gives him more, and pours more water on the sheet, which is almost dry again. It is as if the boy is drinking the water through his skin. She does it a few more times and then sits down beside him, leaning back against the bed.

The body under the sheet starts to breathe a little more calmly. His hand is cooler and when she touches it, his fingers take hold of hers.

"Sleep, Fish Boy," she sings quietly.

> "Boy who's a fish
> Boy who's so quiet
> And harmless and small
> Boy who's no monster
> At all, at all."

Not a monster. But what is he then?

The pirates used to tell stories about them. Before. Back when the pirates still came by. When she was little and everything was fine.

They were called Crow and Jules, and there were other ones she has forgotten. They smelt of drink and of sweat, and Lampie was allowed to help them put pieces of fish and shrimps onto sticks. They used to cook them and eat them all up, with scales and whiskers and everything. They threw mussels into the fire until they went pop. They sang and chatted away, played ferocious card games and told stories that the girl listened to open-mouthed.

Of course it always got far too late and she should have been in bed long ago. But she kept quiet and went to sit on the sand just outside of the circle of firelight, where the dark shadows flickered wildly.

It was all about sunken ships, lost booty, bad luck. About fights with sea creatures, bloody battles with fish the size of houses. And about fights with each other of course, because they were no softies. Hack! A hand. Swish! A nose, an eye, a couple of fingers. All of them were missing something or other.

Her own father was missing most, of course. A whole half a leg!

But he never wanted to tell that story, and if anyone tried to insist, he would get angry and her mother went very quiet, and then Lampie always had to go to bed.

But sometimes, sometimes one of them had sailed far beyond where all the others had sailed, even beyond the White Cliffs. And that was where he had met them, the Children of the Sea:

Women like fish.

Women with tails.

Women with eyes that…

The babbling would stop then, as the men began to whisper, or they said nothing at all and just stared at the one who had seen them.

But he would not say much either, becoming tongue-tied and stammering a few words.

"Tell us about them," they said. "Go on."

And he tried to, but he stumbled over his story and it ended in gibberish and shoulder-shrugging.

"It's not a story that can be told," he would finally admit.

And the pirates would all nod, and then sit in silence and let the fire go out.

That sort of creature. Is that what she has found, here in this house?

But what is it doing here?

Lampie leans against the bed and yawns. She gently tries to free her hand, but his hand will not let go. So she sits there and sings all the songs from the past for him, one after another.

There are so many songs that she still has not stopped singing by the time it gets light and Nick kicks the door open.

Slowly the little hunting party shuffles closer. Lenny is hiding behind his mother, with the dogs hiding behind him. Nick lowers his rifle, Martha her broom. They look at the creature lying half covered by the dirty sheet. The monster. Monster?

Martha shakes her head, almost laughing. Is that what she has been so afraid of? Is that what all those nightmares were about? Look at it. She could kick it right across the room, just like that, if she wanted to.

Nick turns to her and shrugs.

"See? It's like I've been saying all along."

She instantly feels her anger flare up again. "You? You don't ever say anything at all!"

The boy suddenly sits up, his eyes flying wide open.

They all take a step back. Lenny runs back out into the corridor. Those eyes. That's not a child, that's...

"Hush now, all of you," says Lampie. "Be quiet. He's poorly." She pushes Fish back down and puts the sheet over him. "And the bed's all dirty. I need clean sheets and some food, something hot, and tea or something."

"Yes, of course, of course." Martha is already out in the corridor. It may well be poorly, but she can still feel its teeth in her leg. Time to get away. She pushes Lenny down the stairs ahead of her. The dogs follow, as soon as they have gobbled up all the rotting fish.

"And you too! Come along now!" she barks at Lampie. Now that she can see the child is safe and still in one piece, she just wants to give her a good shake and chase her downstairs, into the safety of the kitchen. What a morning! And she hasn't even had her coffee yet.

"Yes, of course," says Lampie. "I'll be right there."

Nick stands there a little awkwardly, with the big gun in his hands. He looks a little ashamed as he carefully rests it on his shoulder.

"It wasn't loaded, you know," he mutters. He wanders around the room for a while before walking over to the boy, gently lifting the sheet, looking under it and nodding, as if it is as expected. Then he turns around and disappears downstairs.

The boy opens his eyes again. They are so strange, so black. Lampie can see herself reflected in them.

"Do you want some more water?" she asks. "No? Then go back to sleep for a bit, Fish." She leans over him to straighten the sheet.

"MY NAME IS NOT FISH!" he shrieks and then he bites into her wrist. Deep. The blood comes streaming out and Lampie stumbles backwards.

"Piss and bile!" curses Lampie.

The boy slips out from under the sheet and disappears beneath the bed.

"Ow, that was mean! Why did you do that?"

"Serves you right," he whispers from the shadows.

"What for? I was only trying to help you!" yells Lampie. She grips her wrist tightly, the blood dripping through her fingers and making red splashes on the carpet.

"Do not anger the monster!"

"Monster? You're not a monster!" Lampie whispers back. "I don't believe a word of it. You're just a nasty little boy." She stomps out of the room and slams the door behind her. Bang!

Inside the room, she can hear him protesting. Quietly at first, then louder. "Hey. I wanted to… Come back. I need to… Hey!"

Lampie can hear him, but she just keeps on walking. A trail of blood follows her down the stairs.

Once the blood has stopped, the wound does not look too bad. A semi-circle of little red holes. With her rough fingers, Martha rubs ointment onto it, which smells a bit and stings a bit, and then she wraps a white piece of cloth tightly around Lampie's wrist. She cleans the wound with a mixture of kindness and anger, muttering to herself as she does so: "This just won't do," and "How is it all going to end?"

"So… who is that, up there?" Lampie asks when Martha is finished.

"You saw it for yourself, didn't you?" Martha says, looking at her sourly. "Well, there's your answer."

"A boy with a—"

"A boy? That's no boy! It's a monster!" She holds up Lampie's wrist. Red dots appear on the bandage. "Is that what boys do? No. It's what monsters do."

Then she goes to make coffee, bashing around angrily. So she was wrong, again. Just for a moment she had thought this child would make her life here a little easier. But no, of course not. As if Martha would ever get anything she hoped for. She bangs the coffee pot onto the table.

"Sugar and milk?"

"No, thank you," says Lampie. "My father always thinks it's a waste, putting milk in your coffee."

"He doesn't know what he's missing," says Martha with a slurp, pouring an extra dash of milk into Lampie's cup.

Lenny gets a cup too, almost all milk and lots and lots of sugar. He sits quietly at his corner of the table and keeps looking at Lampie's wrist.

They blow into their cups.

"He can't die," begins Martha. "He mustn't smell too bad. And whatever he screams for, we have to give it to him."

"Who says so?" asks Lampie.

Martha points up into the air.

"God?"

"No, the master, the admiral." Martha stares into her coffee. "Joseph always did everything. Knew everything. Fed him, looked after him, kept him up there. No one else was allowed to see him. Of course there was talk, and no one wanted to come and work here, not for long at least. This place gives you bad dreams."

Lampie nods. She wants to say that what she dreamt and imagined, alone in her room, was actually more frightening than the creature in the tower, but she picks at her bandage and remains silent.

"We could only ever get shirkers who cut corners or never did anything at all. Well, you can see what a mess it is here. It's been that way for such a long time. But we always managed,

somehow we always managed. Until last week, until Joseph…"
She swallows. "Until one night he didn't come back. Or
the next day either. Until him up there started screaming
and shrieking. For a whole day and a night. No one could
sleep. No one dared to go upstairs. I had to beg and plead
until they finally agreed to go and look. They carried Joseph
out of there. Dead, of course, as I already suspected. And
then…" She gives a deep sigh. "After they'd brought him
downstairs, they packed their bags. All of them: the maid, the
gardener, the handyman. No one wanted to stay here. Not
even for… Ah, you can't blame them. So I went into town to
ask around and see if they could send someone to help. I was
thinking of a big, strong chap. Someone who could handle
that thing upstairs. But it seems I didn't quite make myself
clear. Well, yes, I was feeling rather upset. Anyway, then
they sent…"

"Me," says Lampie, downing another bitter mouthful.

"Indeed, child," says Martha with a sigh. "Right. I'll pour you
another cup of coffee and then you can go and pack your
things. I'll ask tomorrow if they can send someone else. And
you can just go back to your mother."

For a moment, Lampie imagines how wonderful it would
be if she could do exactly that. But then she sees her father
and the floor covered in broken glass. She thinks about the
seven years. She can't leave. And there is something else. She
wants to know, she wants to find out more about that strange
creature upstairs. She sat with him all night, and she still does
not understand. What is the boy doing up there all alone in
that tower?

Lampie puts down her coffee. "I'm staying," she says.

"Really?" Martha spills half of her coffee on the table. "You can't possibly mean that!"

"But I do," says the girl.

"No, you can't. There's no way a child could…" But she is already giving the girl a look of relief.

From the corner of the table, Lenny is staring at Lampie with big, wide eyes, as if he understood what she just said. In fact, he probably did. He tilts back his head and throws a handful of newspaper pieces into the air. They float down, landing all over, even in his mouth and his nose, and he coughs and sneezes, and then Lampie has to help him pick up all the bits of newspaper. When they have finished, he looks at her seriously and strokes her bandage with one finger.

"It doesn't hurt now, Lenny," she says. "I promise."

"Well…" Martha pours herself another coffee. "I'd be lying if I said I'm not glad you're staying. But are you really sure about that, child? No one ever stays here. I'd leave if I could. And the master's been away so long this time. He might never come home. And we'll be stuck for ever with his… With that…"

"Does he have a name?" asks Lampie. "I called him Fish, but he got angry."

"Um, yes…" says Martha. "What was it again? Come on, Martha. He's called… Oh, my brain's such a sieve. Ah, Edward, of course. Edward Robert George Evans. Just like the master."

"Like the admiral?" Lampie asks in surprise. "But why?"

"Oh, I thought you already understood." Martha looks at Lampie over her coffee. "It's his son."

So it's Edward, thinks Lampie, as she climbs the stairs. Not Fish. Edward. She thinks Fish suits him better. The cup and the plate are rattling on the tray, because she is shaking a little.

Her rabbit had never had a name. She had thought of a lot of different ones: Fluffy, Long Ear, William. But her mother had said, "Don't do that. Don't give him a name. Or you'll only get attached to him."

Which was, of course, what had happened anyway. She had cuddled and stroked him until he was tame and slept on her bed and had stopped trying to run away.

But her mother had just shaken her head. "Don't become too fond of that rabbit."

"I will," she had said. "I already am."

She has to move slowly so as not to startle him. Smile. Talk quietly in a kind voice. That is what she needs to do; that is how she will tame him. He is not a monster – she is certain of that. Her rabbit used to bite her at first too.

Slowly, she slides the bolts.

"Don't be scared. It's just me," she says as she opens the door. It is still a bit smelly in the room. She'll open a window, she'll wash the sheets, she'll—

"Can't you knock?" says an angry voice. She is not sure where it is coming from.

"Um… Well, yes." Lampie looks around. The curtains have been closed again. There is barely any sun shining through the gaps. The room is dark.

"Well, do it, then," says the voice.

"Now?"

"No, it's too late now. Just leave it. You can put that down. Here."

Lampie turns around, but she still can't see anyone. That voice, is that Fish – no, Edward?

"Over here. Hello! Are you blind or are you deaf?"

Then Lampie sees him. He's lying almost completely under the bed, with a book in front of him on the floor, and he is looking at her with his pitch-black eyes.

"Or are you just plain stupid?"

"Oh, there you are," she says in her sweetest voice. "I didn't—"

"What is that? What have you brought?"

"Your breakfast," says Lampie cheerfully.

"Well, it smells absolutely disgusting. Oh, just put it down." He drums impatiently on the floor in front of him.

"You must be hungry." She bends down and puts the tray on the floor in front of the mouldy bed. "You haven't eaten anything for—"

"What's that supposed to be?"

"Um… Well, Martha said you only eat fish but there wasn't any, so she'll buy some this afternoon," Lampie quickly says, still in her sweetest voice. "But you haven't eaten anything for so long, and I thought: how about some eggs? That'll—"

"Take it away." The boy pushes the plate away with such force that the eggs slither off the bread. "And what about that? Is that milk? I don't drink that."

"But you haven't eaten anything for so—"

"I can wait another day. I'd just like some water, please, in a glass. A clean one."

Lampie looks around the room, where everything is grubby and mouldy. "A clean glass," she says. "Right. I'll just—"

"Then you can change the bed. And someone needs to come at half-past three, because that's my bath time."

"Your bath time?"

"My bath time, yes. I have to take a bath at half-past three every afternoon. Do you think you can remember that?"

"Yes. Yes, I can." Lampie stoops to pick up the tray. He glances at the bandage on her wrist, but does not say anything. Close up, she can see that his skin is no longer as grey and scaly. He looks very different to last night, no longer as pale and white and feverish. Now that she can't see his tail, he seems just like an ordinary boy. But one with green hair and pitch-black devil's eyes and a mouth full of sharp teeth.

"What? What are you looking at?"

"Nothing," says Lampie quickly. "I'm not looking at anything at all." She puts down the tray on a big chest of drawers that's covered with books and papers. There are some used cups too – she will take them back down to the kitchen. She starts opening the curtains, one by one.

"Did I tell you to do that?"

"No." Lampie gives him her very sweetest smile. "But the sun's shining so nicely today, so…"

"I hate the sun. Close them."

"Oh," says Lampie. "Fine." She closes the curtains again. Taming a wild rabbit with strokes and cuddles was easier, she thinks. But that took a long time too. She stops for a moment at the fifth window and looks out. There, in the distance, the lighthouse stands, a grey line against the blue spring sky.

"So are you deaf?" says the boy. "Or just slow?" He clicks his fingers impatiently.

"Did you say something?" Lampie turns around.

"Yes. Twice. And I'll say it again. The atlas, please. Just put it down here."

"The what?"

"Don't you know what that is?"

"Of course I do," says Lampie. "I just didn't hear you properly." Talking in her sweetest voice is becoming more and more of an effort.

"The atlas. At-las."

"Um…" Lampie looks around the room.

"Under A."

"A?"

"On the bookshelf." He says it with clenched teeth.

"Oh," says Lampie. "So it's a book?"

"Yes! It's a book, yes!" He starts yelling. "A book! A book of maps! Maps of the land! Maps of the sea! Have you never seen a map before, you… you bumpkin?!" He bares his teeth, and his eyes spit poison.

133

Lampie steps back; she has no idea what to do. There are books all over the room. So she walks over to the wall and looks at the rows of books on the shelves, all made of brown leather, all with their spines facing her, as if they have turned their backs on Lampie and are laughing at her.

"Is it, um, one of these, um, brown ones?" The letter E – that is the only one she can read, but she can't even see that anywhere. The boy on the floor is watching everything she does. Hesitantly, she picks up a book, just any old book.

"This one?" The boy does not reply, so maybe it was a good guess. She turns around to see him looking at her with disbelief.

"She can't read!" he says. "You can't read, can you?"

Lampie does not answer. She puts the book next to him on the floor.

"It's not the right one."

"A book is a book."

"A book is most definitely not a book!" On his elbows, he wriggles out some way from under the bed. She can almost see his tail. "Why can't you read? Have you never been to school?"

"Yes, I've been to school."

"But I bet you were too stupid, weren't you?"

"Two weeks. I was only at school for two weeks."

"Two weeks? And then what happened?"

"Then… Other things happened."

"What sort of other things?"

"That's none of your business!" She picks up the tray, which tinkles and clatters. "Right, I'm taking this back downstairs. And I'll fetch some sheets. And towels. And a clean glass. And I'll come back at half-past three because that's your bath time. And because, yes, I can remember that, and yes, I can tell the time, if you really want to know." Lampie takes big steps towards the door. She completely forgets to move calmly, slowly, but what good would it do?

As she leaves the room, she hears him say something.

"Wait a moment."

"What?"

"It's not you, is it?" He has crawled back under the bed. She can barely see him now.

"What's not me?"

"The one who'll be coming from now on."

"Yes," says Lampie with a nod. "Yes, it's me, Edward. That's your name, isn't it? Edward?" She tries her smile again, but it has stopped working. He can't see her anyway.

"Isn't there anyone else?"

"No," says Lampie. "There's no one else." Then she walks out of the room and down the stairs.

One morning it was gone, of course, her rabbit. Her mother had already warned her though, hadn't she?

It was not on her bed as usual, and she found it that afternoon, hanging up in the shed, head gone, fur gone.

They did not have much money, but they still needed to eat. Yes, Lampie understood.

It was painful, but she understood.

When she has finally gone, he breathes out. How could they do this to him? Such a stupid child, such an illiterate bumpkin.

And she is supposed to take care of him? To do everything that Joseph did? No, no way, never! If she comes back, he will bite her to death.

Did she really sit with him all night, singing to him? Or did he just dream it? Oh well, so what?

No one else wanted to come, or more like no one dared to come, and so they sent that child.

If his father knew about this, then he would, he would... He would never approve. He would throw her out and look for someone else, another Joseph or someone else who was good enough for his son.

Or would he? Would he really be bothered?

Of course he would.

So where has he gone? Why hasn't he come back?

He always comes home a few times a year, doesn't he? Edward has lost count – has it been a year already?

Edward turns onto his side, sees the harness in the corner, his walking bars. He has not practised for days, of course, what with everything going on.

And I'm supposed to come all the way back from Japan for that? he can hear his father saying. *For a son who doesn't do his best, who doesn't even try?*

I was ill, he says, defending himself. I nearly died.

Ill? You call that ill? Seven weeks of malaria – now that's what I call ill. Shaking with fever, red lumps full of pus – that's what I...

Yes! he shouts. You can stop now. I know! Edward has a headache. And of course he still has not had anything to eat. He should have eaten those disgusting eggs after all.

He lies on his back. He'll practise tomorrow. First thing tomorrow morning. And this afternoon, a bath – finally!

At least, if she ever comes back, that stupid child.

Of course she comes back, at half-past three exactly. She has even brought a plate of fish, which Martha dashed to the market to fetch.

"Maybe you could pop that upstairs for him. If you go up there again. I'm not telling you to do it though, mind."

Lampie had nodded.

"I promised to give him a bath at half-past three."

"Pff," Martha had snorted. "A monster that can tell the time?"

"He's not a monster," Lampie had said yet again. But she is no longer so sure about that. He is actually some kind of monster, after all.

"I've brought someone with me," Lampie says to the mouldy bed. She still has not seen or heard Edward, but he must be under there again. "Lenny from downstairs. That's not a problem, is it?" No answer. She puts down the pile of clean sheets on top of the dirty ones. "He's a bit, um… slow. But he's also very strong and he's going to help me. It must take about thirty buckets to fill that bath, and I don't really feel like—"

"No."

"But…"

"No one is allowed to see me. That's one of the rules. Do you understand? There are rules." The voice comes out from under the bed, but the boy himself does not.

"But he's already seen you, Fish. Edward." She bends down and puts the plate of bloody chunks of fish on the floor. "He saw you this morning. He already knows that you have a tail."

He shoots out from under the bed and suddenly he is on top of her. Lampie's head bangs against the floor and she gives a gasp of fear. His pitch-black eyes are so close; she can feel his breath on her cheek.

"It!" he hisses. "Is! A! Deformity!"

"What? What do you mean?"

"Not a tai— Not that other thing! A deformity! My legs are just deformed! Say it!"

She tries to wriggle out from under him, but he is holding her arms too tightly.

"Um… But…"

"Say it!"

"Right," she says. "Fine. It's a deformity. Now let go of me."

He lets go and slides back under the bed. "I could still grow out of it. It's possible. If I practise lots. A doctor said so."

"Oh," replies Lampie. She rubs her sore head with her sore arm. What a wonderful job she has. "So what exactly do you have to practise?"

Edward does not reply.

*

Lugging thirty buckets of water is as easy as anything for Lenny. He keeps looking nervously around the room and splashing big puddles of water on the floor, but when he realizes that he cannot actually see the monster, he calms down. He empties bucket after bucket into the big iron bath. Flakes of black dirt float on the surface of the water, and dead insects. Everything here is dirty, thinks Lampie. Silently, she changes the bedclothes. Does he ever actually lie in the bed?

From under the bed she can hear the boy eating, tearing off pieces of fish with his teeth and chewing away.

"Rule number one: my head must not go under the water. Rule number two: I have to stay in for one hundred and thirty-five seconds. Exactly one hundred and thirty-five seconds, no more, no less. And you have to count the seconds. Can you do that?"

"Yes," Lampie says with a sigh. "No problem. But why is it such a short time?"

"Short is good, shorter is better." The boy is still lying halfway under the bed. He has taken off his shirt. He is white and thin, and his shoulder blades stick out.

"But isn't it nicer to—"

"Can't you just do as you're told?"

"Yes, I can."

"Good. And you have to count, because I'll forget to do it."

"Forget? But why?"

"And don't look. When I'm in the bath, you're not allowed to look. That's rule number three. Is that clear? You turn around, with your face to the wall, and you count. Out loud."

Lampie nods. She smiles at Lenny, who is waiting just outside the room.

"And when it's time, you have to help me out of the bath. Even if I don't want to get out. I still have to get out anyway. Is that clear?"

"Yes, it is."

Then he comes out from under the bed and shuffles across the room, his dark tail – no, his deformity – twisting behind him. At the edge of the bath, he takes a deep breath and tries to pull himself up. It does not work. He tries again. And again.

"I can do this," he pants. "I can always do this."

"Shall I help you?"

"You're looking."

"So that's a no." Lampie turns around and listens to him struggling and quietly cursing himself.

"Come on, you weakling, you wimp. Come on."

"You've been ill," she says. "You almost died last night – remember?"

"So? That's no reason to…" She hears him slipping from the bath and back onto the floor. "I have to be able to do this. No! Turn around! Don't look!"

Lampie does not listen. She walks over to the boy and grabs him around the waist. He is so light that she lifts him into the bath without any difficulty. His tail brushes again her, as cool and smooth as a frog's skin. Then he plunges into the water and surfaces, spluttering and shrieking.

"No! My. Head. Must. Not. Go. Under. The. Water! That's what I said! Listen to me!"

"Oh yes. I forgot."

"Or I'll drown. I already told you that! Don't you have a brain in your head?"

Lampie sighs. Stroke the rabbit. Sweet little rabbit.

"And look away! And count: seven, eight…"

"What? Already?"

"Yes, you stupid child. Ten, eleven…"

"But why? What's the point? Fine, I'll do it. I'm counting!" His dark eyes always make her shiver. "Um… thirteen, fourteen…" Counting slowly, Lampie walks to the door, where Lenny is watching from around the corner.

"Sixteen, seventeen…" she counts. "Thank you, Lenny. That was really kind of you. Eighteen, nineteen. I'll be finished here soon. You can go back downstairs if you like. Twenty. Twenty-one." She smiles at him, but then she sees that the big boy is not looking at her at all, but is staring past her and into the room, with his mouth wide open. Lampie turns around.

Edward is floating in the bath, his head half above and half under the water. His eyes are slowly opening and Lampie watches as they change colour.

Black, brown, dark-green, ochre, orange, gold. Eyes full of gold, with gold flowing from them.

Her mouth falls open too. Beside her she hears Lenny sigh, and together they stare at the dark corner of the room, which has suddenly become much lighter. She forgets that she is not allowed to look. She forgets to count.

I'm falling, thinks Edward. I'm falling and no one will catch me.

He does not trust her one bit, that child. Joseph must have said it a thousand times: short is good, shorter is better. Don't stay any longer in the water, lad. Never. Longer is dangerous.

She probably can't count. She is sure to make a mistake. There is no one to take care of him. He will have to do it all himself. He needs to keep his wits about him. He clings onto the edge of the bath. How long has it been? How far has he gone?

Finally he can feel water on his skin again. So cool, so soft. It's been such a long time, maybe he could stay a little longer, just this once? *Forget her, that stupid child. Forget the counting, forget everything, forget who you are… Feel how cool, feel how soft…*

No! That's it, that's why! That is not allowed! He strains to hear how many seconds have gone by. Surely it must be time, so why isn't she getting him out?

He can feel himself falling – falling, and no one is going to catch him.

I'll catch you, the water whispers. *Just let yourself fall. Go on.*

It is only as the boy's head slowly sinks under the water, chin, mouth, nose, only when the golden eyes are about to be extinguished with a hiss, that Lampie comes back to her senses. How many seconds has it been? She has no idea, but it must be more than…

"Um… a hundred and thirty-five!" she cries. "You can get out now!" The boy does not move, just sinks a little deeper, his hands sliding down the side of the bath. Lampie hurries over to him, reaches her arms into the cold water and tries to lift him out. She can't do it; he seems much heavier than before. "Help me, Lenny!"

Lenny does not really want to – oh, he really, really doesn't want to! – but when the girl asks him a second time, he very nervously ventures back into the room and lifts the dripping boy out of the water. Lenny keeps his head as far back as possible, squeezing his eyes shut as if he were holding a pile of venomous snakes in his arms. With a thud, he throws Edward onto the bed and dashes back onto the safe landing.

The golden eyes have shut, and the boy lies on the sheet, his chest calmly going up and down. His tail is so obviously a tail, thinks Lampie, now that she can see it properly. A thin white scar winds along it, from top to bottom, as if someone once tried to cut him open. She lays the clean white sheet over him.

"That was longer." His voice seems to come from a long way off.

"No, it was—"

"It was longer."

"I forgot to count for a moment, just for a moment. I was looking at—"

"You can't even do that."

"Next time I'll… Tomorrow I'll…"

He throws off the sheet and slides under the bed, into the darkness. "Just go away," he whispers. "Leave me alone."

So this is how it works from then on.

She brings breakfast every morning, waits for him to finish, and takes the tray back downstairs.

She is still as friendly and cheerful as possible, even though she has almost given up any hope of taming him. She tries to give him whatever he wants to have, but usually it turns out to be the wrong thing. The wrong book, the wrong map. Africa when it should be Japan. Greenland instead of Indonesia. What does she know? "You're not the brightest of lights, are you, Lampie?" her father always used to say. Well, she seems to be proving him right again.

"Shall I just teach you how to read?" the boy has already asked irritably a few times. "It's the easiest thing in the world."

"No, thank you."

"Unless you're stupid, of course."

Yes, unless you're stupid.

Whenever she gets the chance, she slips behind the curtain and peers into the distance, at her old house and at the sliver of sea, which is a different colour every day, green, grey, grey-green, blue-grey, and she longs to feel the wind blow around her head, the cool steps of the lighthouse under her feet.

"Are you still here? What are you doing? What are you looking at?"

She does not tell him.

In the afternoon, she goes upstairs to put him in the bath. Lenny helps, taking dirty water downstairs, bringing clean water upstairs and lifting the boy in and out of the bath when needed. It is always needed. Edward announces every day that there is no longer any need, that his muscles are getting stronger and he can do it himself, but every day it is still needed.

Lenny does not mind though. He waits obediently outside the room, looking around the corner of the door at the girl, for as long as he can.

Lampie counts properly to one hundred and thirty-five, without making any mistakes. She remembers to call his deformity a deformity and not a tail. She calls the boy Edward and not Fish. She blows the dust off the books on the shelves and puts them back – in the wrong place, of course. She picks flowers in the garden, puts them in a vase beside his plate. And then takes them away, because he thinks it is ridiculous. He is not a cow. She washes the dirty windows, very slowly and carefully, particularly that one window. She thinks about her father and worries about him. Sometimes she walks into the garden and looks for a while at the tree, the tree with the branch that grows up close to the fence.

So this is how it works from then on.

She comes upstairs every morning, that child, and every morning he has to get used to the fact that she is there, and not Joseph. And to the fact that she is not calm and quiet and does not know exactly what he needs, but that he always has to explain everything to her and still she usually does not understand. And to the fact that she is stupid and can't even read and wanders around his room until it drives him crazy and she refuses to leave, but goes behind the curtain to look out of the window or whatever it is that she does. Until he shouts at her, and then she generally goes.

When she has gone, he practises. He does not want her to see.

He practises until he turns blue in the face, strapping himself into the harness, hoisting himself onto his walking bars and galvanizing his muscles into action, shouting at them that they need to be stronger, that they should stop complaining, that all they have to do is carry him! But it all happens so, so slowly – in fact, it does not happen at all.

Before Joseph… When Joseph was there, Edward could take five steps in a row. Sometimes even six. And now? Two, three at most. They are clumsy hops that do not even look like steps. And then she comes back, skipping around with those legs and those feet of hers, as if it is nothing special, as if she is mocking him.

When she does that, he just wants to bite her and bully her and to make her cry.

He does not actually make her cry until he says she is no longer allowed to look out of that window. He has decided that the curtain is to stay closed from now on. And when she has finished her work, she has to go straight back downstairs. She can look out of another window, a window that is somewhere else.

"I can look at whatever I want to look at," she shouts. But he can already see the tears – ha ha.

"No, you can't," he says. "You have to do whatever I say."

"Oh really?"

"Yes, really. I'm your boss." And it's true. The house does belong to his father, after all.

"Well, a fine boss you are!" she yells. "Locked up in a little room! A fine boss, hiding away under the bed!"

He shrieks and comes after her, his teeth seeking her feet, and she jumps back and out of the room.

"Monster!"

Yes! That's right. That's what he is! He's a fearsome monster! His chest swells triumphantly. Who does she think she is? Such a stupid child. So stupid.

The next morning, for the first time, she does not come. All day long. And not in the evening either.

Lampie has been wandering around the garden for an hour now. Everyone thinks she is upstairs, but she is not. Not today. Not tomorrow either. She kicks at the nettles as she walks through them. Never again. She is so tired of this place. There is the tree she was looking for.

She is abandoning everyone, of course. And Martha is not going to like it. Lenny… Lenny certainly isn't. Oh well. They'll find someone else. Someone who is better suited to that horrible boy upstairs. Someone who does not mind being yelled at. Someone who can read and write, not an idiot like her.

The tree has lots of handy side branches. She perches on one of them before carefully climbing up to the branch that grows close to the fence, almost up to the high metal points at the top. If she is careful, she should be able to get over it without hurting herself.

Lampie slides to the point where the branch is almost too thin, and then takes a deep breath, grips the fence and tries to swing herself over it.

She can tell right away that it is not going well. Instead of swinging over the top of the fence, she finds herself hanging down on the inside, and all she can do is hold on tightly to the flaking iron rails beneath the points. She kicks her feet, but finds nothing to stand on.

So she just hangs there. If she lets go, she will fall. If she does not let go, she will dangle here for a while – and then she will fall. She does not need to look to know how big the drop is and how spiky and thorny the bushes on the ground far below are. And she is still not even on the right side of the fence.

She tries again, uttering a furious cry to give herself strength and reaching her foot up as high as she can, but it is not high enough, nowhere near.

"Emilia? Emilia Waterman! For goodness' sake! What are you doing up there?"

Lampie can't believe her ears. She recognizes that voice, doesn't she? Surely it can't be? But then she hears rapidly approaching footsteps and she sees, far below, the tall figure of Miss Amalia, who is running up to the other side of the fence.

"Have you gone insane? Come down here! At once!" she shouts. "Wait, no! Stay there! You're going to break something!"

Lampie really has no other choice than to stay hanging there.

"Hello, Miss Amalia," she mutters. Her fingers are cramping. She will not be able to keep this up for much longer.

With her long arms, Miss Amalia attempts to grab Lampie's foot through the bars. The girl yelps as she feels herself being pulled down. Miss Amalia quickly lets go.

"Hello!" She anxiously rattles the gate. "Can someone come and help? Can anyone hear me? You stupid, ungrateful child. And I was coming to bring you something too. I should really take it straight back home." She is pacing up and down on the other side of the bars, like a tiger in a cage. "What is the matter with the staff here? Appalling! So lax! As I have previously noted. Oh, I would really like to give you a good hiding – do you know that, Emilia? Why is no one coming? Hello?"

Lampie's fingers are hurting so much that she cannot hold on any longer. She looks down. There is nothing to break her fall.

Well, here I go, she thinks. Catch me, Mother! She squeezes her eyes shut.

"Go on," says a voice, just behind her. "Just let go."

She falls, just a little way, before her feet land on the shoulders of a big brown leather coat. Nick takes hold of her ankles and, when she lowers herself, her arms shaking and her hands now painful red claws, he takes hold of her, climbs down the ladder that has suddenly appeared against the fence and gently sets her on her feet. Lampie looks in surprise at Nick and then at the ladder. Where did he appear from?

"Well, that wasn't a minute too soon!" Miss Amalia says, rattling the gate impatiently. "I've been calling for half an hour. Were you asleep?"

"Are you all right?" asks Nick quietly.

Lampie nods, wiping her hands on her dress. They leave behind rust and flakes of paint – and even some blood.

"You have been luckier than you deserve, Emilia. Perhaps it would have been a better lesson if you had indeed broken something. You have thanked the man nicely, haven't you?"

"Thank you," mumbles Lampie, as she is indeed very happy to be in one piece.

"Oh, don't mention it," says Nick. Then he takes a bunch of keys from his pocket and dangles it in front of Lampie's face. "If you ever want to leave again," he says quietly in her ear, "just come and get these from the carpenter's hut."

From the what? thinks Lampie.

"Hello?" Miss Amalia is shaking the gate again. "So are you actually going to come and open this gate, or not?"

It is as if no time has passed at all: Lampie is once again walking along the path between the hedges, with Miss Amalia's cool hand on the back of her neck. There they are again, together on the doorstep of the Black House and, again, there is the sound of barking and shouting from the corridor, before footsteps approach the door and a surprised Martha, her hair oddly flattened from her afternoon nap, opens up. Lampie can see that she is thinking the same thing too: again?

"You obviously have absolutely no idea," Miss Amalia says, immediately launching into a lecture, "what is going on behind your back." She pushes Lampie past Martha and into the house.

"I was asleep," says Martha. "I have a nap at around this time every afternoon."

"As Emilia clearly knows very well. Is this the kitchen? Good."

Martha follows the two of them. "What is going on? Lampie?"

Lampie suddenly feels ashamed. She likes Martha. She should just have stayed here.

"Emilia was attempting to break out," declares Miss Amalia. "At least I assume it was not her Wednesday afternoon off. And she clearly had not finished her work." She looks around the kitchen, where the dishes are still unwashed, the table has not yet been cleared, and the smell of wet dog fills the air.

Martha picks up a cup, but then does nothing with it. "If she leaves, she leaves," she says. "This house is not a prison."

"Maybe not…" says Miss Amalia. "But you are responsible for this girl. I shall have to report this, you know."

"Oh, really?"

"Yes, really. I'm afraid, when the time comes, I shall also have to inform the admiral himself."

"Fine. Go ahead."

Lampie tries to catch Martha's eye and to signal some sort of "I'm sorry", but Martha is not looking at her.

"And now I'll tell you what I actually came here for…" Miss Amalia slides a plate and some cups aside and places a brown parcel on the table. "I should just take them away with me, Emilia, because you don't deserve them. But I'm not that kind of woman. Now go on – open it up!"

When Lampie does not move, Miss Amalia tears off the paper herself. Inside the parcel, Lampie sees a pile of dark-brown checked material. With white collars and buttons.

Martha looks furious. "Oh, there's no need. Really. I'd already made a start on something myself."

Miss Amalia takes a dress from the pile and holds it up to Lampie's shoulders. It looks far too big.

"We can all make a start," she says, her smile remaining perfectly friendly. "But what counts in life is actually finishing, is it not?"

Lampie had noticed that Martha was sewing something in the evenings, but she did not know that it was for her. How kind! Lampie has never had a new dress before. But now she has a whole stack of them. She strokes the dark-brown fabric, which is rather itchy.

Miss Amalia pushes her hand away. "Don't make them all dirty. Come on, off with that dress." Her smile grows even wider. "We're all girls together. I'm sure the housekeeper won't mind."

Martha does not smile back.

Miss Amalia hangs Lampie's dress, with the blood and rust stains, over the back of a chair and pulls a new one over her head. The dress is hard and stiff. Lampie is drowning in the dark material.

Martha takes hold of one of the sleeves, which is so long that it is dangling inches beneath her hand, and grins. "She could fit into this twice over."

"Nonsense." Miss Amalia takes the other sleeve and folds the cuff over. "Anyway, a girl of her age will grow into it in no time at all. At least, she will if she's being fed properly."

"You have no need to worry about that," says Martha, pulling the sleeve even longer. "She's just small for her age."

"She certainly is."

Lampie looks left and right at the two women, who are both holding a sleeve of her dress and looking at her as if she is a calf at the market.

"I can still picture her in the hallway when we first came." Miss Amalia suddenly laughs. "She was so terrified of the monster!"

Lampie gasps and feels Martha stiffen beside her.

"So how did that turn out, Emilia?"

"Um…" mumbles Lampie. "Well…"

Martha lets go of the sleeve and turns to the sink.

Miss Amalia straightens the dress. It almost reaches Lampie's ankles. "Very nice, even though I do say so myself. Well? There aren't any monsters, are there? Admit it."

"I, um…" begins Lampie.

Martha slams the kettle onto the stove. "Coffee. I'm going to make coffee."

"Isn't that a job for Emilia?"

"I make my own coffee," says Martha, with her back towards the woman. "Lampie, show the lady out, will you?"

"So kind of you to offer," says Miss Amalia. "But I never drink coffee." She takes one last look around the messy kitchen. "So now you have no need for concern about Emilia's clothing. Which will give you more time for… other necessary tasks. I'll be sure to visit again. Good day to you."

Martha mutters something that does not sound very much like "good day" at all.

Lampie realizes that walking is not very easy in her new dress. The heavy fabric wraps around her legs and the sleeves have slipped back down and are swishing to and fro as she walks.

Halfway down the corridor, Miss Amalia stops.

"However…" she says, "in spite of…" She waves her hand around, at the cracked tiles and the cobwebs in the corners. "I still think I've found a good place for you. Of course you were only at school for a very short time. But long enough to see that it wasn't really for you, hm? Eh? Writing. Reading."

"Oh," says Lampie. "But that was because… I had to leave because my mother…"

"Learning is not for every child. That is just the way of the world."

Lampie stands a little straighter. "But someone in the house wants to teach me how to do all that. How to read and write, and everything." It popped out before she even realized, and she really hopes Miss Amalia is not going to say, "Oh, yes? And who might that be?"

But Miss Amalia's laughter fills the entire corridor. "Oh, Emilia! Don't get ideas above your station! It'll only end in disappointment." Then she turns on her heels and walks to the front door.

Lampie is so angry that she can see spots before her eyes. She wants to run down the long corridor and kick the school-teacher's legs, as hard as she can, but it is as if the stiff, stifling dress is holding her back. It probably would not be a good idea anyway. So she stays where she is and just glares at the tall woman, who by now is almost at the front door, still shaking her head at the girl's impertinence – and then Lampie remembers something. Something much more important.

"Wait!" As quickly as she can in her dark-brown straitjacket, she runs after Miss Amalia. "My father!" she calls. "How is?… Where is?… Do you know how my father is?" Now she could almost kick herself. That was the first thing she had wanted to ask. The only thing.

Miss Amalia pauses on the doormat. "Oh," she says. "Really? You want me to tell you that now?"

"Yes," pants Lampie. "Yes, I do."

Her head heavy with thoughts, Lampie walks back to the kitchen, with the dress chafing her legs. She does not think she has ever disliked anything quite so much as the schoolteacher and her gift. What she really wants to do now is to run upstairs. She wants to look out the window, whether that boy likes it or not. But first she has to face Martha. Who must be angry with her.

Martha is sitting at the dirty kitchen table with her coffee. When she sees Lampie, she shakes her head, but then she starts to laugh. Really loud.

"My goodness, child, what an awful dress that is. You look like a nun. Please, just take the thing off!"

She throws Lampie's old dress to her. "Another couple of evenings and you'll have a new one from me. I'm sure madam will have all kinds of comments to make, but let her."

Relieved, Lampie drops the heavy dark dress onto the floor and pulls her dirty, soft, old one back over her head. Then she looks at Martha.

"I wasn't really trying to run away," she says shyly. "Or, well, um… I don't know, it was all suddenly so… I'm sorry."

"No need." Martha pushes a cup over to her and pours some milk into it. "I'd leave too if I could. But that's not an option."

"Isn't it?" asks Lampie.

"With Lenny? Where would we go?" She looks at the girl. "Is it so bad upstairs? Does he?… What does he do?"

"Oh, nothing," says Lampie. "It's actually fine. Mostly."

"What if I, um… took a turn going up there now and then?"

"No need." Lampie thinks it is kind of Martha to offer though. She knows just how much the housekeeper does not want to go upstairs.

"Fine. Would you just go and call Lenny?" says Martha. "He's been shaking in the pantry for an hour."

Lampie opens the door and the dogs storm in, barking, with a scared-looking Lenny peering after them.

"She's gone now, Lenny. You can come on in." The boy lumbers into the room, nervously sits down at the table and picks up his scissors.

"I'm going to pop upstairs," says Lampie when they have finished eating.

"What? Now?" asks Martha.

"Yes," says Lampie. "Just for a minute."

She thunders up the stairs, barely even knocks on the door and doesn't wait for an answer before running into the room, heading straight behind the curtain and looking out.

It is twilight, and the darkness is slowly creeping up out of the sea. *The mouth of the night* – that is what her mother always used to call it. As she is looking, there, in the distance, a light goes on. It grows brighter and slowly starts to turn. That is where he is, she knows that now. He is not allowed to leave. He might not have enough food and he certainly does not have anything to drink. Perhaps he is cursing everyone, her most of all, but that light – it is her father. He was the one who lit it.

"What are you doing?" The voice that comes from under the bed is grumpy and sleepy, as if she has just woken him up. "I told you that you're not allowed to look out of that window. But you're still doing it anyway. And where were you today? I haven't had my bath. Don't you know what happens if I don't—"

"Tomorrow," says Lampie. She stays behind the curtain for a little longer, watching. "First thing tomorrow morning. I promise."

"But it always has to be—"

"And do you know something, Fish?"

"Edward."

"Do you know what you're going to do after that?"

"What?"

Lampie jumps off the window sill. There he is, lying on the floor, half under the bed, the thin white little creature with the head that is too big. She can't help but smile.

"What?" he says again, angrily.

"You're going to teach me how to read." She nods because she is suddenly absolutely certain about it. "How to read and write."

Part Four

SUMMER

Augustus dreams of her face every night.

He can see it so clearly that he can almost touch it. Her hair over her eyes. Her soft cheek. The tiny hairs on it, like down.

Then he whacks the dream with his stick and it bursts apart.

He wakes up, full of regret and gasping for air. Every single morning.

Augustus squeezes his eyes shut to block out the light and listens to the thoughts racing through his head. Thoughts about what he should never have done, about what he should do now, about what he would always do from now on – if he only had the chance. Which he knows will never happen. And that is his own fault.

He cannot drown his thoughts, as there is no drink in the house and the door is nailed shut.

Everything he could break is already broken.

Every insult he could hurl at himself has been said a hundred times. Bungling fool. Good-for-nothing. Failure.

Failed as a man, as a sailor, as a father. Failed as a lighthouse keeper.

Although perhaps that last one is not entirely true. There is still something he can do to make up for his failure, just a little. Not for himself – he does not care about that. No. For Lampie.

So he hauls himself upstairs, every afternoon, step by step, on one leg and a stump. It takes half an hour. Sometimes longer. He makes light in the darkness, and stands and watches as it glides across the black water.

Swish on, swish off, swish on. It is there and then it is gone, as if no light had ever shone.

Swish on, swish off. Swish light, swish dark. First you have a wife, swish, and a child, swish, a job, a leg. And then you have nothing. As if they had never been there.

At daybreak, he extinguishes the light and stares out across the sea at that rock. That damned rock.

Usually he stays up there all day long. He watches the sun move across the sky above him, sees the shadow of the tower growing shorter and then longer. Until it is time to light the lamp again.

In the evening, a neighbour brings him a pan of food. An iron pan, one that cannot break. But not for want of trying.

She has to walk all the way along that slippery sea path, so he always says politely, "Thank you."

"I hope you enjoy it," she replies, and that is it. She is not a good cook.

As she climbs upstairs the next morning, Lampie does not feel quite as certain as she did last night. When she gets to the room, she puts down the tray of food on the floor in front of the bed.

"Breakfast," she says. She sits in the chair to wait until he is ready.

Behind her, on the shelves, are the books with their brown spines. She can hear them quietly shuffling around. They are clearly nudging one another and whispering about her.

Her? That child with the mop? She's going to learn how to read? They rustle their pages, chuckling at her. *Whatever is she thinking? She'll never be able to learn. As if! Can you imagine?*

Lampie sighs and looks at the floor. Maybe they're right, she thinks. She will just have to wait and see.

I'll just have to wait and see, thinks Edward as he crawls out from under the bed, if I'll ever be able to teach her something, that stupid child. He has laid out some things on his desk: paper, ink and a book with strips of paper marking the easy sections. But then he sees her sitting there, dangling her legs, in Joseph's chair.

"Not in that chair!" he shouts. "Get up! This instant!" She must not sit there, absolutely not.

Shocked, Lampie jumps up and sits on the floor. With her legs crossed, and her arms too. Then she puts one finger up to her lips.

"What are you doing?"

"That's what you have to do at school, isn't it?" she says. "That's how you're always supposed to sit."

"Oh." He has no idea. "Right, then. We'll start with… Um, you were at school for two weeks. So what do you already know?"

She puts her hand in the air and points a finger at the ceiling.

He looks up.

"What? What's up there?"

"If you want to say something, you have to raise your hand."

"There's no need to do that. You can just speak to me."

"E."

"E?"

"Yes," says Lampie. "The letter E."

"You went to school for two weeks and you can read the letter E. What else?"

She shrugs. "That's it."

"Fine, the letter E." He writes an elegant flowing letter on a sheet of paper and holds it up. "The letter E is the fifth letter of the alphabet. Our alphabet, the Latin alphabet, is based on the ancient Phoenician script, which in turn developed from…"

She puts her hand up.

"What?"

"That isn't the letter E."

"Yes, it is."

"Isn't. The E is made out of lines." She draws in the air with her finger.

"Ah," says Edward, nodding. "You're talking about the capital letter, the upper-case E."

"The what?"

"This is the small letter, the lower-case version. But it is most definitely an E."

"Oh," Lampie says. "But…"

"It's very simple," Edward explains. "Every letter of the alphabet can be written in two ways, depending on its function in the sentence. If it's at the beginning, then…" He is starting to enjoy himself a little now.

She whispers something.

"What did you say?"

"Never mind," says Lampie. "Doesn't matter."

The books on the shelves are helpless with laughter. *It's difficult, isn't it, little girl?* they giggle. *Oh yes, reading's not for everyone, you know. It takes years and years of study. Look at her, that little mop girl who thought she could learn how to read and write in no time. Whatever was she thinking? Don't get ideas above your station…*

She stands up.

"Where are you going?" shouts Edward. "We're not finished yet!"

"Downstairs. To help Martha in the kitchen or something. To mop the floor."

"But I was going to teach you to read."

"Forget about it. There's no need." She is already at the door. "I'm too stupid anyway."

Edward throws his pen down. "Good grief!" he says. "You coward. You… defeatist! No wonder they threw you out of school."

"They didn't throw me out."

"No? So why did you leave?"

Lampie stops, but she does not turn around. "Because… because I had to look after my mother."

"Oh," says Edward. "What about after that?"

"She died."

"Well, then you could have gone—"

"And then I had to help my father. And then… then something happened and I came to live here. And now I have to take care of you."

Edward sits up straight. "You don't have to take care of me. No one has—"

"Oh really?" Now Lampie turns around. "No one has to take care of you? So are you going to do everything for yourself from now on? Fetch your food, your water, get yourself into the bath, out of the bath, count to one hundred and whatever—"

"One hundred and thirty-five."

"Yes, I've actually got the hang of that now! Do you think I enjoy doing it? Getting bitten and shouted at by a… by a… nasty reptile!" She knows she should not be saying it, but right now she does not care.

"And do you think, do you think?…" the boy begins. He is stumbling over his words, almost spitting because he is so angry. "Do you think I like to have you doing all those things? A brainless bumpkin like you? Who doesn't know anything, who can't even read?"

"Well, teach me then!" yells Lampie.

"That's what I'm trying to do!"

"But I'm too stupid, eh?"

"Maybe," says Edward. He looks at her with his pitch-black eyes. "But maybe not."

He stares at her as she stands there in the doorway. At her ragged dress and that wispy hair, at the bruise on her cheek, which has almost faded away, the bandage on her wrist. Then he turns to look at the chair, the desk stacked with books. That chair is where Joseph sat. That book, *The Three Musketeers*, is one that Joseph often read aloud to him – Edward knew it almost by heart, but that was what made it so good. That atlas, too, had given them hours of pleasure – leafing through it, tracing maps and tracking his father's travels, with neat dotted lines and crosses to mark the harbours. There is the book about birds and the one about flowers, full of dried petals and leaves that the old man brought for him. Exactly the right flower on exactly the right page. It is nowhere near full. It probably never will be complete now.

He takes a sheet of paper from the desk and draws two lines on it. A horizontal one and a vertical one.

"Let's just start again. I'll make it easier." He points. "Look, child. This is a T."

"My name is Emilia," says Lampie. "And you're a child yourself."

"Emilia, then."

"But you can call me Lampie too. That's what they—"

"Look at the letter!"

Lampie looks. "Er. Eh?" she says.

"No, T," says Edward. "*This* is an A." He takes another sheet of paper and draws a shape on it. He makes the sound of the letter. "A. That is the letter A."

"Mm," says Lampie thoughtfully.

"Excellent. We can do that one too!" He takes a third sheet of paper.

Four lines with two points at the top. "Mm. That's the sound of the letter M. Look. Let's start with those letters, shall we?"

He places the three sheets of paper on the desk, on top of Alexandre Dumas. They will not be getting around to that book for a while.

"So we have a T, an A and an M."

Lampie shrugs. If he says so. She still has not stepped back into the room.

"So what does this say?" asks Edward.

"I don't know," says Lampie. "They're just letters."

"M-A-T," says Edward slowly. "What does that spell?"

"No idea."

"Just look at the letters."

"But I'm too stupid."

"No, you're not. Read it. M-A-T. What does that say?"

"How should I know?"

"Go on. What does it say?"

"I DON'T KNOW!" yells Lampie. "Mat or something!"

"Exactly," he says. "Mat."

"Really?" She comes closer to the desk and takes another look. M-A-T. She feels quite lightheaded. She understands. She can read a word!

Lampie is speechless. Mat. She thinks of all the mats she has ever walked on or swept or beaten... There are so many mats in the world, and now she can read all of them. M-A-T. This is easy!

"And now let's continue," says Edward in a very important voice. "We'll take another letter. This is the letter C. You see? It's a C. And I'll take away the M and put down the C instead. Now what does it say?"

Lampie frowns. Her mat is gone, her lovely mat, which she understood. That mean boy has turned it into something else, something she is too stupid to read. With a letter C or something. C as in, "You see?" Yes, she sees that she can't read C.

"C? Like the sea, with the waves and?..."

"No, no. I see where you're going wrong. That's the name of the letter, but that's not what it sounds like in this word." Then Edward pronounces the sound for her, very clearly. Lampie stares at him, feeling more stupid than ever.

But then suddenly she gets it. The light goes on. She sees the C!

"Cat," she says. "C-A-T."

"Cat," replies Edward. He looks almost as happy as she does.

And now the world is made up of letters, of letters that she can read. Everywhere she looks, she sees the letters C and A and T and M.

On the spines of books, inside the books, on Lenny's scraps of newspaper. In the kitchen, the C is on the coffee tin, and the T is on the packet of tea.

Lampie skips along the corridors all afternoon. She wipes

a clean T in the dirt on the windows. She mops the slowest M ever in the longest corridor of all.

Tomorrow she is going to learn how to write her name.

Then she will finally belong in this world.

E-m-i-l-i-a. She can do it – just look, she is writing it with her finger on the tablecloth. She also learnt M-a-r-t-h-a in no time at all, and L-e-n-n-y, with two Ns. You see? She writes it down for him and even though he cannot read it himself, he looks at it as if it is one of the wonders of the world.

F-i-s-h, she writes.

"Edward," says Edward.

By the next day, she has learnt how to spell that too. As if the letters were ready and waiting inside her head. All she had to do was learn them.

She quickly grabs Lenny's newspaper, while it is still in one piece. A whole new world opens up: *Rob-ber-y*, she reads. *Cow dead. Fair com-ing to town.*

Lenny sits there with his scissors, looking bewildered. What is he supposed to cut up now?

*

But then, one afternoon, Nick comes into the kitchen at lunchtime and walks up to Lenny. His shoes are muddy and he is carrying something wrapped in a dirty cloth.

"Not on the table," barks Martha. "What on earth is it anyway?"

Nick puts a finger to his lips, unwraps the cloth and places the contents in Lenny's lap. "For you."

"Oh," says Martha. "Just look at that, son."

Lenny does not look though. New things are far too scary. He looks up at the ceiling, where there is nothing. Nothing new in any case.

"Go on, Lenny. Take a look," says Lampie. "It's a pair of scissors."

Lenny takes a peek. Yes, scissors. But these are very big scissors indeed. Nick lays a hand on his shoulder.

"They're shears, Lenny. You'll be able to cut lots and lots of things with them," he says. "You have no idea."

With frightened eyes, Lenny follows Nick to the garden. The dogs go too, with Martha anxiously following. She does not know what is going on. Whatever is Nick up to? Lampie quickly slurps down the rest of her soup and runs after them.

In the garden, Lenny is already snipping away at a black-berry bush. Gently at first, one branch at a time, but before long the shears are taking great big bites. After all, cutting is what Lenny does best. Nick points out where: brambles, nettles, big prickly bushes and then the green hedges behind them, taller than two men put together. Branches fly every-where, and the dogs run around with big pieces in their mouths.

When Lenny sees what they are doing, he throws the shears onto the ground, runs after the dogs and takes back the branches. With the branches in his hand, he searches for the right spot. He takes hold of a twig, a leaf, and tries to match it to what he is carrying. Where did it go? Was it here? Or there? He looks despairingly at the mountain of green. How is he ever going to put it all back together again? How can he solve this puzzle?

Lampie places a hand on his arm. "There's no need to do that, Lenny. A hedge isn't the same as a newspaper," she says. "It can just stay as it is."

The boy looks at her in surprise. There's no need?

"It'll grow back by itself," Lampie explains.

Nick nods as well. "Go on, Lenny. Cut it. You can cut whatever you like."

And Lenny cuts.

The weeds around the Black House are blooming in so many different colours: pink, yellow, the white flowers of the blackberry bushes, the purple spikes of the thistles. The soft plumes of grass scatter their seeds all around and even the nettles are wearing crowns.

Lampie has been given her new dress and she is so pleased with it that she only wears it when she is sitting quietly at the kitchen table and not touching anything dirty. And as she sits there, learning the whole world, one letter at a time, Lenny is outside, clipping the tall hedges around the house. They become rounder and smoother, developing bumps that look like backs, and like heads. Slowly they turn into animals: two dogs, a rhinoceros, a swan.

All day long, everything smells of grass and cut leaves, and Lenny takes wheelbarrows full of clippings to the compost heap. The days grow longer and warmer.

Martha notices that she sometimes bursts into song as she is doing the dishes, and that she feels like making complicated soups. The kitchen belongs to her all day. And in the evening, when her son has drowsed off over his dinner and so she has sent him to bed, Nick no longer runs away straight after eating, but stays at the table to talk. Sometimes they even play a game or two of cards. Because she asks so nicely, Lampie is allowed to join in. However, you can't spend half of your life around pirates without learning how to play poker like a champion, and she bluffs brilliantly, making mincemeat of them and winning all Martha's savings that very first evening. She gives the money straight back though, and after that they play for matches.

Martha pushes a quarter across the table to Lampie. The girl can take it to the fair on Wednesday afternoon, she says, feeling unusually generous. And then she sends Lampie to bed too.

Lampie creeps up the stairs and heads to the room in the tower to look out at the lighthouse. She opens the window just a little way, closes her eyes and listens. Down there, at the foot of the cliff, she can hear the sea gently splashing.

"Goodnight, Father," she whispers. Then she tiptoes out of the room and back down the stairs. She does it so quietly that Fish does not wake up. Or so she thinks.

So that's it, he thinks. Her father is out there somewhere, and that's why she always goes to that window.

The boy is lying in the darkness, looking up at the underside of his mattress. His own father is out there somewhere too, far away at sea. Cutting through the ocean on his white ship, defying the waves and so on. He has no idea where. But no matter how far away he is, his eyes always find Edward, even in the darkness under the bed.

What are you doing there? Resting? Why? After all your hard work? All your progress? And what progress would that be, boy?

He can picture him so clearly, sitting at his desk, like the last time he was at home.

"Just a little progress. That is surely the least a father can expect of his son. For him at least to try his best."

The way his father had looked at him… He was not even angry. If only it had been anger.

"But it would seem that I was mistaken about you. You are not made of the right stuff after all."

"Stuff?" Edward had feebly replied. "What kind of stuff?" He honestly did not understand what his father meant.

"Oh, goodness, boy! Don't always take things so literally."

The rusty springs coil up into the darkness to where he can no longer see them. He can smell the summer night; she forgot to close the window.

And this is how Lampie finds him the next morning, when she comes for her reading lesson. Edward is still on the floor, not lying under the bed now, but in the middle of the room. He is struggling and kicking like a rabbit in a snare. There is a kind of leather harness around him, with belts and straps, and at the bottom a clumsy leather shoe that is sticking out at an angle. His tail is hopelessly entangled; the belts have buckles and holes and he keeps tugging away at them, but he cannot undo them.

"Fish? What are you doing?"

"My. Name. Is. Not. Fish!"

"Do you need some help?"

"No. Go away."

"Couldn't I?… If I just undo the buckles on that… What is that thing you're wearing?"

"Go away, I said!" His hands keep fiddling with a prong that he cannot get out of a hole. The whole rotten contraption is twisting his back and he cannot take it off, he simply cannot take it off.

"Are we going to do some reading?"

She is still standing there. "If you don't go away this instant…" he pants. "I'll bite you in two. I'll bite your stupid head off. I'll…" He struggles and kicks, but he only gets even more entangled.

"If you'll just let me…"

"No! How many more times do I have to tell you? No!"

He hears her put down the tray on the chest of drawers and then she is suddenly standing there behind him. He feels a small tug and the harness slides off him and onto the floor. He is free. He wants to slip straight under the bed, but he has no strength left in his arms. So he lies there, with his cheek on the carpet.

"What on earth is that thing?"

He groans. She can't just go away and leave him in peace, can she?

"Are you learning to walk with it? Are you trying to walk on your, um… deformity?"

She can see for herself, can't she? She's not blind.

"But why?"

"Because I made a promise."

"Who to? Your father?"

He gives a little nod. She picks up the breakfast tray and puts it down beside him on the floor. He smells the fish and it makes him feel sick.

"Take that away. And take yourself away too. I have a headache."

"But you have to eat," she says. "You know, a bit of strength for the day ahead."

What nonsense, thinks Edward. He lies on his back.

"My father," he suddenly hears himself saying. "My father has a box in his desk." He was not planning to tell her, but that little box has been on his mind all morning. "There's an arrow inside it, he showed it to me once. A tiny little poisoned arrow."

"Oh yes," says Lampie. She sits down on the floor beside him. "The kind that the Bushmen use."

He looks at her. "How do you know that?"

"Oh, I heard it somewhere."

"Who from?" She can't read, but she knows that?

"From Crow, from… from a pirate I know."

"You know a pirate?"

"I know plenty of pirates."

"Oh," says Edward. She knows pirates? He can't imagine that at all. So she must be lying. He sits up a little straighter. "But, anyway, that arrow – it came out of my father's leg. Someone shot him with it, somewhere in the jungle. It was an ambush, of course. The cowards. His men took him straight back to the ship. Poison arrows are really dangerous, because…"

"Yes," the girl says with a nod. "They give you blood poisoning."

"Um… Yes. Well, anyway, the ship's doctor was ready and waiting with a saw. But my father was still conscious. Any other man would have fainted from the pain, but not him. He took out his pistol. 'Anyone who attempts to saw off my leg is a dead man,' he said. No one dared to go any closer. The poison was slowly creeping higher. 'But, captain,' they begged. 'You're going to die. You have to—'"

"I thought he was an admiral."

"That was later. Do you want me to tell the story or not?" She nods.

"'You're going to die, captain,' they said. 'Let us do it.' No. My father shook his head. 'A man with one leg is no man at all,' he said. And then his leg turned completely black. Any other man would have died. But not my father. He sweated it out. You can only do that if you're really strong. Two weeks later, his blood was clean. A month later, he could walk again. Mind over matter."

Edward sighs. It is the best story his father has ever told him. It is pretty much the only one too.

"Then it can't have been actual blood poisoning."

"Yes, it was, you stupid child."

"Blood poisoning always kills you. Everyone knows that."

"Not my father," replies Edward. He does not care if she believes him. He just feels so very, very tired.

The girl lies down beside him on the floor and together they look up at the flakes curling off the ceiling.

"My father has only one leg," Lampie says after a while.

He raises his head and looks at her. "You're lying."

"No, I'm not." She shakes her head. "Honestly. He has one whole leg, but the other one is just half a leg. He walks with a limp. Which causes all kinds of problems with… with his job."

"Because he's a pirate too, of course." It's all lies – he's sure of it.

"No, he's a lighthouse keeper."

"So how did it happen, then? His leg, I mean."

"I don't know, he wouldn't tell me."

"Oh." He lies back down again. "Does he mind?"

The girl thinks for a moment. "Yes," she says. "He does."

Augustus would never talk about it. And he never wanted anything that might help either. Not a strong crutch, not a wooden leg.

"Gone is gone," he used to say. "Dead is dead. I'm not going to go out and get myself a wooden wife, am I? So I'll just have to do without. It's not a problem anyway, is it?"

No, thinks Lampie. It wasn't a problem. As long as I was there to do everything for him. And what about now? How is he doing it all by himself? Suddenly she really, really wants to go home. Wednesday afternoon, she thinks. Wednesday afternoon off.

The scent of grass wafts in through the window, along with the sound of Lenny's shears snipping away. Seabirds sail around the tower, shrieking happily at the sun.

"What a din," says Edward. "Shut that window."

"But it's nice with the window open. Everything smells so good."

"Do as I say." He rolls under the bed. "I've got a headache. Shut the window and go away."

"Aren't we going to read?"

"Not today."

She picks up the tray and walks to the door. "I'll be back at half-past three for your bath then. See you later."

He does not reply.

When she goes outside, Lampie sees Lenny's ladder sticking up over a hedge. He keeps moving it along just a little way, and then climbing back up and going on snipping. The two hedges at the front are beginning to look a lot like dogs, with open mouths and their ears flapping in the wind. The tall hedge at the back is turning into a rhinoceros, and the long spine that winds between them is getting dragon spikes.

Oh, Lenny, she thinks with a smile.

The air around her is warm and soft and even the house no longer seems quite as angry, now that all those little owl chicks are growing up in its ivy.

Lampie looks up at the tower with its windows so firmly shut. How is she ever going to get that boy to come outside with her?

Nick carefully puts the ship down. It is as long as his little finger and as wide as his thumb, but it has masts and sails, portholes and even a tiny little mermaid as a figurehead. The bottle he is about to slide it into is ready and waiting on the table. Then it can go with the others, which are gleaming away on shelves on the wall. Rows and rows of bottles, all with little ships inside, ships that should never have fitted in through the necks of the bottles, and yet there they are. He has a whole system of little strings to pull, hinged masts, folding sails, and his fingers are learning to work on a smaller and smaller scale, and every ship is an improvement on the last one.

He used to make real ships, big ones, but this is much more fun. A lot less tiring too. He could do it all day, in his hut that lies hidden in the garden, so overgrown and entangled with thorns and nettles that no one knows it is there. Squirrels on the roof, robins at the window, a bit of porridge, a cup of coffee now and then – that is all he needs.

Until suddenly there is something that he has to do. Even though his hut is so deep in the garden, he still hears it when the girl calls. He hears it every time.

Help. How am I ever going to get over the fence? Help, I'm falling. Help, how am I ever going to get that boy to come outside? How am I ever going to see my father again? Help! Will someone help me?

Well, then, that someone would be him.

Perhaps because she is her mother's daughter, perhaps that is why. He had not thought about her for years. But he saw it as soon as she walked through the gate. She looks so much like her.

Nick pushes back his stool and stretches. Then he looks for a few suitable pieces of wood, a saw, a sanding block. He should still have some wheels somewhere too. After brushing down his workbench, he sets to work.

The little boat will have to wait.

Behind his hut, up on two blocks of wood, there is another boat, a real rowing boat, made of green wood. That is for later, but it is already waiting there. Upside down, but you can still read its name: *Emilia.*

Lampie has almost finished the dishes when she hears a shrill whistle from outside. From the kitchen window, she sees Nick on the path, beckoning at her to come out. He is pulling something behind him: it is a cart, newly made, softly sanded, with a handle on the front and a leather cushion inside, which you could rest your tail on, for example, if you happened to have one.

Lampie instantly knows what it is. She runs to the kitchen door, with the tea towel still in her hand.

"Yes!" she says. "That's perfect! However did you know?"

"No," says Edward. Of course he says no.

Whatever is she thinking? Out of his room? Downstairs? And then outside, where it's cold and the wind's blowing, in some cart that will bump about all over the place so that he'll fall out and have an accident? Outside, where everyone can *see* him? He can't imagine anything worse.

"Yes, but…" says Lampie. "You'll finally be able to see everything for real. The trees, the birds, the—"

"I already know all of the birds," says Edward, and that's true. Their plumage, their breeding spots, how they build their nests, the songs they whistle – he knows it by heart.

"But that all came out of a book! And that isn't the same."

He does not see why not. The real world just makes more noise – that's the only difference.

"No," he says from under his bed. "Go away. Come back when it's half-past three."

"Yes, but…" she says again. She can never keep her mouth

shut. "We could even go through the gate one day. To the sea. We could go to the lighthouse if you like. Or go and take a look at the harbour, or…"

"The harbour?" whispers Edward. Where his father's ship always moors? "Really?"

"Well, maybe not today."

"Oh, then forget about it. Never mind."

"But we could do it later. We'll go for a short ride first, just in the garden."

"Hmm. No, I don't think so."

"I'll be really careful."

"No."

"And it's not at all chilly out."

"No."

"And I can put a blanket over you."

"No." He has crawled back under the bed, as far as he can. "I don't want to, and you can't make me. I said NO."

They sit there without saying anything.

"Anyway," he mumbles after a while, "I can't get down the stairs."

Edward blinks. The light is bright, and the air is cool on his cheeks. There is so much light here, and lots and lots of sky. It is enormous, with clouds floating across like gigantic monsters, and the trees are towers with grabbing branches and they are green, everything is so ridiculously green, and there are so many smells all at once and so many sounds: rustling and whistling and barking, and on the other side of the garden there is a thin man in a big coat, and huge dogs are running by and everyone is staring at him, of course, at Edward. He buries his nose under the blanket and squeezes up closer to

Lenny, who responds by holding him more tightly and that helps a bit.

"Come on," says Lampie. "Down these steps and we'll be there. We'll just go for a little trip this afternoon, just a tour of the garden. Lenny, you can be the horse."

Lenny nods seriously. Yes, he will be the horse.

The cart has been crafted for Edward. His body fits snugly inside, and his deformity can rest on the cushion. Lenny carefully lays him in the cart, and Lampie puts the blanket over him. The horse takes hold of the handle and starts to pull.

Edward squeezes his eyes shut. Why did he let her persuade him? He is so stupid, so stupid. This is going to be so painful and uncomfortable. So he braces himself. But the wheels turn smoothly, the blanket is warm, and the cart hardly bumps at all. Off they go, down the path.

Edward takes in his surroundings, bit by tiny bit. A piece of bark. A tuft of grass. There: a branch with a hundred leaves that are moving in the wind. Maple, he thinks. Or a lime tree, or… He can't see very well, because everything is intertwined. The birds are not taking it in turns to squawk and whistle either; they are all singing away at the same time and he cannot identify a single one of them.

All of this has been here all along, he thinks. All of it belongs here.

All of it except for him.

He looks up. There is his tower, with his window, and his bed inside. If only he were back up there right now.

"Are you all right, Fish?" asks Lampie. "It's not bumping you about too much, is it?"

"I'm fine," says Edward grumpily. He can handle it, he really can.

Lenny is a good horse. They go as slowly as anything. Around the smelly pond, past the half-finished hedge animals: the dogs, the dragon, the swan, which still has a bit of a lumpy neck.

"Not bad for a horse, eh?" says Lampie, gesturing towards the animals with a smile.

"What? He didn't make those, did he?" Edward can't imagine it.

"He certainly did," says Lampie. "Lenny is a wonderful clipper."

Lenny looks back, both proud and shy. Then he gives a little skip and a whinny.

"Shall we go to the gate? Or do you want to go back inside already?"

Edward shakes his head. Just a little longer. He is already sitting up a little straighter. He can do this. He is brave enough. There is nothing to it, in fact.

Lampie brings him whatever he points at, so that he can take a closer look: a strange clump of fluffy moss, a flower that looks like an umbrella, which he intends to find in his flower book later, a stone with a vein of gold running through it. He gently places them under his blanket.

The dogs are curious and come over to take a look. The bolder of the two even sniffs at his hand. Edward is brave enough to hold out his hand – it's easy, in fact. You just have to let them know who's the boss – that's what his father always says. He knows their names: Douglas and Logwood. When he calls, they come to him, just as they come to his father. Well, they do if Lenny gives them a bit of a nudge.

He pulls the blanket down a little. "We'll go out again tomorrow," he decides.

"Great," says Lampie. "Where would you like to go? To the sea? To take a look at the harbour?"

His dark eyes widen. "Tomorrow? Can we do that?"

"Why not?" says Lampie. "I can ask Nick for the key. We'll just go out through the gate and then we'll…"

"Whatever are you doing? Have you all gone completely mad?"

Martha is standing on the path with shopping bags full of fish and leeks. "No, no, no. This simply will not do. Go on! Back inside with the lot of you. Right now."

"Why?" asks Lampie. "We weren't doing anything wrong."

"Lenny, do as I say. Now."

Lenny always does whatever his mother tells him to do, and so he turns the cart around, so quickly that Edward almost rolls out. He gives a squeak, but then ducks back under his blanket. With a sniff, Martha walks past. She does not look at the boy in the cart.

Lampie does not understand. "But what's the matter? Why aren't we allowed?"

"Because you're not! He's not allowed outside, he can't be on display for everyone to see. You understand that, don't you?" Martha pushes her son ahead of her through the garden. She strides on with her bags, looking at Edward as little as possible. Lampie stomps angrily after her. She had thought it was such a good idea.

"And certainly not…" Martha stops walking for a moment and gives the girl a stern look. "Certainly not outside the fence. Not ever. Never. Do you understand, child-who-never-listens?"

"But why not?"

"Do you understand?"

"Yes, I understand."

When they get inside, Martha shuts the door with a bang. The sun remains outside, and the long corridor is dark and cold.

"Go on," she says. "Upstairs with him." She points, but she still won't look at the boy in Lenny's arms. "No, wait. This affects him too." She puts down her bags and takes something out of her pocket. "There was a telegram at the post office. Finally. The master's coming home."

Edward's face turns pale. "When?" he says. "When's he coming?"

"I don't know. He didn't say. Soon. A few days? A week? Who knows?" Martha irritably beckons Lampie. "You, come with me to the kitchen, right now. When I think of all the work we still have to do, I feel quite faint, I really do."

Edward does not want to go out in the cart. Never again, he thinks. How did he let himself be distracted from what is most important? He stops giving reading lessons and he skips his baths. He has to stand – to stand and to walk. He practises all day long. Pulls himself up and falls and pulls himself up again and falls again. He goads himself on. Weakling, wimp, don't give up! He does not give up.

Not that Lampie has any time for reading. Martha is trying to squeeze a year's work into a week, and everything needs to be clean. Now. She sends the girl into rooms where she has never been before, and Lampie sweeps out fireplaces, blows dust off rows of books and waves dusters out of windows.

Martha tells Lenny and Nick to clip the ivy from around the windows and then clean out the filthy pond. The house smells of swamp and rotten leaves for two whole days, and Lenny and Nick have to eat their lunch outside, because the mud is dripping off all their clothes and they only have to look at something to get it dirty.

Lampie runs around with tea and sandwiches. She does not really care if the house is clean in time for the admiral's return. But she does have a plan.

On Wednesday morning, Martha comes into the kitchen, all hot and bothered.

"I completely forgot to peel the potatoes. I should have…"

"Already done it!" says Lampie, dropping the last one into the water with a splash.

And the soup is already simmering, Martha notices. She goes to make tea, but it is already there. Lampie pours two cups and gives her one. Martha sits down to drink her tea and catch her breath. She can still remember how disappointed she was when this skinny little girl turned up at the house, and how she would have preferred a strong man, who would be of some use to her. But she could not do without Lampie now, she has to admit. She will have to tell her as much, one day, when she is in the right frame of mind.

"I, um, I was wondering if I could… leave now," the girl suddenly announces.

Martha gasps. "What? You want to leave?"

"Yes."

"For good? You can't do that, you know."

"No, no, just for this afternoon. It's Wednesday, isn't it? And didn't you say I could go to the fair?"

"Did I now?"

Lampie nods. "Yes," she says. "You promised."

"Yes, but I didn't know then that…" Martha glowers at her.

"Before we know it, the master will be here, and I haven't even started on his room yet."

"I've already done it."

"What about the bed?"

"I've put clean sheets on it. And dusted everything, all those cages with beetles and stuff. And if I go and do the windows too, can I leave after that? Please?"

Martha downs her tea. This is all she needs. She wants to say no, because she always wants to say no. But then again. She was only just thinking: the house is brighter, him upstairs is keeping more or less quiet, and Lenny is clearly crazy about the girl. A bit too crazy… Far too crazy, in fact…

"What about the outside of the windows?"

"I'll do that too! If Lenny can help me with the ladder. Please?"

How can she say no? "Hm…" says Martha. And then, a little later: "Maybe."

"Oh, please," says Lampie again. "I really, really want to go."

"To the fair, eh?" Martha can't help smiling a little. When was the last time she went to the fair herself? So long ago. First alone and then arm in arm, and then later…

"Um… yes," says Lampie. "To the fair."

But Lampie does not want to go to the fair at all. Why would she?

As soon as she has left the house, as soon as she has promised to enjoy herself and to be back by six, and has skipped through the gate like a girl who is looking forward to an afternoon of fun, as soon as she has gone around the corner, she starts to run.

Lampie runs stumbling downhill to where the forest stops and the sky opens up. She stops there, just for a moment. Finally. She sees the distant grey water and smells the salt. And there in the distance is the town, the harbour, the path to the lighthouse... She runs on.

The streets are almost empty; here and there small knots of people are hurrying to the field where the fair tents have been pitched. She can hear snatches of music coming from that way, and some laughter and screaming. Good, then no one will pay any attention to her this afternoon. She goes around two more corners and then she is at the harbour.

The afternoon is grey and the sea breeze chases drops of water along the quayside and then upwards, like rain in reverse. Lampie wipes her cold cheeks and licks her hand. Salt. It tastes good.

And there is the lighthouse. Grey against the grey sky. Lampie stands and looks. She wants to drink it in.

She runs up the sea path, the tide is out and it is dry enough, so it is easy today. But the closer she gets, the more she sees that everything has changed. Her house no longer looks like her home. Big, rough planks have been nailed over the green front door with the copper knob, crisscross, so many of them that she can hardly even see the green. The window next to the door has been covered with a splintering sheet of wood. The bench outside is gone, the vegetable garden has been flattened. Only the prickly grass that she always tried to weed out is still growing there and has finally found the space it needs to spread out its tough roots and to overrun everything else. As Lampie stands there, she feels her eyes start to sting.

Come on, Emilia, she says to herself. Hey, it's just grass. You can get rid of it in no time. She wipes her nose, her tears, seawater, all so salty, and then she walks on. She keeps looking up at the windows above and at the railing around the lamp room. Maybe he is in there right now. Maybe he will see her. Maybe he will even wave. She peers up, but she does not see anyone. Nothing moves.

"Father!" she calls, and again, but no face appears at a window. At the house, she rattles at the hatch and tries to bang on the door through the planks. "Father, it's me! Can you hear me? Or not? Father!"

The wind blows her voice away and the planks give her nasty splinters; in no time, she has three of them jabbing into her. She pulls out two with her teeth, but the third one breaks off and a big chunk of it stays there, deep in the fleshy mound of her hand.

"Father!!" She yells again, as loud as she can. No one comes. Nothing moves.

What did you think would happen? mutter the planks on the door. *Think you could just pop round for a nice cup of tea? This house is a prison now. It's our job to guard it. When will he be allowed to leave? In seven years' time. Seven. Have seven years already gone by?*

No… sighs Lampie and she sits down on the doorstep.

So long to go, so long to go! scream the seagulls circling around the tower. *Whatever were you thinking? What did you want?*

I just wanted to see how he is, and…

That man? hisses the prickly grass. *That man with the stick? The one who hit you?* tease the waves rushing by. *The bruise has only just faded, hasn't it? Forget about him. He's forgotten all about you.*

It's not true, it can't be, he would never…

Oh, no, of course not, everything around her whispers. *Because he was always so kind to you. Child, he loved his bottle more than you. You knew that, didn't you?*

Lampie can picture her father, stumbling around the house, looking for that one bottle he could have sworn he had left, or the money he thought he'd hidden away. And, whether he found the bottle or not, he always disappeared.

What are you doing here? You have a new home. Go and live there. Forget about him.

Yes, but he wasn't always like that. It really was different, once upon a time. This beach, this doorstep, she can see it all as it used to be. The pirates pulling their boats up onto the sand, the shrimps over the fire. Her father making jokes, her mother… Her mother, her mother…

You know, the thing about the past, the whole world whispers in her ear, *is that it's over.*

Lampie rests her head on her knees and feels herself getting slowly colder and wetter.

Yes, but, she thinks, Miss Amalia told me. He is here. And the lamp was on, I saw it. So why won't he come to the door?

"Hello there. You're Lampie, aren't you?" a voice says suddenly. "I suppose you must be, eh?"

Lampie looks up. There is a woman standing on the sea path. She has a pan in her hand.

"Is it your afternoon off? Did you decide to come and visit? Oh dear, I'm afraid you're out of luck." She climbs up onto the doorstep, and Lampie feels the soft fabric of her skirt brush her cheek.

"Mr Waterman!" the woman shouts through the hatch. "Look who's here! Your daughter! And your food too, if you want it! So you come down here, do you hear me? Mr Waterman?"

Lampie has stood up now and is listening. But she does not hear anything, just the rain tapping on the door, because it really has started pouring now.

The woman shakes her head. "He came down yesterday," she says. "So we won't be seeing him for a while. It's not your lucky day."

Lampie wipes her cheeks. Ouch, that splinter is really deep. Her whole hand is throbbing.

"But he is there?" she asks, shivering. "He is upstairs?"

"Where else would he be?" The woman has a wide, friendly face with wind-and-weather cheeks. "He's not going anywhere. But sometimes he doesn't come downstairs for days on end, even if I call up there a hundred times and tell him his food's getting cold." She takes the lid off and shoves the pan under the girl's nose. "Look, it's good now, but it won't be for much longer." Drops of rain splash into the grey mush.

"But sir will come down in his own good time. What's he doing up there? Nothing, I reckon, because there's nothing up there, is there? Light on and light off again, and that's it. You might think eating would break the day up a bit. But no, he's as stubborn as an old…" She looks at Lampie and does not complete the sentence.

"Oh well," she continues in a friendlier tone. "What a palaver, eh? And what about you? I've thought about you too, you know, all alone in that Black House. Is there really a monster? I guess not, eh, because you're still here. And it looks like you're still in one piece. You remember me, don't you?"

No, I've never seen you before, Lampie wants to say, but suddenly she is not quite so sure.

"I live over there. Remember?" The woman points to the end of the sea path, where there is indeed a small house, half hidden behind a rocky outcrop. "I haven't been there that long, just since my husband… I've waved at you so many times, but you didn't ever seem to notice me. Always so worried, always talking away to something…" She looks back into her pan. "Well, it doesn't look like he'll be wanting this today. Would you perhaps like to, have you already?… Oh but, child, you're soaked through! Come on, come with me, for a cup of tea at least." She takes Lampie's hand. When the girl says, "Ow!" she stops to have a look at the splinter and then goes on talking as they walk.

"And I have a nice clean needle for you too. We'll get that splinter out in no time. It's from those planks, I'll bet. Ouch, yes, splinters can really hurt. Not that long ago I got a—"

Lampie tries to jump into the conversation as if it were a skipping game. "But, but," she says, "how is he? My father? Is he well?"

The neighbour stops and looks back at the lighthouse. "Well? Hmm, I wouldn't say that. But he's still alive. And I think he's missing you terribly."

"Really?" asks Lampie. "Has he said that?"

"No, not in so many words." The neighbour pulls her onwards by her good hand. "But, even so, it's still true. Come on, and then I'll give you some tea. What a shame you had to come today of all days. Are you going to the fair? Do you still have enough time? Would you like to sleep over? Oh no, of course you can't," she says when Lampie shakes her head. "I'll tell him you've been. I'm sure he'll be… Wait a second, I have an idea."

She stops halfway along the sea path and gives the girl a grin. But then a cloud passes over her face.

"Oh no, of course not. I thought you might be able to… But that won't work. Or will it? Can you write?"

For the first time on her afternoon off, Lampie smiles.

Part Five

THE MERMAID
IN THE TENT

Everything costs twenty-five cents and Lampie has exactly that: one quarter, the quarter from Martha, hidden away in the depths of her pocket.

She can go on the Big Wheel or on the Swashbuckling Swing Boat, or she can have one attempt at fighting the strongman in his red-striped shirt, who seems to be angry with everyone – well, she certainly won't be doing that. One sausage with sauerkraut, one go on the shooting gallery, where you can win bottles of scent and paper roses, one spoonful of the miracle oil that will cure all ills… But Lampie already knows what she wants to do.

Among the jostling crowds and the splashing beer, she has already spotted the candyfloss tent. She is going to buy some and carefully take it home, all wrapped up, for Fish. As a surprise. He always looks so grey and tired. Maybe it will help.

But first she wants to look around – there is so much to see.

A watery sun has broken through the clouds and is turning the sky purple and green and gold. Lampie's hand does not hurt any more and this evening or tomorrow or by the next day at the latest her father will have read her letter and will be thinking about her.

Dear Father, she wrote. *How are you? I am good. I can see you from the windoe of the house where I live. Will you wave to me? You have to eat. I will come agen soon when I can have time of.*

Lampie smiles and pushes her hands deep into the pockets of her new dress. Writing – it really is a miracle.

People are screaming and whirling around, and groups of children are chasing each other, on their way to the next attraction and the next. *Look at that! And that! Look over there!* No one is paying any attention to her, thank goodness, everyone is looking at the parade that is marching straight across the crowded field.

Stripy clowns on long stilts are pulling along small white dogs on strings. Jugglers are tossing all kinds of things into the air: scissors, bottles, apples, oranges, rabbits. Stacks of acrobats are swaying and sweating and swinging their flags. Fire-eaters are breathing flames...

Here it comes! Here it comes! It's the elephant!

What? There's an elephant coming? I have to see this, thinks Lampie. She climbs onto a barrel and tries to look out over the heads of the crowd. Yes, here it comes, from behind that tent over there, the elephant, waving its trunk.

But suddenly she sees something else. She sees a pair of eyes. Fish's eyes.

Fish's eyes? It's impossible, but she really can see them. The same shape, the same colour. Gold with gold flowing from them. These are not really his eyes though; they are painted on a sign outside a tent, over there behind the circus parade, which is still passing by.

Lampie jumps off her barrel and runs between legs, past fire-eaters and stilt-walkers, she squeezes past warm, drunken bodies, jumps over someone who is lying on the ground – maybe sleeping – and then she is there.

Phe-no-men-al Freaks, she reads slowly; the letters are yellow and black and flaming red. Beneath the letters are painted pictures of a fat lady with a beard, a dwarf with a head that is far too big, and a woman with Fish's eyes. She has wild green hair and a fish's tail. It's a mermaid. A real one! Could she be inside the tent?

In the ticket booth, a very fat man is resting his head on his hands and shouting in a hoarse and bored voice: "Monsters and frrreaks… Only a quarter… Phenooomenaaal frrrreaks… Roll up, roll up! Come and see the freaks!" He has a strange eye and his arms are enormous and covered in tattoos. "Behold the quirks of nature! The bearded lady, the Siamese twins, two heads, oh yes, all the way from Russia. The bird-woman and a maiden of the sea. Don't put your fingers in the water! Only a quarter!"

Lampie fingers the quarter in her pocket. She hesitates. What about the candyfloss?

Inside the tent, her eyes take a moment to get used to the semi-darkness. On the floor, a path of canvas leads past various alcoves, each illuminated with a lamp. She is all alone – everyone else is outside, watching the parade. Lampie can hear the shouts and laughter.

In the first alcove, there is a cage with a small, feathered woman inside, perched on a stool. She looks like a child, but she is old and almost bald. Her dark beady eyes look straight into Lampie's face.

"Hello," whispers Lampie.

"Hello, child." She has a piercing, high-pitched voice. "Feel free to take a look. That's what I'm here for."

"Um, I'm looking for the mermaid," says Lampie shyly.

"Oh, her. Down the corridor on the left, in the tank at the back. But there's not much to see, and she doesn't talk either. I do. It's nice to have a chat, eh? Or would you like me to whistle something for you?"

"No, thank you," says Lampie, quickly walking on, past the next alcove, where the fat bearded lady is sitting in a chair, quietly snoring. She reminds Lampie of someone, but she can't quite remember who. As Lampie tiptoes past, so as not to wake her up, the woman suddenly opens her eyes and looks at her. She stands up and it seems as if she is about to say something, but Lampie hurries on, past a sad-looking black man who is so tall that his head is touching the top of the tent, past two old ladies who have only one pair of legs between them and a hairy creature that is sitting at a desk, writing. She feels naked and uncomfortable; the Phenomenal Freaks are all looking at her too.

Fish would fit right in, thinks Lampie. Sitting here all day and being gawped at. She gets angry at the thought of it. People just have to take the time to get used to him. Then he doesn't seem so scary any more and he's almost not really that strange either. After all, she got used to him, didn't she? But people don't come into this tent to change their minds; they come to be frightened. A quick "Eek!" and then off to the next attraction.

Eek! She jumps.

There is a dwarf around the corner. Loose, not in a cage or anything. He is smoking a cigarette and he gives her an angry look.

"Hey, nothing to see here. I'm on my break. Go on, move along." He gestures with his large head.

"Um… I'm looking for the mermaid, sir."

The dwarf points over his shoulder. "In the back. Have fun."

He sucks long and hard on his cigarette.

The aquarium at the back of the tent is surrounded by wild scenes painted on sheets of wood. Mermaids with sharp teeth and swishing tails are fighting giant fish. They are armed with tridents and blood is spurting out from the places where they have stabbed the fish. Golden eyes flash dangerously; scales glisten.

Something is floating inside the tank. The water is dirty and green, so Lampie can't really see very much in there. What she can see though, has a tail and green hair too. Or is it seaweed floating in the water? The skin is grey, the tail is covered with algae and barnacles, like driftwood that has been rotting away in the water for a long time. That's what it smells like too.

Lampie goes closer. She wants to see the mermaid's face. The poor creature only just fits inside the tank, and she has hardly any room to swim or to stretch her tail.

Lampie wants to leave. It's creepy here, and sad. And it smells so bad. But she takes a deep breath, not through her nose, and goes one step closer. There is no movement in the water. She places a hand on the glass.

Go on, turn around, she thinks. I need to know. I need to know for Fish.

"Hello! Wakey wakey! You have a visitor!"

Lampie jumps at the sound of the dwarf's voice. He is standing right behind her with his hands on his hips.

The mermaid jumps too. With a wild movement of her hair, she whirls around. Water splashes out of the tank. She glares at Lampie, with her face right up against the glass. Just as angry as Fish can sometimes look. Because yes, she has exactly the same eyes.

Edward lies panting under his bed. The muscles in his arms are shaking. But there is no time to rest: he has to stand up, he has to stand up. He has to! He slept badly and, when he did manage to sleep, he had strange, restless dreams. But that is no excuse, of course.

Finally, for once, he has to walk downstairs by himself. On his own legs. And his father will stand at the foot of the stairs, his mouth wide open with surprise. No, no, he won't be surprised; he'll just nod and smile at his son.

A man's job! I had my doubts, but it turns out that you're made of the right stuff after all. Bravo, Fish.

Edward! Edward! He has become completely used to the stupid name that the stupid child keeps using. But it is not his name. His name is the same as his father's! Another week to go, or maybe three days, or it could be tomorrow.

*

His father has grey eyes with the sea in them, his cheeks are rough from the wind. Edward would like to look at that face all day long, until he knows every hair, every wrinkle by heart, to make up for all those months when he doesn't see him.

But there was never enough time.

After just half an hour, the admiral would start to become restless again, picking things up and putting them down. Sitting at his desk. Writing something down. While Edward still had so much to tell him, to ask him, to show him.

Behind him, Joseph would start shuffling his feet and mumbling that it really was time to go now.

"We won't hold you up any longer, sir. You must have all manner of things to do, of course."

His father would then mutter back something along the lines of, "Yes, yes," or, "It's sad, but true," and would stand up from his chair. And then the best part would come. But also the worst, because it was always the last part. His father would walk over to him, reach out his hand and take hold of him, just under his chin, and look at him with narrowed eyes, as if searching for something in his son's face. One time he had even briefly placed his hand on Edward's head. He can still remember exactly which time, and how big the hand had been, and how heavy. It did not happen again, no matter how much he hoped.

"Well, make sure you do your very best," the admiral had said. "The next time I want to see you standing."

"I promise, Father," he had said in a voice that was as deep and manly as possible. But he was already talking to his father's back.

"I need to talk to you later, Joseph," said the back.

Taking one last look, Edward would try to remember as much as possible: the figure standing by the desk, the desk itself, the cases full of insects and butterflies, the masks on the wall, the stuffed animals and, oh, the tiger, the tiger on the floor! There was never enough time. Then Joseph would shut the door and carry him upstairs.

Usually the admiral stayed at home for only a few days. He ate there and slept there and had a dinner party or two. Then the boy would listen so carefully all day, trying to catch something of what was happening downstairs. But not much sound reached all the way to the room in the tower.

While he waited, he would take out all his most interesting books, his neatest essays, his finest maps.

"Ah, lad," Joseph would say, when he saw that Edward, pale with exhaustion, was doing extra practice, skipping sleep, and constantly looking at the door. "I'll ask him. But he's busy – you know that."

The admiral never came upstairs.

After a few days, he always went back to sea. For a year, sometimes shorter. Usually longer. Much longer, it seems this time. He has already lost count.

But he must not count, he must not think, he must not be so damned sentimental. He has to act. Get on with it! Practise! Why are you just lying there?

Then the door flies open and that stupid child runs in.

"You have to come with me," she says. "You really have to come with me, Fish. We'll take the cart, but Lenny can't come – it'll be too complicated. I'll get you down the stairs. I can pull you."

He has no idea what she is saying. He is not even listening.

"Stop calling me that," he says. "And go away, I'm busy." He tightens the straps of the harness.

"Edward, then. But you really have to come with me, Edward. If we go now, we can make it before dark. Listen, I've…"

"Are you deaf? I said: I'm busy." He shuffles back over to the walking bars and starts to pull himself up.

"Fish, you can't… Edward, you can't stand. So stop trying."

He gives her his blackest look and shows her his teeth. She takes a step back but does not go away. He concentrates on his arms again. But she does not give up. She walks over to him and pulls at his shoulder.

"This is important," she says. "You really have to listen."

What could be more important than this? It is almost evening again and he does not know how much time he has left. All those days when he did not practise…

"I've seen your mother."

"What?" He crashes to the floor. That girl kneels down beside him. She smells of the wind and of outside; her hair is wet.

"Fish. Edward. Really, I've seen your mother. At least I think it was her."

He does not have a mother. So it can't be true.

"She had eyes just like yours and—"

"So what?" he sneers. "Eyes? What does that mean? Everyone has eyes."

"No one has eyes like you, Fish," she says. "No one at all."

Now what? His eyes?

"And what kind of eyes are those?"

She takes her shard of mirror out of her pocket and holds it in front of his face.

"Haven't you ever seen yourself? Take a look. And when you go into the water, they turn gold."

Edward stares into his own eyes.

And suddenly he remembers what he dreamt about last night.

The wheels squeak and grind and they still have so far to go. Nick and Lenny let the cart out through the gate while Martha was working in the cellar, so she did not notice anything. Nick turned the key in the lock and Lenny stayed behind, watching sadly through the bars as Lampie and Edward disappeared into the forest.

"It's bumpy," says Edward. "And this blanket stinks. Where on earth did you get it from?"

Lampie needs all her breath to pull him.

"Ouch, mind where you're going!" says the boy. "You have to go around the stones. And that wheel's wobbly. I think it's about to come off."

Lampie stops for a moment. "Be quiet," she says. "Someone might come along." For a while, there is silence.

"Is she beautiful, this mother?" Edward asks very quietly.

"She looks like you."

"That's not what I asked."

"But she's more… whole. You're half and half. And she is completely, um, mermaid."

"And her hair is green."

"Yes."

"And her legs are…"

"Yes."

"Was she nice?"

"I don't know, she didn't actually say anything."

"I bet she isn't." Edward stares into the distance. "No one's nice."

"I'm nice. I've pulled you all the way here."

"Then turn around. Take me back home."

He says it, but he is not sure that it is what he really wants. He dreamt about her last night, about this mother, or whatever she is. He does not understand how it is possible; he has never dreamt anything like that before.

He sees her for the first time and he already knows her so well.

Her face is his and his face is hers. Their tails are the same and their hair fans out in the same way.

Laughing suddenly feels so easy. It comes out of their mouths in bubbles. And there is suddenly so much to laugh about.

Then she takes his hand and pulls him along. They shoot forward, into the deep water, deeper than he could ever have imagined.

Big shadows of whales swim in the distance; smaller fish dart past in shoals. All around him everything is waving and glittering and rippling, and she strokes his cheek and swims past him, laughing, and he finally belongs somewhere.

But dreams are just dreams.

"Forget it," says Edward. He is cold and all that bumping has made him feel sick. The road is full of potholes. "Forget it," he repeats. "I've changed my mind. We're going home."

Lampie turns around and stares at him. "You must be mad!"

"We'll go another time. I need to think about it first. I have to practise walking. I want to—"

"We can't! The fair will be gone," says Lampie. "They never stay for long. They might not even be there tomorrow. If it's your mother, then we have to find out now."

"I don't need a mother," says Edward. "I've never had a mother. I'm used to not having a mother. So just take me home."

"No," says Lampie. She is absolutely certain that she must not do that.

"I am your boss!" Edward says in an angry whisper. "My father is—"

"Fish," Lampie suddenly says in a strange voice. "You need to get back under your blanket. Now. And you have to be quiet and not move at all."

Someone is coming around the corner, heading towards them, and Lampie immediately sees who it is.

She looks around. The undergrowth is thick to the left and the right, and there are bushes full of thorns. Can they quickly find something to hide behind? Do they still have time? But the tall figure is swiftly coming closer. Lampie has not forgotten how steadily she always strides.

Her? Again? she thinks. What is *she* doing here again?

Yes, what is she doing here? Miss Amalia? On her way to the Black House? Again?

Nothing in particular, she tells herself. It is Wednesday afternoon, and she has sent those annoying children home. She is just going out for a walk and she is allowed to go wherever she wants. And that just so happens to be here, on the path to... Well, yes. To his house.

It is quite a climb, and she is slightly out of breath, so she loosens the bow under her chin.

Even though she is such a great admirer of the admiral, Miss Amalia is not as keen on that house of his. Far too large, and so draughty and dirty. It is no wonder that people start telling strange stories. About monsters and so on. Of course she does not believe a word of it.

And she also does not like the road that leads there. It is so sinister here, in this dark forest where the sea mist lingers. If someone were to come along... Someone who meant her harm... If she screamed, who would hear her?

She laughs at herself, because of course there is no one else here. That would be ridiculous. Wouldn't it? Ah, but someone is coming.

Miss Amalia peers along the road with anxious eyes. But then her face brightens, as she can see who it is now. Oh yes, her eyes are still in excellent condition.

The girl, Emilia, is walking along, pulling a sort of cart behind her. A cart with something in it. Something that… She sees the girl stopping and trying to turn around. As if she is startled, as if she has something to hide.

Miss Amalia shakes her head. She might have known.

A child like that, from that dirty lighthouse. You could be certain, no matter how well behaved and shy she might seem, that she would steal the cushions out from under you as soon as you were not looking. She has stolen something, that girl. Stolen from the house where she was so kindly welcomed, and this is how she pays it back, the ungrateful brat. She is quickly trying to pull a blanket over whatever is in the cart. But not quickly enough, my dear girl.

The admiral should be grateful, thinks Miss Amalia. At least someone is still keeping an eye on what is going on in his house, as he clearly cannot expect his staff to do so.

It's just as well, she will say to him, *that someone was around with eyes in her head and your interests at heart.*

You are a marvel, Miss Amalia, he will say with that funny little smile he sometimes has.

Miss Amalia would rather have a crowd stoning her in the town square than ever tell anyone what she sometimes hopes for. A man all on his own, in that big house. Someone should be keeping an eye on him, shouldn't they? And why should that someone not be her? She is a woman, is she not?

"Emilia! What a coincidence, meeting you here like this." Miss Amalia holds out her hand.

"Hello, miss," says Lampie. She gives her hand a very quick shake.

"You're not wearing your new dress."

New dress? thinks Lampie, and then she remembers. "No…" she says. "It, um…"

"Were you on your way into town by any chance? Is it your free Wednesday afternoon?"

That was yesterday, wasn't it? Oh no, it's still today. Lampie gives a little nod. "I'm allowed to go to the fair."

"To the fair? How nice. Is the admiral home yet?"

"Not yet, but almost, I think. We're busy cleaning everything."

"And they just let you have the afternoon off?"

"Yes, I have to, I mean, um, I'm going to…"

"To the fair, you said? And you're taking something with you?"

"No," says Lampie.

"So what's that, then?"

"Nothing." Lampie can't think of anything to say. She sees Fish move a little under the blanket. Oh, please just let her walk on, she thinks. Why won't the woman leave her alone? Why won't she mind her own business?

"You're probably wondering: why won't this old woman mind her own business?" She laughs but it does not sound very friendly.

Lampie shrugs.

"But I really would very much like to know what you have there. Will you show me?"

Lampie shakes her head. She sees the blanket move again. Stop it, Fish.

"Are you sure about that?"

Lampie nods. "Yes, and I really have to get going, miss. I'm sorry."

She tries to pull the cart past the schoolteacher.

Miss Amalia looks at her badly sewn dress and her worn-out shoes. It is not that she does not understand… A child like that, she has never owned very much, and now she is in such a big, wealthy house. It is tempting fate, it really is. Of course it is her duty to inform the admiral and she plans to do exactly that; in fact, she is already looking forward to it. But if anyone in the world has a tender heart, thinks Miss Amalia, then it is her. A big heart. So big that she can't help but smile at the girl.

"Emilia, do you know what? Why don't you show me what you have in the cart and confess to me honestly that you stole it, and then we'll take it back together?" She looks at Lampie with a serious expression on her face. "Honesty is the best policy, child. Of course the admiral will punish you, as is only fair, but I shall personally ensure that it is not too…" Then Miss Amalia realizes that the girl is not listening to a word she is saying and that she is trying to pull the cart past her.

"Emilia Waterman, I have given you a chance and, if I were you, I would take it! Show me what you have under that blanket. This instant!"

"No, miss." Sweating away, Lampie struggles to pull the wheel over a stone. "I can't."

"I know very well what you have in there, girl."

224

"Goodbye, miss," says Lampie. Finally managing to free the wheel, she starts to run. But Miss Amalia has been expecting that.

"Emilia," she says sharply, "the game is up."

She reaches out one long arm and yanks away the blanket.

In a flash, she sees it coming for her: pitch-black eyes, sharp teeth. There was a monster under the blanket!

That's not possible, thinks Miss Amalia. Monsters don't exist. But there it is, slithering towards her, opening its jaws to bite…

"Fish! Don't do it!" shrieks Lampie.

And Fish does not do it, not really. His teeth graze the arm of the woman, who stumbles back and falls and opens her mouth to scream. But by then Lampie has thrown the blanket over him, grabbed the handle, and she is running onwards, so quickly that the cart almost tips over and Fish only just manages not to fall out.

"The m—" Miss Amalia gasps. "That was the m—"

Lurching and stumbling, Lampie runs on. She glances back over her shoulder, but Miss Amalia is not coming after them. She is still sitting on the ground with her skirts spread out around her. She watches them go, clutching her wrist, until they turn the corner.

Lampie runs on around another two corners, and then she has to stop to catch her breath. She spots a shed that they can hide behind for a while. Fish pulls the blanket down a little and peeps out.

"Wh-who was that?" he stutters. His face is completely white.

Lampie takes a few deep breaths. "That," she says, "was the teacher from the school."

"From the school? Which school?"

"My school."

"You've never even been to school."

"I have! For two weeks."

"And she was your teacher?"

"Yes, she was my teacher."

"Was that when you didn't learn how to read?"

"But I did learn how to read." Lampie giggles. "I could read the letter E."

"Oh yes, the E…" Edward laughs too, but then he gives her a worried look. "She saw me," he says. "No one's allowed to see me."

Lampie shrugs. There is nothing to be done about that now.

"I hope you give her nightmares," she says. "Really bad ones."

"She's not coming after us, is she?" Edward asks anxiously.

"I can't see anyone."

"Maybe we should just go home."

"No," says Lampie firmly. "It's not very far now. Really."

They can see the first houses in the town already. She can hear the fairground music in the distance.

Staying in the shadows as much as possible, Lampie pulls the cart to the fairground. The tent is off to one side, where there is no music and there are hardly any people.

Edward peeps through a gap in the blanket. "Are we there yet?"

"Ssh! Yes, over there in that tent."

The fat man is still sitting in his wooden booth, next to the painted boards. He is reading a newspaper now.

"Only a quarter…" he mumbles, barely looking up.

A quarter. She had forgotten about that. She does not have a quarter left.

QUARTER

The fat man has only one eye that can see; the other is a dark hole with something blue glinting at the bottom. His pale tattooed flesh is pressed up against the glass on every side; he only just fits into the tiny booth. Anyone without a quarter can already admire his entire troupe on his arms: the bird-woman is whistling out of his armpit, the mermaid is coiled around his upper arm and, on his neck, the dwarf is playing cards with a skeleton wearing a top hat.

Lampie takes a deep breath and walks over to the booth. "I've already paid once this afternoon, sir," she says. "But I'd like to take another quick look. Can I go in for free?"

The man does not even look up from his yellowing newspaper. "In is in," he mumbles. "And out is out. Only a quarter."

"I don't have any money," says Lampie. "But I still need to go in, just for a minute."

The eye glances up from the newspaper and at her face. Then the man shakes his head and goes on reading.

"What if I promise to bring it tomorrow?"

"We're leaving tomorrow."

"Well, what if I…"

"Pay up or clear off."

Lampie looks at the man in his filthy shirt. With all his tattoos and with that eye, he could easily be a pirate. They used to give her money sometimes, when she sang sailors' songs for them. The sad ones worked best, the ones about someone who was longing to be where they were not: at home or at sea. Then the tears would run down their cheeks and they would give her everything they had in their pockets: copper, gold, pearls, they did not even look first to see what it was. Sometimes it was pieces of string and fish hooks. She used to have a whole chest full of treasure, which was all hers, her mother said, for when she was older. But one day her father had found it, and the next day it lay empty on the floor. She clears her throat.

"Sailor, sailor, where do you roam?" she begins to sing. It is far too quiet; he does not even look up. Again. "Sailor…"

"What are you doing?" whispers Fish, sitting up a little. "When are we going inside? We were going to go into the tent, weren't we?"

"Shh!" hisses Lampie. "And don't move an inch!"

The man in the booth is still looking at his newspaper. Did he really not notice anything? She stands up, taps on the glass and starts again, louder this time.

"Sailor, sailor, where do you roam?

Have you no mother who's waiting at… um…"

He looks at her as if she has gone mad. She does not see any tears in his eye or rolling down his cheeks.

"The lips of the sailor's bride taste like salt…" Lampie

begins, because that one always worked. But it is no good – she can see that already.

"Well, well," says the man, with a strange laugh. "A serenade for Uncle Earl. Fancy that! Why would you?…"

"I wanted… to make an exchange…" whispers Lampie, with a very red face. "I thought, um… a song for an entrance ticket, or… but never mind." She looks around. If this won't work, what else can she do?

"Oh, it was a swap you wanted, was it?" Now the man has put down his newspaper. His eye looks the girl up and down, from head to toe, and he leans as far forward as he can, with the counter pressing into his stomach. "Sweet and silly songs are no good to me." He smiles, but it is not a very friendly smile. "But I can think of something else…"

He beckons Lampie closer. Curiously, she takes a step towards him. What could she have to swap? What does she have that he might want?

The big man purses his lips like a fish. He points at them with one fat finger. "How about a little kiss? Just one? Here?"

"What?" It takes Lampie a second to understand. "Oh," she says, taking a step back. "No, thank you."

"Two. Two kisses. One for you and one for your cart?"

"No, I'm sorry." Lampie bends down to grasp the handle of the cart, but instead slips and falls down in the cold mud. The fat man laughs so much that the whole booth shakes.

"Don't be scared, sweetheart. Just one would be fine, and you can leave your little cart here. Uncle Earl will keep an eye on it."

Lampie walks away, slipping along in the mud, pulling the cart behind her.

"Ohhh…" she hears from behind her. "Ohhh, what's just one little peck?" Then he bursts out laughing again. "Mwahaha! The look on her face! Oh, they love me, they do, all the girls! They love me!"

Three tents on, she can still hear him laughing. She drags the cart roughly over a clump of grass.

"Ow! Hey!" Edward calls from under the blanket. "Ow, stop it! Careful!" Then he bangs his chin on the cart and falls silent. Lampie finds a spot between two tents, with no one else around.

"Bleurgh," she says, shivering. "Oh, bleurgh. Yuck."

"What?" asks the boy. He is sitting up now. "What happened? What did he want?"

"A kiss," spits Lampie.

"A what?"

"A kiss."

"From you?"

"Yes."

"Why?"

Lampie shrugs. "He just did," she says. "That's what men want, isn't it? That or a quarter. But I don't have any quarters."

"But you do have kisses?"

Lampie sighs. Yuck, oh, yuck.

She rubs her hand over her lips. What should she do? How are they going to get inside that tent? It is getting darker and colder and before long everything will be closed. And she does not want to go back home. Fish will see his mother today – and that is that. So should she just do it? She sighs. Just one, two, three, eyes closed – and hup, they can go into the tent. She thinks about Uncle Earl and she feels a bit sick.

Inside the cart, Edward is wondering what he is actually doing here. He feels cold under his blanket and the world around him is suddenly so big: music, noise and shouting on every side. Someone might come along at any moment and pull off his blanket, and look and point and scream. He is tired of all the new things around him, tired of getting frights all the time, and his head is suddenly filled with all sorts of thoughts about things he never had to think about before. Mothers. Lips. Kisses.

He fidgets around; the cart is terribly uncomfortable. Why would anyone want to do that, to kiss someone? To have someone else's spit on their cheek. On their mouth. In their mouth…

"Bleurgh," he says, just like the girl. He peers up at her; in the semi-darkness he can just about make out her face, her mouth, her lips, which look pretty soft, and pink, and spit-free too.

"Fine!" he says, so loud that it makes her jump. "Then we just won't do it. We're going. Take me home. Now."

He wishes he was already there, under the bed as usual, where he belongs.

"No." Lampie shakes her head. "We have to do this. I'll do it. Come on, it's only a kiss."

She pushes Edward back under his blanket, even though he still has a lot to say, and pulls the cart back across the field, past a group of slurring men who almost stumble over her.

"Hey, look out!" she barks at them.

"Look out yourself, chickie!" one of the men shouts while the others go on singing:

"Oh, down on the quay where the red lights shine,
We'll drink our fill of whisky and wine!
A night of good cheer, with flagons of beer,
And…"

"Hey, wait a moment, chickie," the same voice calls again. "Where are you off to with that cart?"

Get lost! thinks Lampie. All of you, you can just get lost! She is going to walk on, straight ahead, and go over there to the man in the ticket booth. She'll give him a kiss, or even two if she has to, and then Fish will get to see his mother. It is going to happen, even if…

"Lampie?"

She almost bumps into someone again. But then she is not looking where she is going. She sees a tall, thin man leaning over towards her. He is standing with his back to one of the torches that are being lit all over the fairground now, but she still recognizes him instantly.

"Hello, Mr Rosewood," she says.

"It really is you!" Mr Rosewood reaches out his hand as if he wants to stroke Lampie's head, but he does not do it. "Lampie!" he says. "How good to see you, child. I've thought about you so often. How are you doing?"

Lampie shrugs. How is she doing? She is angry and she is worried, here with Fish in this big, open field, and she is cold and she is about to do something she really does not want to do, just to get some money.

"I'm fine," she says.

"And how about your father? I haven't seen him for so… People are saying that… Is it true that?…"

Before Lampie can hear what people are saying, a small woman comes striding quickly across the dark swamp that the fairground has become. She pushes her husband to one side and stands right in front of Lampie.

"Ha!" says Mrs Rosewood. "So here she is! At the fair!" She looks Lampie up and down and then stares at her cart. "You see!" She thumps her husband's arm. "And after what everyone said… Locked up in that terrible house, that's what they said. Eaten up by that monster, my goodness. Well, I said, I don't believe it, not one bit, but if it's true, I said, if it's true, then I'll tear up the bill for what they still owe us. Because that's what I'm like, you know—"

"Hilda," says Mr Rosewood with a sigh. "Do calm down, my love. We're just happy that Lampie is still alive, aren't we?"

"Yes, delighted!" cries the grocer's wife. "And with all her arms and legs still attached, or so it would seem. Walking around here, having fun. With *our* money. That's right. You might not think so, but it's true. We've never seen a cent, so—"

"So nothing." Mr Rosewood hooks his arm around his wife's elbow. "So we'll leave Lampie in peace and we'll go home now. You did want to go home, didn't you?"

But Mrs Rosewood does not move an inch. "So, whatever you have there in that cart, it actually belongs to us. Whatever it might be." All three of them look at the lump under the blanket. "Actually… what is it?"

"That is none of our business!" hisses Mr Rosewood. "We're going, Hilda. Now."

"And so are we," says Lampie quickly. "Um, I mean, so am I. There's something I need to…"

Mrs Rosewood pulls her arm free and walks up to the cart. "What is it? What do you have in there?"

"Nothing." Lampie is suddenly sick of the whole adventure. Why won't everyone just leave her alone?

"Nothing that is any of our business," Mr Rosewood says.

"Nonsense, it is very much our business!" Mrs Rosewood

reaches out her hand to the blanket, under which something is clearly breathing.

"Oh, Hilda, please! Just stop it, let things be, leave this child alone, leave me…"

But Mrs Rosewood has never listened to her husband before – and now is no exception. She wants to know. She wants to talk about it tomorrow in the shop, and "something mysterious under a blanket" is not much of a story. What is it? What is under there? She reaches out to touch the blanket, which slowly starts to rise. Something growls and in the shadows she sees what she already suspected.

"Eek!" she shrieks. "It's the monster, the monster from the Black House!"

No one can scream quite as well as the grocer's wife. The sound slices through the evening air, and the entire field of fairgoers looks in her direction. What a story this is going to make tomorrow! She can't wait. She wants to pull off more of the blanket, to take a better look, but the child is already dragging the cart away.

"Oh, help! Help me!" cries Mrs Rosewood. "It bit me, the monster bit me! I'm bleeding, I'm bleeding to death. Oh, oh, just look!"

From under his blanket, Edward stares at Lampie with dark, scared eyes. He shakes his head.

"I didn't do anything. I didn't bite her! Not even a nip!"

All around them, more voices start screaming. Everywhere people are screaming: "The monster! It's the monster!"

"The what? Really?" People come running to see. Lots of people.

"Which monster is this?"

"That monster from the Black House! It just bit off half of her hand. I saw it with my own eyes!"

"Where? Where is it?" Most of them are looking in the wrong direction, or up in the air, as though they are expecting to see some giant creature. Mrs Rosewood disappears into the crowd. Lampie tries to push her way through, but she keeps getting jostled to and fro and the cart almost topples over.

"Let me past! Let me through!" she shouts. No one hears her, no one gets out of the way. But suddenly the cart feels much easier to pull. A big hand has taken hold of the wooden handle and is helping to tug the cart.

"This way." Mr Rosewood takes charge, steering the cart straight through the curious crowd. He points back over his shoulder.

"There it is! Over there! It's terrifying. Go and take a look!"

The crowd excitedly runs in the wrong direction.

"Come on," he says, beckoning Lampie and pulling the cart across the field. He stops in the shadow between two tents. Lampie, unable to keep up with his big strides, runs after him, puffing and panting.

"Fish," she says. "Fish, how are you doing?" She places her hand on the blanket, which the shivering boy has pulled tightly around himself.

"Home," says the blanket. "Home, home, home."

"Of course," whispers Lampie, stroking his head. "We're going. We're leaving soon." She sighs. It's failed. The whole plan has failed. And tomorrow the fair will be gone, and it will not be back for another year.

And she still doesn't know if the mermaid is…

"If you go that way," says Mr Rosewood quietly, "you'll hardly bump into anyone."

Lampie can see him looking at the cart with Edward in it. But he does not say anything.

"He's not a monster," she says. "He's really not. He's…"

Mr Rosewood shakes his head. "I don't need to know." He looks at the crush in the distance. They can hear shouting and screaming. People are still looking for the monster or for some other form of entertainment, because the last evening of the fair is always one big chaotic mess.

"Right then, I'm off to see if Mrs Rosewood needs rescuing," he says with a sigh. "Which she probably doesn't." He takes a few coins from his pocket and gives them to the girl. "And I'm sorry about… For… She's not really like that, you know. Or she never used to be. Or maybe…" He sighs again. "Or maybe I just wasn't looking properly."

Lampie opens her hand carefully, so that nothing falls out. She sees a pile of coins, including some quarters, at least three of them.

"Can we go now?" whines Edward from the cart. "Can we go home?"

"Hmm…" says Lampie. "Maybe not right away."

Inside the tent, it is mercifully quiet. Earl barely looked up
when Lampie put two quarters on the counter but just raised
an eyebrow and waved her through. Finally.

It is darker than the last time. Candles are burning in the
alcoves to the left and right. The Phenomenal Freaks look up
in surprise as Lampie walks by.

"Another one?" mutters the bird-woman. "Isn't it dinner
time yet? Go on, then. Just a quick look." She climbs down
from her stool and flutters around a bit: the thin black feathers
attached to her costume dance about.

The fat bearded lady stands up and stares at the girl with
the cart, but Lampie passes right by. The Siamese twins are
playing cards with themselves. One of the heads glances up.

"Hello, child. Have you come to feed us today?"

The other one does not look. "Who's coming to feed us?"

"I don't know."

"Well, go and ask."

"Ask who?"

"That girl."

"Which girl?"

Their voices fade away as Lampie turns the corner. Then she stops. Edward has pushed his blanket down a little. She can see his eyes.

"Here?" he whispers.

"Shh! Yes, in that tank. Do you see?" She pulls the cart a little closer. There they are again: the glittering mermaids, the tridents, the fountains of blood and the dirty aquarium beneath.

Edward sits up and the blanket slides off him. "In there?" He wrinkles his nose as he looks at the tank of brown water. "I can't see anything."

"Stay under your blanket!" hisses Lampie. "Someone might come in!" She pulls the blanket a little higher over the boy and drags the cart closer to the tank. "She's in there. Can't you see? At the back, that dark—"

Suddenly the mermaid's face appears, looming out of a cloud of algae, and pressing up against the glass. Her green hair fans out, her big pitch-black eyes seem to be searching for something – and they find Fish. He looks at her. His jaw drops. She presses herself even closer to the glass, her nose, mouth and cheeks becoming white and flat. A stream of bubbles flows from her mouth.

Fish makes a quiet sound. He stares and stares. The blanket has slipped off again.

"I thought so," says a voice. Lampie is so startled that she actually jumps. "I thought you'd come back. I could tell by looking at you." The dwarf is inside the dark tent now, hands on hips, a cigarette in the corner of his mouth. But he looks friendly enough, and he is smiling. "And not alone, I see."

Edward tries to pull up the blanket as quickly as he can, but he gets himself in a tangle.

"Peekaboo! I see you!" says the dwarf cheerfully. "I'd already spotted you in there. So where on earth did you find *that*?" he asks Lampie. "Under your bed?"

"Um…" Lampie tries to help Edward with his blanket, but it slides onto the ground.

"Stupid child! Idiot!" the boy hisses at her. "I can bite, you know. I'll bite you to pieces!" He growls at the dwarf and shows his teeth. "Just ask her!"

"Oh, I believe you, Fishtail." The dwarf calmly picks up the blanket off the dirty floor, shakes it out and lays it over the boy again. "So have you come to visit your family?"

Fish looks back at the mermaid. Is that what she is?

"In my case, it's a deformity," he says with an angry nod at his legs. "They're already getting stronger too. I just need to do a lot of practice."

"Oh, lad," says the dwarf. "Of course. I can see that." Then he holds out a hand to Lampie. "Hello, my sweet girl. My name's Oswald."

Lampie takes his hand. "Emilia," she says shyly. "But people call me Lampie."

"Lampie," says the dwarf with a grin. "Perfect. And this is?"

"Edward," says Lampie.

"Fish," says Fish. He can't take his eyes off the aquarium.

There is a ladder behind the canvas, for when Earl feeds the mermaid. Oswald fetches it.

"Would you like to go in there with her?" he asks Fish. "I can get Lanky Lester to lift you into the tank. The tall one. And you can go for a little swim with your auntie, eh?"

"We think she's his mother," whispers Lampie. "Or, um, that's what I thought anyway."

The dwarf narrows his eyes. "I doubt it," he says. "Shouldn't think so. But we can always ask. Well?" he asks. "Do you want to go swimming?"

Fish frantically shakes his head. "No! I can't!" He gives Lampie a shove. "You know that! I can't let my head go underwater!"

"Fine, then," says Oswald, and he climbs the ladder himself. "She'd enjoy it though."

"How do you know that, Mr... um?..."

"Just call me Oswald."

"Can you understand her, um... Oswald? Do you talk to her?"

"Sometimes," says the dwarf. He rolls up his jacket sleeve and puts one hand in the water. "She nearly always says the same thing."

A white, almost transparent hand comes from below and takes his. But through the muddy water the mermaid's eyes go on staring at the boy in his cart. There are bubbles coming from her mouth, which burst as they reach the surface of the water.

"No, not your mother," says Oswald. "But she does know who you are. She's your, um... some kind of aunt, I believe. They looked for you, she says."

Fish's eyes grow big and round. "But who? And when? And wh-where?"

The dwarf on the ladder closes his eyes. "Sparkling Diamond," he says. "That's her name."

Lampie looks at the greenish-brown thing floating in the water. Sparkling Diamond?

"She is a long way from home," says the dwarf. "For so long… Homesick, homesick."

He starts talking in a different voice, a voice deeper than his own. It is the voice of the mermaid. Lampie feels Fish's hand grab hers and squeeze it. A bit hard, but that does not matter. In the semi-darkness she can see a few of the Freaks leaving their alcoves and coming closer. The bearded lady, the very tall man, the ragged bird-woman: they all shuffle quietly up to the aquarium and listen to the voice coming from the dwarf.

"She came… I came… I came to seek my sister, my beautiful, my sweet sister. She was the most beautiful of all the Children of the Sea. And one day she was gone. They said she went with a two-legs, went with a ship. But I could not believe it. Who would want that? Who would want to be above water? The longer I am here, the less I understand. This is no world for us. We cannot live here. But we don't die either, so it is even worse. Look at me here. Around in a circle, and then another circle, never going further, never going anywhere…" The mermaid swims up and down a few times before grasping the hand again.

"It was my own fault. I wanted to wave to my sister, only to wave, only to ask why. Or maybe to ask very quietly if she wanted to come back with me. Because I missed her so much. But I did not find her. They said one of us sometimes swam in the bay, around and around the rock, but when I went there, I did not find her. Just some stupid, gossiping fish. They talked about a fat mermaid, fat with a child inside. But a child does not stay inside, and one day I knew it would come out, and I waited for that to happen. But I waited too long and came too close to the coast, and then I… Then a…"

She thrashes her tail and the water sloshes over the edge of the tank and splashes onto the floor. A wave sweeps over Oswald and he tries to hold on to her hand, but she goes furiously around and around in circles. The dirty water bubbles and brims over, her head bangs against the glass, until she jerks and swims in the other direction. Bang, she goes, against the glass. And back again. And again.

Lampie looks at Fish, who is sitting upright in his cart, his eyes wide open. He can't tear them away from the writhing mermaid for a second. She feels his hand, still squeezing hers, feels how cold it is.

After a while, the mermaid's fury seems to ease and she lies still in the water. When the dwarf holds out his hand again, she takes it.

"I do not know if they ever came to look for me too. I hope so. No, no. I truly hope they did not. I hope they stayed there, beyond the White Cliffs, where two-legs do not go. Or… or are there more of us, in tanks everywhere, on display for the two-legs? That's what I sometimes dream, that all my sisters have been fished out of the water, one by one, and…" She shows her teeth. "All those faces in front of the glass, every day. The things they say. The things they put in the water."

"I don't think so," says the dwarf, in his own voice. "I've been to plenty of fairs, all over the place. And you're the only one I've ever seen."

"Only me," whispers the mermaid. "Then they didn't come." She looks terribly sad. "It's just as well."

Then her eyes fix on the boy in the cart again.

"And what about you?" she asks. "Is it you? Are you my Nephew Neverseen?"

She looks at Fish. Everyone looks at Fish. He shrugs. How can he be? He is, he isn't... Or is he?

"Take that blanket away," the dwarf says to Lampie. "She wants to look at him."

Lampie takes hold of the wet blanket and pulls it from the cart. The mermaid presses her face flat against the glass again. She starts talking with such force that Oswald almost falls off his ladder. Fish does not need the dwarf in order to understand her; he can feel the mermaid's voice thundering through him.

"GO! GET AWAY!" she screams. "What are you doing here? Get away! Leave before it's too late! Why are you sitting there in a cart, like a cripple? Don't you know what you are? Jump into the water! SWIM!"

Fish shakes his head. "I can't! My head's too heavy, it's not allowed, I'll drown in a second, I can't even swim!"

"Oh dear," says a voice behind them. They all turn to look.

A big, tattooed man has appeared at the back of the tent. He is carrying two buckets, which he quickly puts down. Then he steps forward and, with one movement, he hauls Fish out of the cart and dangles him by the tail.

"Well, that's no good, is it?" sniggers Earl. "It's about time you learnt – and fast."

Earl is lazy. He always has to take down the entire tent every time, load it onto the train, put it up again... The Freaks do most of the hard work, but someone has to keep an eye on them, so that they do not sabotage the tent or run away or simply drop down dead.

They are a bit of a shabby bunch, to be honest, his troupe. The bearded lady is looking less and less like a lady. His Siamese twins have been insane for years now, his mermaid on the verge of death... She used to be his biggest attraction. But that has not been true for a long time.

She sometimes used to bite the occasional fairgoer. That clearly could not be allowed and so he would punish her by giving her no food for a week, but it always gave the public a proper fright. People would throng around the tank, and at the slightest movement from the mermaid they would all scream. She has not bitten anyone for months though, not even when people prodded her with sticks. A crying shame.

His top attraction is nothing more than a waste of space now. No matter how many shimmering tails he paints by the tanks, and signs saying BEWARE! FEED AT YOUR OWN RISK!, none of it helps.

Boring, people say, and some of them demand their money back. *Anyone can put a dead fish in a tank of water.*

"She's not dead," he always replies. "She's just resting, she's pining for the open waves, that's what mermaids are like."

Excuses! the people say. *Catch a new mermaid, a nice fresh one – that's what we want to see!*

Did they even know what they were asking for? His father, as tall as a tree and as strong as a bear, had told him the stories. About how he had fished this one up out of the bay, purely by chance. How she had fought and fought and never gave up. Gnawed through thick ropes. Smashed glass tanks with her tail. Catch a nice new fresh one? Not likely. But sadly monsters do not just come trundling into his tent for free, of course. At least, not until today.

"Hello, my little stroke of luck," says Earl to the dangling boy.

Lampie screams. Fish screams. The Freaks chunter and hiss.

"I thought you were sneaking something in here in that cart of yours. Very cunning, my girl, but Uncle Earl is just that little bit more cunning. So, little fishie, go and join your mother in the brine, and I'll have two for the price of one." He holds Fish above the dirty water, as the boy twists and screams and desperately tries to bite the hand that is holding his legs.

"No!" screams Lampie. "Don't do it! Please! Don't do it! He can't swim. I've seen it with my own eyes. Let him go!" She kicks the fat man's shins, but he does not even seem to notice.

"You can't do this, Earl," says the dwarf. "This is a free boy."

"Free? A boy? This?" Earl holds the wriggling child in front of his face. "If I've ever seen a monster, it's this one here. Ooh, lad, what an ugly head you have." He turns to the dwarf, who is slowly climbing down from his ladder.

"What do you think, Oswald? A new tank? Or two in one? Reckon they'll bite each other's throats open?"

Lampie looks around desperately. More of the Freaks have left their alcoves now, the old Siamese twins are slowly shuffling closer on their wooden walking frame, moving it forward a few inches at a time. Their heads are looking curiously at the dangling boy. The Freaks are nudging one another and shaking their heads. But they do absolutely nothing, no one flies at the fat man, no one pulls the child from his hands.

He can't stay here! screams a voice inside Lampie's head. With people staring at him every day. That's even worse than being under the bed all the time. Fish will either go mad or die.

"Help him! Why won't you help him?" She tugs at the dwarf's jacket. "You need to do something!"

He looks at her sadly. "Yes. I know," he says quietly. "But what? Earl…" he tries again. "Please…"

Lampie looks around: the tall man is cowering shyly at the back of the little crowd, the bearded lady is holding her hands in front of her face, as if she does not want to look.

"Is it dinner time yet?" asks one of the Siamese twins.

"Yes, what are we having?" asks the other.

Head first, Lampie rushes at the big fat man. He is holding Fish above the water, about to drop him, and studying him, as if he has all the time in the world – and of course he does, doesn't he? He has the troupe completely under his thumb. No one ever dares to try anything. They know what will be in store for them if they do: cages, chains, no food for a week, and he is sure he can come up with a few even nastier ideas.

The girl's head thumps into Earl's lower back. It hurts a teeny tiny little bit, but most of all it makes him laugh.

"What's this, girlie? Have you changed your mind? Have you come for a kiss after all?"

Fish has wriggled his way up now and he bites the pale arm as hard as he can. His teeth sink in deeply. Earl lets out a scream and drops the boy into the aquarium with a splash.

"Taking a bite of the boss?" he shouts after him. "I'll soon teach you, just you wait." Blood slowly wells up out of the red dots on his arm.

Wide-eyed, Lampie stares at the aquarium. Fish sinks like a stone, his head banging against the bottom. She claws herself up the fat man's body, scratching and biting, but he just grabs her by the scruff of her neck and holds her at arm's length.

"And now get out of my tent, girlie. I've had enough of you."

Lampie glares at him with her most poisonous look. She wants to cut off his head, she wants to shoot poison arrows straight into his… And then she notices someone slowly coming up behind him.

The mermaid is rising up from the dirty water. She is much taller than the fat man and she grabs his neck with her arms and pulls him against the glass. Earl gives a high-pitched scream, staggers backwards and drops Lampie, who tumbles head over heels. Oswald the dwarf reaches out his hand to help her back up.

"Fish!" she screams at him. "He has to, he can't… He's drowning!"

"Shh," whispers Oswald. He puts his arm around her shoulders and points with his other hand. *Look!*

The mermaid is no longer a grey sponge, but a predator, just like in the paintings behind her. Even worse. Her teeth are flashing, her eyes are spitting fire. Black fire. Gold, orange fire. And she does not let go. Water splashes everywhere. Earl's eyes are bulging out of his head. With limp arms, he flails around, trying to free himself, trying to signal to his troupe that they have to help him, please, hasn't he always been such a good boss?

But the Phenomenal Freaks just watch, they watch as all the air is slowly squeezed out of his body.

Lampie attempts to peer around the fat man who is fighting to survive. She is trying to spot Fish, somewhere inside the aquarium, but the dirt in the water is billowing up and she cannot see a thing. I need that ladder, she thinks, I have to get into that tank, I have to get him out of there!

Earl is almost dead when he remembers what his father always used to say: "Nothing will help you against those monsters – they never give up. Don't let them take you by surprise, always make sure that you…" With difficulty, he lifts one leg, and his hands search for his boot. If only he could reach it, but he can't – he comes up just short. The mermaid's steel arms stay in place around his neck, the world around him is getting darker and hazier. But his fingers keep grabbing and eventually he finds it – the knife in his boot.

He stabs, somewhere behind himself, and now it is the mermaid who screams. As he feels her grip loosening, he stabs a few more times. She struggles and writhes, her tail thrashing in the water and smashing against the glass of the aquarium. Cracks appear, an entire cobweb of cracks – and then it breaks with a bang. Everything comes pouring out: water, pieces of glass, a fat man gasping for breath, a mermaid who is bleeding, and finally a boy with a fish's tail, who rolls across the floor and then lies there limply.

Lampie runs over to him, the water splashing around her feet. The whole tent stinks of filthy, stagnant seawater. She kneels down beside him.

"Fish? Are you?… Fish?"

His eyes are shut, but he is coughing and gagging. And if you are coughing and gagging, then you are not dead. She helps him to sit up a little and he vomits up some water, and then some more water, and the scraps of food that were inside his stomach. Lampie is so relieved that she starts to shake. She rests the boy's head in her lap and she strokes his wet hair. When he needs to be sick again, she just lets him.

"That's good, Fish," she says quietly. "Well done, go on."

It is only then that she looks up.

Half of the tent is flooded. Everyone is soaked. The bearded lady is wringing out her pinafore, the bird-woman is frantically splashing about and the old Siamese twins are standing in the corner, both heads sobbing. Lanky Lester and the dwarf are leaning over the two bodies that are lying in the middle of the big, deep puddle. The body on the bottom is panting and coughing. The body on top is not moving. When they lift the mermaid off Earl, Lampie sees that she is as grey as ash, her hair hanging in strings over her face and her arms and tail dangling limply.

Lampie puts her hand over Fish's eyes.

"What's wrong?" says the boy.

"Ssh," Lampie replies. "Nothing. Just don't look."

It is a dark night, the last night of the fair. It is cold and clear, and the moon is a thin line.

Julie, the bearded lady, has made a fire, and Fish watches the light of the flames casting shadows on the faces of the Freaks around him. They are eating chicken and bread, and there is even some cake. Oswald the dwarf has raided Earl's supplies; they do not usually have so much good food to eat.

Lampie has given Fish a plate of food too, but he pushes the chicken around, without eating anything. He just looks. At Julie, who needs two chairs, one for each buttock, at how she bites and chews and makes a mess of her beard. At the bird-woman, who is pecking her food like a chicken herself. At the tall man, who always hunches his shoulders but still sticks up above everything else. The Siamese twins are eating from a single plate on their lap and squabbling over the tastiest morsels.

Everything is so strange for Edward. Sitting here in the evening air is strange. Not being in his room, not being hidden away, everyone being able to see him – all of it is strange. No one is paying any particular attention to him; only Oswald the dwarf catches his eye from time to time and gives him a wink. His wife is sitting beside him. She is a completely ordinary woman, not fat, not thin, not small. She has a baby on her lap, which she keeps kissing and cuddling. Edward can't help staring at that too.

When most of the food is finished, Lanky Lester fetches a small guitar, which seems even smaller in his big hands, and he plays songs that drift into the night. All around them, everything else is quiet; the only other sound is the crickets' chirping. The fairground is empty. The locals went home long ago. Lampie and Edward are the only ones who have been allowed to stay, because they had such a fright and because Edward almost drowned. Earl is recovering inside his caravan, snoring away, with the door locked tight.

"We won't be seeing him tonight," the dwarf had said. "So there's no need to be afraid."

Edward is not afraid. And that is another strange thing. He feels so odd, and there is suddenly so much to think about (like why he did not drown). About how he briefly had an aunt – and now he doesn't. And maybe a mother – and what was the truth about that? And how he nearly got caught and put on display for ever and ever, just like these people around him, who have crowds gawping at them every day. How do they put up with it? Why don't they run away?

Lampie is sitting beside him, quietly singing along to the songs she knows. She knows nearly all of them. She has put her arm around him, and that is strange too. He just lets her. They are telling stories about the mermaid, about what she was like when she first came, and about how she changed.

Lester strums a sad song, which Lampie knows too:

"Sleep with the fishes, roll on the deep,
Let the kind waves rock you to sleep."

But she is not sleeping, she is dead, he knows that. She is wrapped in a blanket inside the dark tent. In *his* blanket – the dwarf's wife has given him a dry one, which smells quite different. He pulls it tightly around himself, even though it is not too cold this close to the fire.

"My beautiful baby," the woman whispers as she cuddles the child. "Yes, you are. Oh, yes, you are."

Edward has already noticed that this is not true. The child has a harelip that twists its whole face and it is completely bald. How can she think it's beautiful?

But maybe all mothers think their children are beautiful. Except for his own, that is.

Lampie is having a wonderful time. Her cheeks are warm from the fire, she is breathing in as much as possible of the delicious smell of woodsmoke, and the tall man seems to know all the songs she remembers from the old days. It is almost like being back there; if she half-closes her eyes, the strange people sitting around the fire could easily be pirates, and the fairground could be a beach by the sea. She listens to the stories they tell, she gnaws on chicken bones – she was starving! – she sings along and sometimes, as she sings, she cries a little too, but that doesn't matter. It's that kind of evening.

The dwarf's wife makes up a bed for them, on the floor of the caravan. It's already far too late to go home, says Oswald, and besides they have something to do tomorrow morning.

Lampie feels soft from the singing, and glowing from the cup of mulled wine she was given, and so she snuggles up next to Fish and goes straight to sleep.

The boy does not sleep, but lies there, looking into the unfamiliar darkness. He has slowly rolled away from the girl, as he is sure that she does not want his cold legs touching her. Tail. Tail – yes, maybe you could call it a tail. His aunt had a tail, the aunt who he had for a moment and has already lost. He thinks about Earl with his grabbing fingers. And he thinks about his father too, and what he would say if he saw him lying here. With the fairground folk, with the dregs, the failures, where his son does not belong. He thinks a thousand things, about the whole day, about his whole life.

And among all those thoughts, there is one, as steady as a heartbeat, which will not go away: what it was like, that instant before the aquarium exploded, when he was completely underwater, and how it felt.

Back at the Black House, Lenny is sitting and waiting by the gate. He will not come inside, not for tea, not for dinner. Martha can call as much as she likes and she can threaten him too, but he does not come. His eyes wide, he stares through the bars and into the darkness, looking in the direction they should be coming from.

But she does not come, the girl, all night long. It gets cold and dark and the dogs went inside long ago, but not Lenny. Lenny stays and waits.

Augustus's eyes are closed, but he is not asleep.

He can still see her standing there in front of him. Every day. Every hour. Every minute.

She is in the middle of the room, with her hands up to her cheek. And her mother is behind her. Both of them are looking at him. They can see him everywhere he goes: in his bed, on the toilet, in the lamp room. Up on the walkway is the only place where the wind blows them out of his head, just a little, and so that is where he spends most of his time.

How could you? their eyes say. *How could you?*

There is a knock at the door. That woman again with her mush. He does not need anything; his throat is clamped shut.

"I don't need anything," he shouts hoarsely. "Just forget about it today."

"Mr Waterman!" she persists. What a shrill voice the woman has. "I've got something special for you. Come down and get it!"

What could it be? A pudding, something sweet maybe. He has no idea, but he is not getting up out of his chair for that.

"I don't need anything!" he shouts again. Why won't she just leave him alone?

"Your daughter was here this afternoon."

What? Lampie? He feels his heart skip a beat. But how? She is where she is and she can't leave, and even if…

"That's impossible!" he rasps. Don't go getting my hopes up, woman! he thinks. I don't want any maybes or what ifs – that just makes it worse.

"It's true! Lampie, right? Well, she left something for you. Will you come down and get it? And you can take the soup while you're at it!"

Something white slides through the hatch and flutters to the floor. A piece of paper. He limps over to it.

"And here's the soup! Careful though. It's dripping!"

And indeed, a hot drop of soup splashes onto his neck as he bends down to pick up the paper. Augustus barely notices. He can hear her, the woman, rattling on, waiting for an answer and then, after a while, walking away. He stares at the piece of paper in his hand. There are letters on it, big lopsided ones. For a moment he allows himself to think that it could really be from her. That she has come all the way here from goodness knows where to push this through his door. Which means that she still thinks about him. That she does not want to spit on his name.

258

He crumples the paper into a ball. Because it's impossible. It can't be from Lampie. His daughter can't read or write; she has never learnt how. And neither has he.

He throws the ball of paper into the cold fireplace and slowly limps back up the stairs, to where the wind is blowing.

FISH SWIMS

Through the early morning mist they walk to the harbour, very first thing, even before breakfast. Lanky Lester and Julie, the bearded lady, lead the way. They are the strongest, so they are carrying the dead mermaid in her blanket. The others follow silently behind. All of them except for Olga and Olga, the elderly Siamese twins, as it was too far for them to walk. Lampie brings up the rear, pulling Fish in her squeaking cart.

Mermaids do not go into the ground. They have to become sea foam, to return to where they came from.

There is no one at the harbour yet and they do not stay for long.

At the last jetty, they stand in silence for a while.

Then the dwarf says, "Farewell, Sparkling Diamond."

They drop the body into the water. It makes a quiet splash. Two quiet splashes.

When Lampie looks back at Fish, the cart is empty.

*

He is swimming after the body. He can see it dissolving in a flurry of bubbles, as if it is disintegrating. The dull skin, the green hair like seaweed, the black tail – they all dissolve in a fizzing cloud, like the headache powder that Joseph sometimes used to give him. Then something swims out of the cloud, as thin and twisting as a sea snake, but sweeter, more beautiful, with soft hair and a smile. She swims towards him, winds around him, brushes the hair out of his face, puts her mouth up to his ear and doesn't speak a word. But he understands her anyway.

Go and look for them, boy. Go and let them find you.

Then she turns greener and more transparent, and shimmers away.

He just hears a quiet *Thank you*, before her voice disappears too. *Thank you so, so much.*

Fish turns around and around, but there is only water now, green and murky. The light falls through it in slanting rays and, in the distance, he can see the dark shadows of ships' hulls floating above.

She was his family, the dwarf had said. Some kind of aunt?

Fine. So he had had an aunt for about half an hour. And then she was gone. Of course. No one ever stays with him, not ever. No one is coming to rescue him either. See? He could just as easily drown in this filthy…

Water.

He has been in the water for some time now but he still has not drowned. He is breathing as normal.

Or something in him is breathing, something knows how, somehow or other.

He touches his neck, but does not find any gills. When he breathes out, a stream of bubbles comes from his mouth and his nose.

But how?…

And also…

He can't swim!

He looks down at his legs, at that deformed, clumsy clump of legs down there. He sees it swishing gently back and forth without any conscious effort on his part. That pointed white foot has unfurled into a fin, which is slowly, effortlessly moving in the water.

He is not doing anything at all. It is happening all by itself.

He closes his eyes.

He pinches himself.

He feels the pinch.

He looks again – and he still has a tail.

Then swim, he says. And his muscles obey.

Which they never did up there, up above, where he end-lessly cajoled them, cursed them, prodded them: Stand up! Carry my weight! Be strong!

No, here they simply work.

Swish! And he shoots through the water. Turn! The other way. He swims and swims. Through the forest of slippery green jetty posts, left, right, left, he winds his way between them, smoothly, without touching a single one.

He is so fast!

He is so strong!

He is so happy!

He had never imagined that…

No, he had imagined it, just for a moment, in that dirty aquarium; he had felt how calm his mind became under the water. Through all the panic, he had noticed, just briefly, that… And then everything had gone crazy.

Could he even?…

He shoots through the water, his tail one big muscle, and with a leap he is up above, his arms open wide, as if he is flying. In a flash, he sees Lampie and the other very short, very tall, very fat silhouettes on the jetty.

"Look!" he yells, getting a mouthful of water as he dives back beneath the surface. He turns and jumps again. "Look at me!" The silhouettes are moving, he does not know if they have seen him, it is still quite dim and misty. He shouts and fills the air with splashing water.

"Look! Lampiieee! Look what I can do! Look at my tail! Lampiieee!"

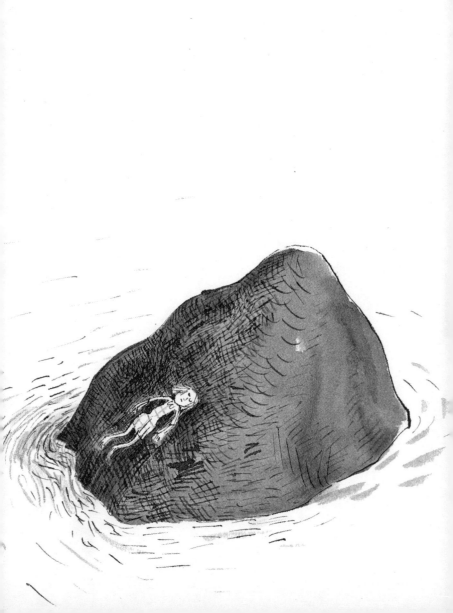

Fish does not want to come out of the water. He just keeps doing circuits between the jetty posts and then somersaults and seeing how deep he can dive and how far he can leap, but when Lampie calls him, from the high jetty, Fish slowly comes swimming towards her.

"Why don't you just leave him here?" says the dwarf. "Isn't it better for him to be free?"

"I don't know," says Lampie, and it's true – she has no idea. What would happen if she went back with an empty cart?

Where is the admiral's son, girl?

Oh, somewhere in the sea, I don't know.

At the very least she'd be fired. And then what about the money, and the seven years, and her father? But what about Fish? Would he have to go back under the bed, in that tower?

"And you can come with us, you know," says the dwarf a little shyly. "If you like. Not as a Phenomenal Freak, you turned out far too neatly for that. But just for fun? For the company?"

"The *Black M* would go in a heartbeat," the fat lady with the beard suddenly says. "She's not scared of anything. She used to sail to the White Cliffs and beyond."

It is the first time Lampie has heard the woman speak. She has a deep, husky voice and again Lampie has the feeling that she has seen her before. But she can't remember ever having met a woman with a beard.

"The *Black M*? What's that?" she asks.

"She should be over there somewhere," says the woman, her bare arm jiggling as she points. "You're her daughter, aren't you? And your father was the ship's first mate."

"No," says Lampie. "My father's a lighthouse keeper."

Through the mist she can see the light slowly turning, far off in the distance.

"Yes, that's who I mean," says Julie. "But she doesn't sail any more, the *Black M*. That's what they say. I wish I could…"

"Julie," says the dwarf impatiently. "Shut up about this *Black M* of yours. Well, what are you going to do?" he asks Lampie. "Do you want to come with us? It'll be fun. Every place you go is different but still the same. And everyone's always so happy to see us. So happy not to be us."

Lampie shrugs. Maybe, she thinks. Being part of a troupe. Travelling all over, making fires in the evening. A postcard from every new place, addressed to the Grey Lighthouse. No, she can't do it. She shakes her head. She doesn't want to leave.

"What about Earl?"

"Oh, Earl," mutters the dwarf. "He won't do anything. He just sits inside his ticket booth and thinks he's the boss."

"Lampie! Did you see me, Lampie? Did you see me?" At the bottom of the jetty post, Fish is shaking the drops of water from his hair, and his golden eyes are gleaming.

"Amazing," says the dwarf. "My goodness, lad! That's beautiful."

"What?" Fish looks over his shoulder to see if there is something beautiful behind him.

"You," says Oswald with a smile.

"Oh. But did you see it? Did you see me? I did a double somersault, as easy as anything, and I think if I practise I'll be able to do a triple one and maybe even…"

Lampie sits down on the edge of the jetty. "Fish," she says. "Do you want to come home with me or not? Would you rather stay here?"

Here? Fish looks around, at the slimy jetty posts sticking up far above him, at the water around him, with the dead seaweed floating in it, and all the rubbish and the fish heads.

"Well, you know," says Lampie, pointing out to sea. "Or you could go further out to sea, to the White Cliffs, where the mermaids live. That's what she said, isn't it?"

She looks at the small bobbing head below. She would miss him so much. "But it's quite a long way, I think."

Fish looks back, across the surface of the water and over the sea, out of the bay, to the distant horizon, to the endless sky. There? Him? All on his own? Suddenly he just feels tired and he really wants to go home, to rest, to sleep in the familiar darkness under his bed. And his father is supposed to be coming home soon, and he mustn't be here then, he should be… Maybe though, maybe he could even, yes, maybe he could show him that… But he hardly even dares to think that thought.

Beside one of the tall jetty posts, there is a slippery wooden ladder. Fish pulls himself up, as far as he can, and then Lester reaches out a long arm and drags him up the rest of the way. Up on the jetty, Lampie helps him back into his cart.

All around them, the harbour is waking up. Ropes and pulleys are rattling, sails are being hoisted with a swish, and fishermen call out, "Ho!" and, "Hey!" Some of them stare in annoyance at the strange group. What on earth are those freaks doing here?

The dwarf takes hold of Lampie's hand. "So the answer's no?"

The girl shakes her head.

"That's a shame," says Oswald. "But we come back here every year. So who knows?" He gently pulls her down to his height and gives her a kiss on the cheek.

"Who knows?" replies Lampie. She hugs him and then Lester. She kisses the bird-woman and sends her best wishes to Olga and Olga and to everyone else, except for Earl.

"Come on, people," says the dwarf. "Time to get this show on the road. Hey, Julie, come on!"

Julie is still standing on the tip of the jetty, staring out to sea, her skirt fluttering in the breeze. Slowly she turns around.

A fisherman walking by spits on the planks, right at her feet. "Disgusting. A man in a dress."

She clenches her fists, but then steps neatly over the blob of spit and gives Lampie a kiss on the top of her head.

"Don't forget," she whispers quietly into her hair. "The *Black M*. If only I could come too…" Then she quickly scurries after the troupe.

Lampie pulls the blanket all the way over Fish and turns the cart around. The planks rattle under the wheels, and through the gaps she sees one bit of sea after another.

When they are out of the town, they can talk.

"What did that man say to you?" asks Fish. "Um… that woman, I mean."

"I don't know," says Lampie. "Something about a *Black M*."

"A black what?"

"I think it's a ship."

"Oh. The *Black Man* maybe? Or the *Black Mainmast*, or the *Black Marlin*?"

"Or the *Black Monster*."

"The *Black Mermaid*," says Fish.

"She said: she sails to the White Cliffs. Maybe we need to go there in a ship."

"To go where?"

"To your mother."

"The *Black Mother*," says Fish with a shiver.

Lampie struggles to tug the cart up the last part of the hill. Fish seems to have become heavier now; his tail looks fuller and she has to pull really hard. But before they reach the top, Lenny comes running through the gate, like a very big puppy, hopping and skipping around Lampie, laughing and crying, all at the same time. He wants to hug her but he is too shy. She gives him Fish to carry and so he cuddles him a bit instead before striding towards the Black House with giant steps. Lampie follows, pulling the empty cart.

Lenny keeps looking back at the girl, to make sure she really, truly has returned.

Martha is angry. She heard them coming from a long way off, the crunching of the wheels, Lenny's happy cries and the barking of the dogs, but she does not go to look. She keeps on angrily washing dishes, with her back to the kitchen. Even when she hears them come inside and the girl hesitantly says, "Hello?" she still does not turn around. Her hands keep sloshing suds over the plate she is holding, even though it is already clean.

"That," she says slowly, "Was. Not. Our agreement."

"Um… did we have an agreement?" asks Lampie.

"Of course we did. An afternoon off is an afternoon off. Not an evening. Not a night. Not one and a half… Whatever were you thinking, staying away so long? Now of all times, when the admiral—"

"Is he already here?" Fish almost screams the words. "Is… is he upstairs?"

Martha goes on washing the same plate. Behind her back, Nick silently shakes his head.

"Oh, yes. Wouldn't that have been something! Where's my son, Martha? No idea, sir. He's off gallivanting with the maid."

"That's not true," says Lampie crossly. "We weren't… gallivanting."

"He is not allowed to go through the gate, I told you that. Not allowed outside. N. O. T. Not! Do I speak too quietly or something? Is that the problem?" Martha throws the plate onto the draining board and takes another one.

Nick puts Fish in a chair and slides two cushions under him, so that he can sit comfortably.

"There's no harm done, woman," he mutters. "Don't get yourself all fired up."

"We just had to go and figure something out," says Lampie. "I saw something that…"

Martha turns around and glares at the girl.

"Oh, really? You saw something, did you? Well, I've seen a thing or two myself. In fact, I see plenty. But I keep my mouth shut and do my work, and you should do the same. Where are we supposed to go, eh? Lenny and me? What will happen if I get fired? Have you ever thought about that, eh?"

Lampie is about to answer, "No," but Fish speaks first.

"If, if… If my father dismisses you, then…" The boy is sitting up very straight. Lampie has never seen him like this before. "But he would never do that. My father is a fair and decent man."

"Huh!" sneers Martha. "And what would you know about that, monster?"

"He is not a monster!" Lampie screams the words. Lenny, who is crumpling up pieces of newspaper into balls, does not dare to look at his mother when she is so angry, but he shakes his head too.

273

"Oh really?" Martha says, waving the wet plate around. "Then I'd like to know what it is. Look at it sitting there, half human, half…" But then she stops waving her hands around and does not say the word. "Oh. What do I know? Never mind."

"Mermaid," says Lampie.

Clatter – there goes the plate.

Before long though, the shattered plate has been swept up and there is tea on the table. Nick makes sandwiches and passes them around in silence. Everyone is waiting for Martha to speak. And after a while she does.

"Oh dear," she says. "Oh well. It's such a long time ago now. When she lived here, when she… No one was allowed to know. That was the agreement. She was… Well, of course she was beautiful. Strangely beautiful, with green hair and very peculiar eyes. But yes, beautiful. We just weren't all that keen on her. Such a strange race. Unnatural. Our dear Lord can never have intended for something like that to live among us, among normal folk, let's say. But we didn't say anything. For the master's sake. We never spoke to her. She didn't say much herself either. Nothing, in fact. I can't remember her ever saying a word. And when she walked past, we made the sign of the cross behind her back and spat on the ground to ward off the evil. It has to be bad luck, that kind of thing. Who knows what unholy bargain she made to turn her tail into legs?

"At first she could still walk like normal, so it wasn't even that noticeable. But we knew. Of course we did, all of us did. That she used to go swimming at night. That Joseph would unlock the door for her. That she was going out more and more often. And that the master said it wasn't allowed. Whenever he yelled at her, we could hear it through the wall.

"'You are not a fish!' he used to scream. 'So stop behaving like one!'

"She was hardly ever allowed to have a bath either. She was forbidden to go in the pond and certainly not allowed in the sea. But whenever he went off on his travels again, she did it anyway. She slipped out of the house more and more often. Until he got her pregnant, and then she hardly ever came downstairs. We sometimes saw her, just her silhouette, at the window up there, but no one went up to see her. No one but Joseph. Yes, I felt sorry for her. But well, you can feel sorry for anyone, can't you? Not my business. You know how it is. And after that... well, I actually never saw her again after that."

"Yes, you did," Nick says, nudging her. "For that photograph."

"What photograph?" asked Lampie. She notices that Fish looks rather pale. He has not even touched his sandwich.

"Photograph? There is no photograph," says Martha.

"It's over there, isn't it? In that drawer?" says Nick, pointing helpfully.

Martha rolls her eyes and walks over to the kitchen cabinet. She slides open one of the drawers, rummages around, takes something out and throws it onto the table. It is a sheet of thick, yellowing paper.

"It happened just the once," she says. "This man came to the house. They said he was a photographer. Had one of those machines with him, under a sheet. It was because... they'd made the master an admiral, that was why. It had to be announced in the newspapers, and they needed a photograph to go with the story. The master wanted it to be a picture just of

275

him, but no: what about your beautiful wife? You're married, aren't you? And that was that. And then he decided that the house and the staff and everyone had to be in the picture. What a disaster."

Lampie gently picks up the photograph off the table and turns it over.

"They had to carry her downstairs. She couldn't take a single step herself by that time. We sat her in a chair, and we had to cover her in blankets, and put a pair of sunglasses on her, so that no one could see anything. The master was really annoyed. He was furious with everything all day, especially with me. Because the photographer wanted to have Lenny in the picture too. Goodness knows why. And back then Lenny kept running away all the time. He couldn't stand still for a second, but you need to be still for a photograph, for a really long time. The sweat on my forehead! I must have aged ten years in one afternoon. The picture never even ended up in the newspaper. They used a portrait of the master instead. All that fuss for nothing!"

Lampie slides the photograph across the table to Fish. On the steps, in front of a much neater house, stands a young, angry Martha, gripping an arm that is attached to a white whirl of movement. She sees the admiral, his eyes in the shadow of his cap. Beside him is a very pale woman in a chair, wearing a pair of dark glasses. There are some other members of staff, people Lampie has never seen before, except for Nick, who seems to have even bigger ears than he does now. And behind the chair is a man with tousled white hair and a lopsided smile on his lips.

"Joseph," whispers Fish.

Lampie did not think that Martha could get any angrier, but it seems she was wrong.

"Yes, Joseph. Yes," she says with an icy chill in her voice. "The man who always solved all our problems. Joseph, yes, who was always upstairs, at first with her, and then with that… With you. Always up in that tower, never with us, never with Lenny. I had to deal with everything by myself. Up there all the time, day after day, until one day he didn't come back, until…" She looks at Lampie. "And you think he's not a monster, do you? Go on. Tell her what you did to Joseph, monster!"

Lampie looks at Fish, who is so horrified that he is gasping for air. He's not a monster, she wants to say, but Fish is already speaking. Shakily at first, but not for long.

"N-nothing. I didn't do anything. He just…" He sits up straighter and looks at Martha with his dark eyes. "He always explained things to me. Lots of things. Everything. Books and maps and stories. Until he started to forget what he'd already said, and he told me the same things again and again. N-not that I minded. But he kept falling asleep too, and I had to shake him awake. Or give him a nip. Because he wouldn't wake up otherwise. And then… Well, um…" He swallows.

"And then… what?"

"Then he just fell over. Suddenly. It was such a shock. And he was dead. There was nothing I could do about it."

Martha looks into the boy's strange eyes and realizes that she believes him. Yes, that must be what happened.

She nods.

"It was awful," says Fish. "Everyone just dies. I hate it."

"So do I," says Martha. She can feel a tear coming, but she blinks it away. "Well," she says, "you can, um… Just keep the photograph. I look funny in it anyway."

Fish looks up. "Really?" he says. "Thank you. I really appreciate it, Mrs…"

"Call me Martha," she says. When she gets up to go and make coffee, she sees that the boy is holding the photograph right up close to his face, so that he can take a better look.

"Ah," she says. "Oh. Hmm." She turns around. "What I wanted to say… I'm sorry for you… that you came out so… um, wrong. I mean…"

Lampie swallows down her last bite of sandwich. "But he didn't. Not at all," she says. "Really. I thought the same at first, but it's not true. You should have seen him this morning. You have to show them, Fish."

Soon they are standing together beside the cleanish pond, which is of course not a harbour, let alone a sea, but there is still just enough room for a backwards dive and a somersault or two. It works even better when Nick comes along with two wooden hoops for him to jump through.

Fish jumps and dives as high as he can, his skin gleaming and his eyes golden, and with such ease and skill that even Martha claps her hands. And Lampie smiles so brightly at the boy that all Lenny can do is stare at her and wish he had a tail of his own.

"When your father sees this…" says Lampie, when Fish has stopped to catch his breath. "He has to see you!"

"I need to do that somersault better," pants Fish. "It's not good enough yet, and that backwards…"

"We still have time. He's not here yet, is he? Oh, or do you still need my help with the housework, Martha?"

"Most of it's done," begins Martha. "But…"

"Well, then maybe we have a whole afternoon to practise. Or are you too tired, Fish?"

"No, not at all." Fish pushes away from the side for another series of leaps.

"Lenny," says Lampie. "You have to help too. We need someone to hold the hoops. Can you do that?"

Lenny nods happily.

"Lenny was going to pick a bucket of blackberries this afternoon, weren't you, son?"

Lenny gives his mother a look of dismay. He would much rather hold the hoop.

"Never mind," says Nick. "I'll pick them."

"Yes, but…"

"Let them do it," whispers Nick, gently pushing Martha back to the house. "Let them give it a try."

Martha shakes her head. "I don't think the master will approve…"

"No," says Nick. "Neither do I. Come on, give me a bucket."

The rest of the afternoon, the sound of splashing, screaming and laughter fills the garden of the Black House. The windows look down in surprise. They thought that life here was long over, that this was a dead house, a dead garden. But that is no longer true: two dogs are barking and running circles around the pond. Drops of water splash over the hedge animals around the lawn, a twisting dragon, a swan, half a rhinoceros and two big green dogs that look a lot like their brown brothers. In the long shadows of the late sunshine, they almost seem to come to life.

The deck is packed with men saluting, standing neatly in line. The admiral returns their salute, as straight as a ramrod, as always. It is more of an effort now though. His old bones are getting stiff and beginning to protest as he gets older, but he has never listened to them before and he doesn't plan to start now. His faithful lieutenant, Flint, towers over him, his shoulders almost twice as wide as the admiral's. But height alone is not enough to make an admiral, as the admiral is well aware. And muscles alone cannot win a man respect. His fingertips tap his forehead. That is what is important. Mind over matter.

He clicks his heels, turns around and walks down the gangplank with Flint.

They are waiting for him down there, the mayor and the sheriff, for some routine formalities. Oh, you've been away for so long. It's good to have you back with us, safe and sound. Yes, yes. A ship on the rocks, a lighthouse keeper found guilty. The admiral is only half listening. He is tired and he feels old. After a while, they let him leave.

"I'll take you home, sir."

"Hmm," says the admiral. "Home."

He has put this off for as long as possible, but now he has to go there. To his house that is not a home and has not been for a long time.

It is packed with old junk, objects he used to like and would bring to the house from far-off places. But what good are they to him? The house is also much too big, and he cannot find any peace there.

That child, the eyes of that child who is his son and yet – God in Heaven! – not his son at all.

He should start afresh. Maybe get married again, have a woman in the house, so that he no longer has to rattle around the place all by himself. A woman who would hang curtains here and place cushions there and who would bring him something in the evenings, a glass of port or whatnot.

Flint leads over two horses, and the admiral mounts his smoothly. He has to grit his teeth as he swings his leg up, but no one notices.

"Another hurrah for the admiral!" the men call from the high deck. "Hurrah!"

Yes, yes, hurrah, waves the admiral. He is so very tired of the sea.

They turn the horses and ride out of the harbour. A large crowd has gathered. It is not every day that a ship like the *Excelsior* comes sailing in, his magnificent white *Excelsior* with her steel bow, which cuts through ice floes like a knife through… blah, blah, blah. He sighs.

A pleasant woman. She does not need to be beautiful. He has had enough of beauty.

*

They ride in silence over the cobbles and out of the town. Suddenly his horse rears up. Someone is standing in the road, right in front of him.

"Whoa, boy. Easy now," says the admiral, patting the horse's warm neck. It is a woman, and she is not getting out of the way. Not a beautiful woman, getting on in years, and dressed entirely in grey. She begins to talk.

"I'm so glad to have bumped into you, admiral," she twitters. "I came as soon as I heard your ship was here. I thought you would want to hear this at once and…"

He doubts that very much. God, he is only just back on land and already it is beginning. He is in no mood to listen to women's chitter-chatter. He needs to look for one who at least knows how to keep her mouth shut. But the woman is still standing right in front of his horse; he can hardly ride into her and knock her down.

"You have my attention, madam."

Flint's horse snorts, right beside her, and she jumps back in fright. The admiral coughs to hide a smile, while giving his lieutenant a look of disapproval.

"I really wouldn't tell you this if it were just gossip, you know that. But I've heard it from various sources, from different people. Even so, I wouldn't have come to you if I hadn't seen it myself, with my own two eyes."

Doesn't he know her? Isn't she a schoolteacher? Yes, that's right. What does she want with him? He just wants to end the conversation, to ride on.

"As any right-minded person knows, those kinds of creatures don't exist. At least they really shouldn't. You know that, and so do I."

The admiral is so taken aback that he almost falls off his

horse. What is the woman saying? What exactly is she talking about?

"But if they do exist – and I'm saying 'if' – then they most certainly do not belong in our town, among civilized folk. Yes, at the fair, one hears rumours, of course, but it's only to be expected in places like that – unbelievable freaks, abominations. Anyone who goes to that kind of place, well, they're just asking for it, that's my opinion."

My God, thinks the admiral, it's starting again. For twelve years, it has been quiet, and now it is starting again. He tugs on the reins, so hard that the horse rears up a little. The woman jumps and takes a few steps back, but she does not leave and she does not shut her mouth either.

"But when it happens on the public road. Right near your house. Your own house, admiral!"

"Madam, I still don't know what you're talking about." But he does know, he knows very well and he is trembling with fury as he sits there in his saddle. Has the boy been outside? Has he allowed other people to see him? This has never happened before.

The woman takes a small step closer, but remains at a safe distance from the horse's legs. "I never wanted to believe it," she says seriously. "I want you to know that. People gossip all the time, but I never let myself be swayed by such talk."

"That does you credit, madam."

"But now, now I've seen it with my own eyes. And felt it with my own flesh!"

"Your flesh, madam?" He hears Flint snort beside him. But the admiral does not feel like laughing, not at all.

Solemnly, Miss Amalia pushes up her sleeve and shows him the bandage around her wrist.

*

It is not going to be easy to get rid of her, the admiral realizes. She appears to have all manner of things that she wishes to discuss and would clearly be quite happy to come home with him to do exactly that. That will never happen, of course, he would rather be strung up. But when the woman has finally left, taking her wound and her story with her, when he has assured her that such an encounter will never occur again, on his word of honour as an officer, when she has finally disappeared around the corner, with her respectability and her bonnet and her skirts, the admiral turns to his lieutenant. The man is staring at him, eyebrows raised but, like the good soldier that he is, he asks no questions.

The admiral clears his throat. "Flint," he says. "What I am about to tell you is in the strictest confidence."

"Of course, sir."

"And then I have a job for you."

Over the roofs of the city, the admiral gazes at the dark forest and the road that winds through it to his house.

His mind is made up.

Lampie dangles her feet in the water. The sweltering heat hangs over the pond and over the garden, making everyone sleepy, except Fish. He does his double somersault over and over again, until it is almost a triple one. Lampie is terrified that he will hit his head on the marble edge of the pond, but he keeps just missing it.

"Fish," she says. "Shouldn't you have a little rest?"

But Fish shakes his head so firmly that it sprays a shower of water. He has almost got the hang of the third twist. Almost, but not quite.

Lenny has rolled up his trouser legs and is hanging his big feet next to Lampie's.

They have been sitting there since very early this morning, because once Fish gets an idea in his head, then it has to happen. He turns and jumps and darts back and forth, the sunlight sparkling in the water and in the drops that are splashing all around. Lampie can feel herself getting sleepy and she leans a little against Lenny, with her feet on the edge of the pond.

Holding the hoop *and* being a cushion at the same time – Lenny can do that just fine.

They both jump when they hear the sound of horses' hoofs. A black horse comes racing through the gate, sending stones flying in every direction. When it comes to a stop, a man in a dark uniform climbs out of the saddle. He glances at the group by the pond, but walks on, up the steps to the front door, which is half open. The dogs, lying lazily on the slabs in the sunshine, stand up and lumber over to him, with their heads down. He gives them both a quick pat and they lick his hand. Then he turns and walks inside. The dogs follow him.

Slowly, Lampie gets to her feet. "Was that?…" she asks.

The splashing in the pond has stopped. Fish is lying perfectly still in the water, watching his father walk away.

"But he didn't even look."

Fish shakes his head, and slow waves ripple across the water.

"Do you think he saw you though? Maybe he didn't realize it was you. Maybe he thought you were someone else." Lampie looks at Lenny, but he does not know either. "Do you want me to go and fetch him?"

"No, it doesn't matter," gurgles Fish, half underwater.

"Yes, it does. It does matter. We'll go and fetch him."

Fetch him? Fish thinks of all the times he has waited in his room and waited and waited until his father finally had time for him. How long it took. Maybe he had forgotten exactly what his father was like, but it is all coming back to him now.

"He has to see you!" Lampie jumps up and pulls on her socks and shoes over her wet feet.

"I think he already has."

"No, I don't think so. Come on. Get Fish, Lenny, and come with me."

Limply, Fish allows himself to be picked up out of the pond and, tripping over her untied laces, Lampie drags the boys with her to the house.

"Was that really your father, Fish? I thought he would be much bigger."

In his room, the admiral is eating a piece of Martha's blackberry pie. Silently, bit by bit. The dogs are lying obediently beside him on the tiger skin. He does not look up when Lampie, Lenny and Fish appear behind him and stand dripping in the doorway. He just wipes his mouth with a white napkin, leaving behind a small, dark stain.

The admiral nods. "Ah, Martha," he says. "I've certainly missed your blackberry pie. Delicious."

"Thank you, sir," says Martha. She is looking at the three of them in the doorway. When Lampie goes to step into the room, Martha slowly shakes her head. No, don't do that.

So Lampie stays where she is. She can hear Fish's teeth chattering. Probably not from the cold, because it is really hot in here too. She looks around, at the dead butterflies in the cases and the animals' heads on the wall, which stare back with their glass eyes.

"Would you like another piece?"

The admiral nods. "But leave some for my lieutenant. He'll be here soon."

When Martha passes him a clean plate, he gives her hand a quick squeeze.

"I'm sorry about Joseph, Martha," he says kindly. "I know you were fond of him."

"Thank you, sir," says Martha, serving him another slice of pie.

The admiral tucks in.

Does he even know we're here? thinks Lampie. She tries to catch Fish's eye, but he is staring through his wet hair at his father's back. His eyes are pitch-black again. Drops of water are falling onto Lenny's trousers, tapping on the floor. And the admiral eats his pie, chewing and swallowing. When he has finished the second piece, he puts his fork down.

"There are some things I don't understand," he says then, still with his back to the door. "And which I should like to understand. Why my garden resembles some kind of demented zoo, for instance." He takes a sip of the coffee that Martha has poured for him. "But that is not the main issue. Why is it that I have barely even sailed into the harbour before I start receiving complaints that something… *something* has been roaming around the town? *Something* that has apparently been swimming in the harbour and biting decent citizens. How strange, I think. Whatever could that be? Surely not something that has anything to do with my house. Or with my son. That cannot be so. Because my son and I have an agreement. Do we not? He stays up in his room, with his books and his maps and goodness knows what, and he learns how to walk. That is the agreement." Now he turns around, chair and all, and looks at Fish. "So how is it going, my boy? Have you been practising?"

"I've… um…" Fish begins a kind of sentence, but does not finish it.

"But with little success, it would seem, if a halfwit has to help you over the threshold. Do excuse me, Martha, I mean nothing by it. And furthermore…"

Lampie sees Martha's hurt expression, sees Fish pale with misery. A flame of fury shoots through her.

"You should see him," she says. Her voice sounds hoarse and quiet.

"Excuse me?" The admiral turns his head and looks at her with cold eyes.

"You should see him," says Lampie, more loudly this time. "He is so incredibly fast when... when he doesn't have to walk, and he can do somersaults and..."

"Oh, the circus tricks I saw outside? Hmm. My son the... fish." The admiral almost spits the word out.

"Yes," says Lampie, trying to give him an equally chilly stare. "Or you could say merman."

The admiral pushes back his chair, scraping its feet across the floor. "Who are you?" he says. "And why in Heaven's name are you poking your nose into my business?"

Beside him, Martha quickly puts the pie down on the table. "This is, um... The girl who helps me, she comes from the lighthouse, she's here, um, because..."

"Ah. The drunken lighthouse keeper." The admiral stands up and walks over to Lampie. From close up, he looks a lot taller. "So you're his daughter, are you? The daughter of the man who cost me an entire ship?"

Lampie gasps. "*Your* ship?" she says.

"My ship, yes." He looks the girl up and down, from her messy hair to her untied shoelaces. "It was gross negligence, as I just heard from the sheriff. Did you think you could mop away some of your debts in my kitchen? Did you think I would want to have that father of yours in the lighthouse any longer? What do you think the punishment is on my ship, the punishment for drunkenness and negligence?"

"I don't know," Lampie says with a shiver.

"Indeed. And I don't think you want to know."

As Lampie stands gasping for breath, not knowing where to go or what to do, someone else enters the room. It is a man who seems to be made entirely of muscles, with black side-whiskers curling out from under his cap. He pushes past the three figures in the doorway.

"It's all arranged, sir," says Lieutenant Flint with a salute. "As easy as, um, pie. I mean, I've found someone who'll take him. Actually happy to have him, I think." He casts a curious glance at Fish in Lenny's arms, but then looks straight ahead again.

"Excellent." The admiral nods. "Do have a piece of pie, lieutenant."

I need to get away, screams a voice inside Lampie's head. I need to run out of the door, through the gate, down the road, through the town, along the sea path. I need to get my father out of the lighthouse somehow, and we need to run away. She has no idea how, but she has to do it. Before the admiral, before he, before someone... Her muscles are tensing up to run, but then she looks to one side, at her friend lying in the arms of her other friend, and she sees that they are waiting, waiting for something that is going to make everything even worse. So she pauses for a moment.

The admiral has turned and is walking over to where the two dogs are lying on the old dead tiger. He bends down and gives them both a pat.

"There is no need to make a drama out of this," he says. "I've been thinking about it for some time, and I'm sure that

you'll ultimately feel more at home there than among, um…
normal people, shall we say?" He glances at his son and then
back at his dogs. "And having seen you doing all those tricks
outside, I'm even more certain that I'm right."

"No." Fish shakes his head, and then he starts talking really
quickly. "No, really. I know I'll be able to do it, one day, if
I keep practising, I'll learn how to stand and walk, I promise…"

The admiral sighs. "Ah, walking," he says. "I gave up on
that idea long ago. Right, so Lieutenant Flint here will take
you. Where exactly is it, lieutenant?"

"He's waiting for me at the train station." Flint swallows
down his mouthful of pie. "But not for too long, he said. Fellow
with one eye. Earl or something, I think. Yes, Earl, that's it."

Lampie and Fish are both equally horrified. They turn to
Lenny and start yelling in his ears, both as loud as each other.

"Run! Upstairs!" shrieks Fish.

"Outside!" shrieks Lampie.

Lenny looks at one and then the other. Run in two
directions at the same time? But how? That's not going to
work. But he does take a few steps back into the corridor, still
carrying Fish in his arms. Lampie tugs on his sleeve – that
way, downstairs, to the front door!

"Lieutenant," snaps the admiral. "Put down that pie and
do as I ordered."

"Sir!" Flint taps his cap and turns to wrestle Fish from
Lenny's arms. But suddenly a small girl appears in front of
him, screaming in his face and ready to fight.

The lieutenant, who could crush the child between his
thumb and forefinger, looks questioningly at his superior.
Shall I?

The admiral sighs. So there's going to be drama after all. He gestures with his hand. "Just leave it to the dogs. Douglas, Logwood."

Growling, the two big brown dogs stand up and walk over to the girl. Lampie steps back. They have always been nice to her, but now she can see their yellow teeth, as their lips curl back and they snarl at her. She takes another step back, and then another. The dogs bark loudly, right in her face.

And then Lenny says a word.

It is the first word he has ever spoken and possibly the last. The only word in his entire life.

"Dogs," he says.

The dogs instantly leave Lampie alone and go and stand beside Lenny. Their twisted faces become friendly again and they wag their tails to and fro.

"Douglas! Logwood! Here!" The admiral can call as much as he likes, but the animals will not move.

"Upstairs, upstairs!" Fish hisses in Lenny's ear, and the big boy lumbers along the corridor.

"Wait, no! Outside!" calls Lampie, but she still runs after them.

The admiral curses and so does Flint, as he tries to run past the dogs and into the corridor; they will not let him through, standing firm and growling, with their hackles raised. The lieutenant, who is not afraid of a couple of animals, shoves them out of the way – and so they bite him, Douglas the one leg and Logwood the other. They hang on for a while, until Flint shakes them off, yelling and bleeding.

*

From the other side of the room, Martha watches the spectacle. It would be better if she could keep that smile off her face, but she can't. She has never been so proud of her son.

The admiral turns to look at her. "Martha," he hisses furiously. "That moron of yours is leaving my house today."

Martha slowly puts down her tray on the table. "I see," she says. "Well, in that case, I shall be leaving too."

She strides out of the room, past the dogs, who are still growling. They do not touch her.

NICK

Lenny is running in the wrong direction.

"Not upstairs!" Lampie calls after him. "Not to the tower! Anywhere but there!" But he is already on his way, around the corner, down the dark corridor, up the narrow staircase. Lampie looks across the hallway, at the staircase leading down, to the front door, where she can leave the house. But then she turns and runs after her friends.

Fish is shivering, with his arms clasped around Lenny's neck and his eyes tightly shut. As soon as they are up in his room, he drops onto the floor, wriggles under his bed and disappears.

Lampie comes into the room, panting. "Fish, you have to leave with me, we can't stay here. Fish!"

But Fish stays where he is.

Lampie wants to drag him out from under the bed, but she can't reach him.

"Piss and bile!" Lampie curses. "Don't you understand? They'll be up here any minute now, he'll give you to Earl, and you'll end up in the aquarium, just like your aunt. You don't want that!"

It is so quiet under the bed, as if there were no one there.

"And your father is going to… I have to warn my father. Fish, help me. Come on!"

Fish does not respond.

Lampie bends down and looks under the bed, her cheek on the floor. Right at the back she sees a small black shadow.

"Fish," she whispers. "Edward. I really have to go. I need to warn my father. Come with me. Please! But I have to go anyway, whether you come or not." Then she realizes that tears are rolling down her face and dropping onto the carpet. She can't leave him like this, can she?

Lampie looks at Lenny, who is still standing where he dropped Fish.

"Lenny," says Lampie. "What should we do?" The boy looks at her with his round eyes in his round head. He can't help her this time.

Then someone whistles, outside in the garden. The sound blows in through one of the windows. And then again.

Lampie stands up and walks over to the window. Down there, beside the rhinoceros, stands Nick. He looks up at her, waving something in his hand.

Lampie leans out of the window, as far as she dares. "Nick!" she cries. "You have to help us. Please! I need to get to my father, and…"

Yes, nods Nick. He beckons her and points at the thing in his hand. Lampie can't quite see what it is, some kind of short stick with straps on it. What is she supposed to do with that? Nick beckons her again. *Come on!*

Lampie looks back at the bed. Should she do it? And leave Fish behind?

Downstairs she hears the dogs barking away. There is some shouting and then a bang.

"Have you lost your mind, Flint?" says the furious voice of the admiral. "Shooting at my dogs?! You idiot! Lucky you're such a poor shot!"

Lampie shakes her head. That rules out that escape route; she would never dare to go past them.

"Nick!" she screams. "Could you maybe?… Someone has to go to my father and tell him that…" Around her, the wind is rising. The trees and the hedges are rattling and rustling. "He needs to know that… that the admiral has come home!" she yells over the noise. "And that he… he has to…"

Nick shouts something back to her, but she can't hear him.

"What did you say?" she screams.

Again his words disappear into the wind.

Lampie looks around. "Wait! Wait, Nick! I'm going to throw something down!"

He nods. He waits.

Her hands shaking, Lampie takes the top off the inkpot and kneels down at the low desk. I can do this, she thinks. I've learnt how. And maybe this is why. She dips her pen into the ink and immediately makes a blot.

Dear Father, she thinks. *Dear Father, This is your daughter, Lampie. How are you?* No, that's not right. What she has to say is: *That ship was the admiral's ship and he owns this house too, and now he's here and you have to leave, you have to leave right away, because otherwise…* She grips her pen. More blots. *Otherwise…*

It feels as if her brain is shaking too. And she really needs to hurry. Is that someone coming upstairs? And does Nick even know where her father lives? And what exactly did the admiral say? *Do you know what the punishment is for drunkenness and something else?* he said. But he did not say what the punishment was. Bread and water, or something worse than that, much, much worse, but she has no idea what.

Lenny sits on the bed, watching her with frightened eyes.

From downstairs she hears more shouting and bumping and banging. One of the dogs suddenly yelps. Lenny jumps to his feet and is about to run to the door, but Lampie grabs his sleeve and pulls him back down.

"Please, Lenny. Please stay here!" Lenny slowly sits back down, but keeps his eyes on the door.

Lampie looks at the piece of paper again. There is still nothing written on it.

"Fish," she whispers. "What should I write? What is the punishment on board for drunkenness and… and?…"

The voice from under the bed is very quiet, but she still understands.

"Hanging," he says. "From the highest mast." Of course he would know the answer. "Your father needs to run. Right away. That's what you have to write."

Lampie's hands start shaking even more. *Dear Father, dear Father…* She can't even remember how to write a D – what does it look like again?

"I was so good at writing," she cries. "And now I've forgotten everything…"

"Give it here," says Fish. He crawls out from under the bed. "Let me."

*

He starts writing, quickly and neatly. Before long, the page is full.

Will it really help? Lampie wonders. Will her father ever get it and read it and… and?…

Down in the garden, Nick whistles on his fingers again. Lampie runs over to the window. "It's coming!" she calls. "Just a moment!"

Downstairs a door slams; it sounds really close. The key! she suddenly remembers. She digs around in her pocket, shuts the door, and quickly locks it.

"Have you finished? Fish? Please?"

The boy nods, waving the sheet of paper to dry the ink. "Finished," he says. "But how?…"

They hear someone climbing the stairs, with heavy, uneven steps. Someone who is panting and limping and quietly cursing.

Fish finally seems to wake up now. He looks around, at the window, at the door, at the girl.

"Lampie," he says. "Lampie, what should we do? What should I do?"

Lampie wishes she knew, but she only knows one thing at a time. Her eyes find the stone with the vein of gold, which is on the chest of drawers. She ties the note around it, using one of her shoelaces. This first, she thinks. And then everything else. She leans out of the window.

Nick is still standing down there, his coat flapping around him. Lampie carefully throws the stone; it lands some distance away from Nick but then rolls neatly towards him. He puts it in his pocket and then looks up at the girl, far above him. Lampie wishes that she were the stone. She wishes she could go with him.

"Will you really take it, Nick?" she whispers.

He nods, as if he can hear her, and smiles. Then he puts his hands up to his mouth and slowly shouts three words.

"The!"

"Sixth!"

"Window!"

"The sixth window?" repeats Lampie.

Nick nods again and turns around.

"What do you mean?" Lampie yells after him. "What window? Nick! Wait!"

But he does not wait, he turns around and walks quickly across the garden and down the road, on his way to the lighthouse. Or at least that is where she really, really hopes he is going.

Someone rattles the doorknob.

"Are you in there, you wretched little boy?" calls Lieutenant Flint through the keyhole. "Oh yes, you are, aren't you?"

The sixth window? Lampie slowly turns around. The room has only five windows – that is as clear as can be.

But maybe… Maybe on a day when you could think clearly and were not in such a panic and there was no one rattling at the door who wanted to knock it down and come in and do terrible things to you – yes, maybe on a day like that you might just happen to notice that there had indeed once been a sixth window. Over there, behind that sheet of wood that someone has screwed to the wall, and not very neatly. She has never seen it before, but suddenly she spots it – and it is perfectly obvious. And so is what she needs to do.

"Lenny," she says. "Get up. Time to help."

Lenny stands up with a grin on his face. Time to help!

It would be a lot easier with a crowbar, but Lenny forces his shears between the wood and the wall, until he can squeeze his fingers into the gap, and then he starts to pull. It makes a terrible cracking sound.

The door begins to creak and crack as well, as the lieutenant throws his shoulder against it.

"I think he's in here, sir," he shouts downstairs. "With the door locked. But I'll have it open in a jiffy!"

Fish looks from the window to the door and then back at the window. "What are you doing? What are you all doing?" he whispers.

Lenny pulls one more time; the wood splinters and cracks and comes free of the wall. And there it is. The sixth window – it was there all along! Lampie gives it a push and it swings open.

The wind gusts right into the room and the smell of the sea is so strong. From this window you really can see such a long way: not just the part of the bay with the lighthouse, but the whole wide expanse of ocean, where the sea meets the sky. On the horizon, dark clouds are gathering.

Lenny picks up Fish and together they look down below. There, beneath the tower, at the foot of the cliff that the house stands on, there, all the way down below on the dark water, there is a green rowing boat. Someone has tied it with a rope to the steep cliff, and it is bobbing gently on the waves.

"I don't understand," says Fish. "How did you know there was a window there? And how come there's a boat down there? There's no way to reach it."

"I think… I think that it's my boat," says Lampie slowly.

"Your boat? What do you mean? What are you talking about?"

Outside the room, Flint throws his heavy body at the door once again. Then he curses and gives it a kick, but that does not help either.

Fish looks at Lampie, his face completely white. "No," he shivers. "We don't have to… We'll just stay here. That door's

strong, it'll keep him out. All we have to do is wait until…
Until he goes away again, and… Or… or until my father
comes. I need to talk to my father, if I could only…"

Lampie looks at him and shakes her head. Then she looks
out of the window again.

"Yes, I do," says Fish. "Honestly, if I could just tell him,
just show him that…"

"I'm scared too," says Lampie quietly. "But I think we have
to do it."

The door is cracking now. With every kick, the cracking
grows louder.

Lampie feels the fear shooting through her, from the soles of
her feet to the top of her head. Do they really have to do this?
How far down is it? She would have to keep her body very rigid
and go into the water like a spear – that way it wouldn't hurt
as much. And she would have to take a good jump, so that she
would land as far as possible out in the sea, where the water is
deeper. She would have to… she would have to… she would
have to be completely mad!

And Fish looks around, at the room where he has lived his
entire life. The books, the maps, the bath and the bed – and
there is the photograph that Martha gave him only yesterday,
with Joseph in it and his mother. The mother you can hardly
see anything of, the mother who once lived here and looked
out at the sea, longing for the water. Suddenly he can feel his
tail, which is limp and dry and which is eager to get going
again. He hears the water quietly splashing at the foot of the
cliff, so deep, so green, so cold.

*

"Shoes off," says Lampie, and she starts untying her other lace. "You too, Lenny."

The boy makes no attempt to move, just stays where he is. Even when she says it again.

"Lenny…" she says. "You can swim, can't you?"

Lenny looks at her and shakes his head.

"Really?"

Lenny shrugs a bit and looks sadly at the girl. Really.

"Not even for a short way? Just as far as the boat? It's not all that far, and if we…"

The big boy keeps shaking his head.

"If Fish holds onto you, and I do too? We won't let go of you. Will we, Fish?"

Slowly, Lenny puts Fish on the floor. Lampie wraps her arms around Lenny's neck.

"Piss and puke and bile," she curses and she pinches the big boy very hard, as hard as she can, but it does not help.

Another huge kick. The lieutenant roars, the door shakes in its frame. And now there are other feet coming up the stairs.

"We have to go," says Lampie. "Now. There's no other way." She lets go of Lenny and climbs onto the window sill, without looking down. Keep your body rigid. Take a good jump.

"Fish? Are you coming?" She opens up her arms and Lenny lifts the boy off the floor and gives him to her.

"Lenny, if you sink, I'll dive to get you," Fish says quietly in Lenny's ear. "I can do it. I really can!"

But Lenny keeps shaking his head: no way, no way. He hardly even dares to look out of the window.

Fish puts his arms around Lampie's neck and wraps his tail around her.

"You're the one with legs," he says. "You need to make it a good jump."

"Yes."

"And keep your body rigid, so it won't hurt as much."

"Yes."

"And fill your lungs first."

"Fish, I'm frightened. I don't think I can do it."

"Yes, you can," says Fish. "You're made of the right stuff. The good stuff."

"Stuff?" shivers Lampie. "What kind of stuff?"

"The stuff of heroes." He clings extra tightly around her neck. They briefly look at each other.

Then Lampie squeezes her eyes shut. Takes a deep breath. And jumps.

Carrying the bunch of keys from Martha's cupboard, the admiral climbs the stairs of the tower, where he has not been for such a long time. Up at the top, Flint is still pounding against the door. Then he stops to rub his sore shoulder.

"At ease, lieutenant," says the admiral. "Has this door defeated you?"

"My apologies, sir. It's a tough one. Real oak, I think, they're always—"

"Keep your thoughts to yourself. Are they still in there?"

"I haven't let anyone through, sir."

"Good. You can take the boy. As for the other two…"

"Sir?"

"We shall see. Keep them here for the time being."

The admiral opens the door. Inside, the wind is roaring through the open window. Beneath the window, on the floor, Martha's idiotic son is sitting, huddled up, his hands over his eyes. Otherwise the room seems empty. Lieutenant Flint runs in and grabs hold of the boy.

"I've secured this one, sir!"

"Thank you, Flint," says the admiral. "You may release him. I don't think he's a threat."

He walks over to the window and looks down, at the sea far below. The waves have frothy tops, and he sees a small boat floating down there.

Twelve years ago, he stood in this very spot. Looking out, in just the same way, with exactly the same mixture of relief and – yes, what? – regret, pain, something like that.

Of course he had loved her, his beautiful green-haired, golden-eyed princess. But he had never intended for her to follow him, for her suddenly to be standing there in front of him, with legs and without a voice and completely unsuited to life on land.

Under the water he had understood her. Or at least it had seemed that way. She put her head against his and they understood everything about each other, just like that. But once they were on board the ship, she became a mystery to him. Those eyes, those eyes that wanted something all the time. What is it, girl, what? What? He could hardly take her home and stuff her, as he did with his other trophies, his tigers, his rhinoceroses.

But she did not leave.

So he took her home with him after all. Where the situation got completely out of hand. Her legs did not remain legs; they turned back into a tail. She had to go into the water, had to swim all the time. Everyone saw it, everyone gossiped.

No, of course it was not the done thing to become involved with a mermaid. But she was there, and what was he supposed to do? And then she became pregnant too. And the more pregnant she was, the more like a fish she became. She started to bite him. His fierce green-haired princess changed into a lumbering, scaly creature with a huge white belly.

At first he stroked her stomach and whispered to it: "A son, a son, please, a son with sea legs!"

But that was not what he got. It had been foolish of him to think that it might be so.

After the boy was born, she had fled, out of this very window. And he had stood here back then, as he did now. But holding a son. A son with a tail.

Why had she not taken the child with her?

Flint has searched the entire room, but found no one else. So he grabs Lenny again and twists his arm up his back. The boy just lets him do it; he does not even react when the lieutenant gives him a good shaking.

"Where are they? Answer the question!"

From down below comes the sound of Martha's voice, calling her son. "Lenny, lad, where are you?"

"Lieutenant, let the boy go."

"But he's a witness, sir. He knows what happened to—"

"Let him go, I said."

Martha calls again and, hanging his head, Lenny scurries to the door and disappears.

My God, thinks the admiral. Maybe there are worse things than having a child with a tail. At least his boy has a brain. He looks around at the books, the papers, the maps on the wall. He never should have come to live here.

Yes, why had she not taken her son with her?

*

It would never have occurred to the admiral to ask the simple-minded boy that question. After all, he never spoke. Which is a shame, as Lenny knows the answer to that question. And he is the only one.

He was eight years old at the time and he kept running away, especially when he was told not to and especially to places where he was told not to go. One afternoon, wanting to hide from his mother, he climbed all the way to the top of the house, to the room in the tower, where a mermaid was climbing out of the window. Which is almost impossible with a tail. When the door suddenly opened, she was as shocked as the eight-year-old boy, who shrieked because he had never seen her like that before, in her true shape. In fact, she was so startled that she let go of what she had been clutching so tightly, losing her balance and falling backwards into the sea, back to her home.

What she dropped fell to the floor and started wailing.

Lenny closed the door and ran downstairs, to the kitchen, to his mother.

Since then, Martha has found the boy much easier to handle. That was the last time he ran away.

The wind slams the window shut and the admiral locks it. He has just walked around the entire house, from top to bottom, without meeting anyone. Strange, there should be all manner of servants around the place, but he sees no one. Other than the lieutenant and himself, there is no one left in the Black House.

When he looks through the window on the other side of the room, he sees Martha and her son walking down the front steps, carrying their suitcases. As they walk down the path, his dogs come running out of the house too and bound along after them. One of the dogs is limping and dragging his paw. None of them look back, but disappear into the trees. Then there is no one.

This is what he wanted though. Isn't it?

BOAT

She falls so far and she sinks so deep.

The water is dark and as cold as a stone. Lampie struggles upwards, almost suffocating. The surface is so far away. For a moment she is not sure she is swimming in the right direction and a wave of panic floods through her, but then the blue of the water around her becomes brighter and brighter. There is the light, there is the surface. She bursts through it and sucks her lungs full of air.

The grey cliff towers far above, with the house on it, black with ivy, and at the very top the tower with the open window.

She can't believe that she dared to do it. That *they* dared to do it. She looks around. Where is Fish? In front of her, behind her, to the side – all she can see is the sea.

"Fish!" Her mouth fills with salty water. She can't see him anywhere. She can see the boat though; it is floating on the waves, not too far away. She swims over to it, looking around as she goes.

"Fish! Come on, Fish. Fish, where are you?" Fear squeezes at her stomach. This was her idea, so it is her fault. What a stupid plan.

But as she takes hold of the wooden edge of the boat, he shoots out of the water beside her, dives back in and comes up again, doing somersaults.

"This is so much fun," he shouts joyfully. "Isn't it fun, Lampie? You should see all the things I can do!"

He does not need to go in the boat, of course, but Lampie does. She can't stay there in that cold water, but as she climbs into the boat, the wind rises, blasting away at her, making her even colder. She shivers in her wet clothes and, with stiff hands, unties the knots in the rope. What is she supposed to be doing again? Who is she supposed to be rescuing? Oh yes, her father. She has to row around the cliff and hope that the lighthouse is not too far, and that she is not too late and that the admiral has not got to him first… and that Nick… She thinks about Nick waving and about the admiral's furious face. So much is happening all at once.

Trembling with cold, she picks up the oars and slides them into position. They are heavy and were made for much longer arms.

"Start rowing, Lampie," she says to herself. "That'll warm you up." She rows and it does help a bit, but she is still just as wet. There is a rumbling in the distance now, and the wind is blowing even harder. The waves are pushing her in the wrong direction.

Fish keeps leaping out of the water, in front of the boat or behind it, and calling out to her, but she can't understand what he is saying. The boat crawls forward. If Lenny could swim, if he were here, with his long arms and big muscles, then they would reach the lighthouse in no time.

"Fish!" she screams into the wind. "Can you swim ahead? Can you go to the lighthouse and see if… if?…" The wind takes her words and scatters them around. A few of them reach Fish though, and he gives her a wave. "Yes! I'm on my way!"

"Fish," she calls. "You have to say that he… You have to…" But he is already gone.

The horizon surges around her: high, low, high. The wind whistles in her ears.

Ooh, look at this, it roars. *Don't we know each other? Do you remember me? Have you come to play again, lighthouse child?*

"Mr Waterman! Mr Waterman!"

Augustus is sitting halfway up the stairs, catching his breath. That wretched leg! He has never got used to it. It still startles him sometimes, when he looks down, even though it happened so long ago. That was where his foot was; that is where his toes should be.

If that swine of a sheriff had not taken his stick, his good stick, then he would not have to make do with a piece of rotting driftwood that was lying around, which can barely carry his weight.

Yes, yes, his head says. It's your own fault. If you hadn't used the stick to hit your own daughter, your own flesh and blood…

"I know! Just shut your mouth! Shut your mouth for once!" his mouth tells his head.

"Mr Waterman, there's another letter. I think it's really important this time. You need to…"

He stands up, his makeshift stick bending, almost breaking. Everything always breaks here; the wind from the sea, always blowing, makes sure of that. It eats wood – and that includes the planks nailed across the door. If he pushes against it, he knows the door will eventually give way. Landlubbers never think about that kind of thing. If he wanted, he could be out in an instant. But what then? Where could he go?

"Can you hear me? Will you come downstairs?"

He sees something white sticking through the hatch. What is it now? He limps across the room.

"There was… it wasn't your daughter, there was a man here just now and he… I'm sorry, but there was no envelope, and I happened to glance at it and I thought… Well, just read it for yourself. What are we going to do? Um… I mean you. What are you going to do? You can't stay here!"

For the sake of politeness, Augustus pulls the crumpled paper from the hatch and looks at it. Yes, there are clearly letters on it. Neat letters, completely different from last time. He scratches his beard.

"Is it from Lampie?"

"No, that's what I just said, a man came with it, a man who was in a hurry. He was very friendly though. But what do you think? What are you going to do?" The neighbour's voice is shrill and anxious, and she is clearly waiting for him to say something. But what?

"Um…" he says. "Well…"

"You have read it, haven't you?"

"Yes, yes, of course."

"Well?"

"Thanks, then," he says. "See you tomorrow." He hopes she will go away. But she does not.

314

"Mr Waterman?" she says. Her face is close to the hatch; he can see a small part of it. A brown eye.

"What is it now?"

"You did read it, didn't you?"

What should he say? He could lie, of course. Or he could make himself look like a fool.

"Mr Waterman? You *can* read, can't you?"

The most important details are not in the letter, thinks Augustus after she has read the letter to him. Ah, an admiral who wants to hang him, yes, he could do without that. And he clearly needs to get away. But where should he go? And where is Lampie?

"Somewhere in a boat, that man said. She's rowing across the bay, I think he said. Could that be right?"

"What?" Augustus yells through the little hatch. "At sea in this… Now? I have to get out of here!"

"That's what I've been saying," his neighbour replies. "You do. But how?"

Augustus pushes against the door of his prison. A powerful storm is on the way, he can smell it, he can feel it in everything. And he will not let it happen again that his child is out there somewhere drowning while he sits at home, doing nothing. He has to get to the harbour, right now, as fast as he can. He pushes again, even harder this time. The door opens a hand's breadth. Two. The nails have almost released their hold on the wood, but not completely. Outside, his neighbour is also tugging away at the door and showing him where to push.

"No, lower. No, not like that… Hey, if we just had… Hang on, I'll go and fetch my husband's pliers."

Her husband? he thinks. Not that he cares either way.

"My late husband, that is," she says.

"Oh," says Augustus.

"Like your wife, eh?"

"Yes," Augustus replies.

"Right, then," she says. "I'll be back in a moment."

With a pair of pliers, the last of the nails are out in no time. He hears them dropping onto the slabs outside. Then he gives the door one last push and it opens with a shriek of iron. Augustus steps outside.

He holds up his hand to protect his eyes from the light, even though the sun is not shining. Clouds are quickly filling the sky, and in the distance the storm has begun. He has to get to the harbour as quickly as possible, but it is not going to be easy, not like this. He looks around.

"Well? What are you waiting for?" says his neighbour. "Do you need something to eat first?"

"No, no, a stick's what I need. A good, strong stick."

She has a nice laugh. And something in her hand.

"Ah, yes," she says. "The man, he brought something else with him, and now I understand what it is." She produces a piece of wood that is far too short for a stick, but which – surprisingly – fits exactly under his half-leg. And it stays in place. And it does not even hurt. She helps him with the buckles.

"Well, good luck," she says, when the leg is in place. "I'll stay here and keep an eye out for Lampie. And if you're ever nearby and you're in the mood for soup: I live over there."

She almost has to scream, as the wind is blowing harder and harder. As Augustus walks away, he glances back. She is a little older and a little fatter than he thought. He raises his hand. With the wind at his back, he hobbles down the sea path.

Step, tap. Step, tap.

Augustus is walking by the harbour, and it is so ridiculously easy that it feels as if he has his leg back. He suddenly realizes that he is grinning like a fool. Not only because of the leg, but also because of those letters – they really did come from Lampie. He has no idea how that can be possible. But she thought about him, thought enough about him to let him know what she was planning to do. Even though it is a terribly stupid plan, mind you.

All around him the water is heaving and splashing, and the ships are banging against the quayside like restless animals. In the far corner of the harbour, there is a half-collapsed jetty, which no decent fishing boat would go anywhere near. Sinking boats bob and dangle alongside it and there is an old, scorched ship, which no one ever dares to go near, because it is haunted.

If she really is somewhere in the town, then here is where she must be. Augustus peers along the jetty… Yes, there she is, creaking on her ropes, with freshly patched holes in her side.

He walks up to the boat and slaps his hand against her.

"Buck!" he screams at the wood. "Buck, I need your boat. Can you hear me?" He pounds the side with his fist. "Buck, it's me. I need your boat. Right now!" There is no answer, so Augustus looks upwards. The sails are lowered but the ragged black flag is snapping tightly in the wind. So he is there. "Buck!"

From deep inside the hold comes a voice: "I can't believe you have the nerve to show your face here again."

"Buck…"

"Get lost, man, or I'll come up there. You still have one leg left, don't you? You don't want to lose that too, do you?"

"Buck, that's all in the past," shouts Augustus. "This is now. I need your boat."

"Oh, is that right? And I needed my woman. But I didn't get what I wanted either." The captain's voice is suddenly very close; it seems to be coming from right on the other side of the planks. He is unleashing curse words that even Augustus has never heard before.

"It's not for me," he says as calmly as he can. "It's—"

"Clear off, man! Go back to bed with your woman, with *my* woman – she was mine first! Crawl back under the covers and suffocate for all I care."

"Don't you think I'd rather do that if I could? But I can't."

"What are you talking about?"

Augustus does not reply. He means that he would give up his other leg in an instant, and his arm too, if she were waiting back at home. But you can't make bargains like that.

"Aha," Buck says, laughing. "Did she leave you too? Ha, serves you right. Of course she'd never want to stay with a sour-faced soak like you. I always wondered what she saw in you."

Augustus had never understood it either. Buck was far more handsome, had much more hair and he was the captain too.

It was all so dreadfully unfair. But what could you do about it? Nothing – as he knew very well.

So he tried nothing, did nothing and said nothing. He just looked at her, all day long. At how she walked across the deck and worked alongside the men, because she could work just as well as the rest of them, with her skirts hitched up and her black hair tied up with string.

At night he could not sleep because of her. He stayed up on deck, looking at the moon and thinking about her. Every night a little more. Maybe she could feel it too, because one night she climbed out of Buck's bed and came to stand beside him on deck. They spoke for a while, with her doing most of the talking, while he listened and said a sentence now and then. He was happy in the darkness, as he could feel himself blushing like a lobster.

The next few nights she came again, told him all kinds of stories, sang songs and then did not want to go back to bed inside that warm cabin. The night was gentle, and the wind was mild.

Someone found out about them, of course. A ship is small, and nothing stays secret for long. Within a few days, everyone knew, including the captain. He was furious.

"You will leave my ship at the next harbour!" he roared at his first mate. "And count yourself lucky I haven't thrown you into the sea. Backstabber! Woman thief! I thought we were friends."

Augustus did not know what to say. So he went, with his clothes in a bundle, heading down the gangplank.

"Wait," she called. "I'm coming with you."

No one understood why. He was not even handsome, the first mate, and he hardly ever said anything, so what on earth did she see in him? But that's women for you.

Buck did not want to let her go.

"Then we'll fight for her!" he cried. "And whoever wins will keep her."

Among pirates, that was considered fair. The winner takes the spoils. He waved his two cutlasses in the air and threw one to Augustus, who had no weapons. Augustus shrugged. Fine, then. Let's fight.

They duelled across the deck, back and forth. "Ooh," the men cried when Augustus almost tumbled into the sea, and, "Aah," when Buck was driven up against the mast three times, because the first mate was quite a fighter, and passion gives you extra strength. But not enough, because there went his leg. It was half hacked off. A nasty looking wound, even to the pirates, with their iron stomachs.

The captain panted. "That's decided, then. You still belong to me." He went to kiss her neck, but stopped when he saw how cold her eyes were.

"No. I belong to myself," she said and, with her man leaning against her, she walked down the gangplank, along the pier and away. Augustus stumbled along at her side. He was probably going to lose that leg.

The storm is coming closer; lightning is already flashing above the sea. The heavy clouds want to drop their burden at long last. It starts to rain – big, fat drops.

"No, that's not what I meant," says Augustus. "I mean she's dead."

"What? *What* did you say?"

"I mean that she is dead!" yells Augustus above the wind.

"What?!" Above his head, a dozen faces appear over the side of the ship, hairy ones and bald ones, with wet beards and an eye or a nose missing here and there. They all look shocked. Buck leans forward.

"What are you babbling about? When did it happen?"

A hundred years ago, Augustus wants to say, because that is how it feels. "About two years ago."

"But how?"

"She just died. She was sick and then she was dead."

"She just died?" yells the captain. "Rubbish! No one just dies!" But the pirates around him nod their heads sadly. Oh yes, just dying, that can certainly happen, it's true.

"No! No, no, no!" Buck's face is turning red with fury. "I won't accept it. It can't be true. Here I was, eaten up with jealousy because you were having such a fine time. You had her *and* an easy job on land and a child too. There was a child, right?"

"That's the thing," shouts Augustus. "The child, that's why I'm here. For Lampie."

"Oh yes, Lampie. That was her name!" say some of the pirates, nodding their heads.

"The little one who always sat by the fire. She was such a sweetheart."

Buck looks around in surprise. "Fire? Where? I never heard anything about any fires."

"Ah… Well, captain. Sometimes we used to go… We wanted to go and see her, our Em."

"No one told me anything about it. Why not?"

"It wasn't very often. Sometimes, when you, um, went to bed early and…"

"We will have a proper discussion about this later," says Captain Buck.

"She's coming across the bay!" Augustus calls up from the jetty. "On her own! In a rowing boat! In this storm!"

"What? Has she gone mad? Why?"

"She was trying to rescue someone who doesn't deserve rescuing. To be honest, I have no idea if she's even out there right now. But I'm worried that…"

"If she's anything like her mother," says Buck, "then I would be very worried indeed. Climb on board, you idiot! We're sailing."

"In this weather?" cry the pirates.

"Yes, of course. I wouldn't dream of risking it with the useless lump of a helmsman we have now," says Captain Buck. "But if I could get someone else to… Or can't you sail with that leg of yours?"

"I don't steer with my leg, do I?" says Augustus.

The rain is pouring down now, but as the black sail is hoisted, the boat rears up and pulls her ropes tight. She is raring to go.

"Wait!" a voice shouts. "Wait for me! I want to come!"

A big fat pirate in a dress comes lurching along the jetty, as fast as his high heels will carry him.

"Jules!" the pirates cry. "Jules has come back too!"

Now it'll be just like it used to be. What a day!

The wind blows the ship out of the harbour.

The storm has her. It bounces the little green boat back and forth on the waves. It snatched the oars a while ago and all Lampie can do is cling to the bench, feeling sick and trying not to fall into the sea.

Feeble child, storms the wind. *Hey! Fight back a bit. Don't just sit there!*

But Lampie is tired. Tired of pushing against the world; she cannot keep it up. She can no longer see the land; she is already too far away. She looks at the waves, hoping to see Fish somewhere, but all she can see is the sea.

There is no storm beneath the waves, just the silence singing in his ears. He dived a little so that he could swim more swiftly, but now the darkness is drawing him down, deeper and deeper. The water stretches out in every direction, so far, so far, so far, with him in the middle. How deep can he go? What is down there, and beyond, and what lies beneath all that?

Shoals of fish with bulging eyes come past in the darkness; he sees thousands of sparkling lights, one per fish, turning all at once as they swim around him. Above him float shadows of large fish with fins like wings, and there: a crowd of giant jellyfish, almost transparent, almost not there, and yet suddenly they appear all around him. He recognizes them from the pictures in his book about sea life; he knows not to touch the long tentacles, because they can sting you to death. But he swims so smoothly between them that he does not even feel their sting. Or maybe they do not sting you to death if you are a mermaid… no, a merman. His heart is beating very calmly, he feels brave enough to go anywhere, deeper and deeper, to where the water is pitch black, where monsters with devil's eyes lurk, with big white teeth to chase you away and, dangling in front of their mouths, little lights, little yellow lamps to…

Lampie, he suddenly thinks.

Lampie is lying on her back in the cold water at the bottom of the boat. It has not sunk yet, but it will not be long. As the waves pitch her from side to side, she looks up at the clouds that the wind is chasing across the sky. The wind has found other things to play with now: clumps of seagrass fly past, followed by an old piece of sail from a ship that once ran aground here. And look, there is a basket blowing past. Isn't that her basket from before, with a box of Swallow Brand Top Quality Matches in it? But no, that's impossible, she thinks. There is no way it could be hers.

Inside the pocket of her soaked dress, her fingers find the shard of glass. Yes, it's still there.

Mother, she thinks. This is as far as I can go. I'll see you soon.

A wave lifts up the boat and smashes it against the big rock in the middle of the bay. It breaks into pieces and Lampie falls into the sea.

She comes sinking towards him, and Fish races to reach her. He is just in time. Isn't he? Of course he is, he can swim so fast. Just in the nick of time, he grabs the hem of her dress and drags her upwards, lifts her head above the waves so that she can gasp for air. But she does not gasp and she does not move, just looks as pale as a corpse.

"Breathe, you stupid child! Breathe!" hisses Fish, shaking her. But she simply will not do as he tells her.

So he bites her, that is all he can think of to do, and when that does not help, he pulls her through the water to the rock, where he can lay her down and pause to think. He scrapes her knees and her elbows as he drags her over the rough stone, but if she is dead, then that no longer matters, of course.

"Lampie!" he screams into her ear. "Lampie! Lampie, wake up! Please, please wake up!"

He looks around to see if there is anyone who can do something, who can help him, who can help her, but there is no one, not in this whole wide ocean.

Luckily, the storm has finally blown over. The sun shines brightly, just one last blast, before it sets. The pirates are scanning the sea, but they can't see any sign of a boat with a child inside. Probably sunk – what do you expect when landlubbers go sailing? But still, it is a shame.

Crow, who is at the top of the mast, has almost given up. He can't see anyone or anything. Or can he? Is that someone swimming out there?

"Hey?" he says. And then he shouts it: "Hey!" And then: "Hey! Captain!"

"Can you see her?" Buck himself is standing on the lookout on the other side of the ship, shielding his eyes from the sun.

"No, not her. But I thought for a moment that…"

"Keep looking, man. It's getting so dark."

"I… I thought I saw a mermaid. Could that be?"

"No, they never come around here. So no, it's not a mermaid. Keep looking!"

"But I really did think that I… Yes, there it is again. I think it's a young one. Look, captain, over there! Look! She's waving!"

The rock has been there ever since the sea once bit a big chunk out of the land. It sits right in the middle of that bite, as if there was a small piece the sea did not like.

It is an awkward thing. Nothing will grow on it: it is too small and too far away for a fort or a tower. Seals often lie sunbathing there. Sometimes a ship smashes into it. And now there is a little dead girl lying on it.

At least, that is what the little girl herself thinks. Because her eyes are closed and yet she can still see everything.

She sees the fairground train, winding its way through the land like a long snake, with her friends at every window: Oswald, Lanky Lester, Olga and Olga, and also a very angry Earl.

She sees the admiral at the open window, Miss Amalia alone in her room, Mr Rosewood on the bench in front of his shop in the evening sunshine.

She sees the lighthouse with a wide-open door, with planks dangling from rusty nails. Where a red-faced sheriff is questioning the neighbour, who is smiling and pointing into the distance.

She sees Martha with her suitcase, sitting on a post at the harbour. Lenny is sitting on the ground beside her, with the dogs resting their heads on his lap. They are looking out over the sea, as if they are waiting for something.

She can see the White Cliffs in the distance, where the mermaids are on the lookout for their Nephew Neverseen, who has read every book there is to read and so knows everything, and yet knows nothing at all.

And much closer, in his hut, she sees Nick, and in his hands a bottle with a string hanging out of its neck. He gently tugs the string and, inside the bottle, the sails of a tiny ship slowly rise. They are black and a flag the size of your little fingernail is flying from the mast, bearing a skull and crossbones.

"Look," says Nick. "Here she is."

Lampie looks – and she sees her mother. She is as good as new, with her long black hair tied up with a piece of string.

Hello, Mother.

Hello, my sweet child.

I really must be dead this time.

Is that what you want?

I don't know, says Lampie. I don't think I was finished. Or was I?

That's not my decision to make, says her mother. *But I don't think it makes any difference anyway, whether you were finished or not.*

It's so good to see you. Lampie can't take her eyes off her mother. You went away.

No, I didn't. I was here all along.

Where is here?

Here, everywhere.

Oh. But not with me.

Yes, with you. Always. You just have to open your eyes.

Lampie does not like that thought. But then I won't see you.

Oh, but you will. Just do it.

Through her eyelashes, Lampie can see how bright it all is. Through a hole in the clouds, the sun shines into the water, turning everything around her into gold. Moving gold, splashing gold.

So I am dead, she thinks. Because this must be what Heaven looks like.

You're in such a hurry, says her mother. *It's just water. Look! There's a boat sailing this way.*

She's right. There really is a ship coming, a big ship with dark sails and a flag with a skull and crossbones.

Look, says her mother. *The* Black Em *is coming to fetch you.*

The *Black M*... What *is* that? murmurs Lampie.

She can tell from the sound of her mother's voice that she is smiling all over her face. *The* Black Em? she says. *That's me.*

To sail out in the middle of a storm – well, the storm has died down now, but the wind is still blowing in gusts – and to moor a wooden ship so close to a rock that a man can jump down onto it from the deck, and without knocking any holes in the bow – that calls for a very skilled sailor. But Augustus is rising to the challenge. He feels a little rusty, but he is quickly getting the hang of it again.

Lampie is scared half to death when two big boots suddenly land next to her head, when big hands grab her under the armpits, and big eyes look at her from a bearded face, as if he has been waiting for her all his life. Even though she has never seen him before.

"Cannons and cholera!" says Captain Buck. "You look so much like her."

"Um… Like who?" Lampie asks.

"Like Em. Like your mother."

"Really?"

"Oh, yes." Pirate Captain Buck gives her a grin, showing the gaps in his teeth. Then he swings her over his shoulder and climbs back on board. "You've got red hair instead of black, but otherwise I'd think she was all mine again."

"I belong to myself," mutters Lampie.

"Yes, that's exactly what I mean," says Captain Buck with a sigh.

He stands her on the deck, on her own two feet. A pirate in a dress wraps a blanket around her and plants a kiss on the top of her head.

"Julie!" says Lampie with a smile. "Are all of you here? The dwarf too, and Lester and…"

"No," says Jules. "It's just me."

"And us! We're here too!" More pirates come and stand around her. She recognizes faces and remembers names. Bill gives her some ointment for her scraped knees and Crow brings her some dry clothes, which are far too big. But all the time she keeps sneaking glances at the helm.

He was the first thing she spotted. And he has seen her too.

Sometimes, when you really, really want something for a very long time and then you finally get it, a sort of silence descends, a moment of stillness when no one knows what to do.

Lampie has imagined so often what she would say and – well, there he is. He is a bit balder than she remembers and has a lot more beard. And there is that leg of course and the way he is standing at the helm – that's new too.

Buck takes the wheel from him, and Augustus walks over to her. They rest their hands side by side on the rail. The wind blows in their hair.

"There you are," says her father after a while.

Lampie nods. Yes, here she is.

"I've thought about you so, so much," Augustus mumbles. "All those days, every day. And…"

Yes. Lampie nods again. She has thought about him too. And yes, here they are.

"You know, you really do look like your mother."

Lampie nods a third time. "Yes, everyone says that."

Inside her head she hears her mother sigh. *Come on. Out with it!*

Out with what? What is she supposed to say?

Not you, says her mother. *Him.*

"This is our old ship," Augustus says, taking in the whole boat in a sweeping gesture.

"Yes," says Lampie. "It's nice."

"Do you really think so?"

"Very nice," says Lampie, looking out across the sea. What could be better than sailing, than going wherever you want to go? And plundering, because that is what it will come down to. Sleeping in hammocks. Seeing foreign countries. Turning brown all over.

"I can teach you to tie knots. And to sail the ship, when your arms are a bit longer. Or, um… maybe you could cook for us?"

"Definitely not." Lampie has absolutely no wish to do that.

"That's a shame. We don't have a cook, so we'll have to get by on ship's biscuits."

"I might know someone," says Lampie. "If she wants to do it. And if Lenny can come too. If he's brave enough." She thinks he will be. If Lampie is there too.

"Maybe. Your mother never cooked either."

Yes, Lampie remembers that very well.

Her father looks at the horizon again, where the last remaining bit of the sun is sinking into the sea. "I, um…" he says, and then he clears his throat a few times. "I really, really miss her."

"Me too," says Lampie. "But sometimes she's still here."

"What do you mean?" Her father looks at her in surprise.

"I hear her talking inside my head."

"Em? Seriously? So what's she saying now?"

"That she wants you to get a move on."

"Me? What with?"

Lampie shrugs. "I don't exactly know."

Augustus looks into the distance and thinks. Then he nods and looks at Lampie with that expression she knows so well. But he doesn't say anything.

He's sorry, thinks Lampie. But he can't say so. Doesn't matter.

And then a young merman leaps out of the water.

"Lampie, there you are! They found you! But I was the one who rescued you – did you know that?"

"Fish!" shouts Lampie. "Hey, Fish! Do you know what? I'm going to be a pirate. Just like my father!"

"Is that him?"

Lampie nods and looks a little proudly at the man with the wooden leg.

"Hello, sir," says the young merman politely, leaping out of the water.

Augustus nods. "Hello. Yes. Hey, I'm sorry."

"Um… What do you mean, sir?" asks Fish. Panting, because he is having to swim quickly to keep up.

"Not you. Her," says Augustus. "I'm sorry." He rests his hand on her cheek, where the blue has long since faded. "About everything. Really sorry."

Lampie gives him a big grin. The water stretches out behind her father, in every direction. They can do anything, go anywhere.

"It's fine, Daddy," she says. And so it is.

PUSHKIN CHILDREN'S BOOKS

We created Pushkin Children's Books to share tales from different languages and cultures with younger readers, and to open the door to the wide, colourful worlds these stories offer.

From picture books and adventure stories to fairy tales and classics, and from fifty-year-old bestsellers to current huge successes abroad, the books on the Pushkin Children's list reflect the very best stories from around the world, for our most discerning readers of all: children.